The problem with letting down our guard was that no one was aware of the fact until the lead Humvee lifted off the ground in an explosion of dust and flames. Yet, we were far from Fallujah, far from the battle that was our destination.

I grabbed my weapon and ran to a dune, not only for protection but to destroy any threats. Several Marines were already scanning the horizon. In the desert heat, the air danced above the surface of the sand and played tricks on our eyes. Instead of sand, I saw the flowing garments of the insurgents, but when I blinked, the images disappeared. The bomb that took out my fellow Marines had been set long before. The enemy was long gone.

I avoided the vehicle until we were told to head back to our Humvees and move. Inside my mind, I screamed not to look. I begged myself. But when we passed, I stared at the unrecognizable corpses. A piece of me stayed there in that vehicle for weeks to come. Slowly, I would recall those images, and they would become a part of me again like puzzle pieces chewed by the family dog and found under the coffee table. They were the pieces that one might hold in one's hand and wonder if they should be tossed or salvaged. I salvaged them. I put the broken pieces of myself where I thought they should go and slammed my fist into them until they fit.

Praise for T. S. Tripp and Edward Mickolus

"White Noise Whispers in an impressive novel that, by midpoint, becomes a thriller with exciting war descriptions. I highly recommend this story to anyone who enjoys excellent twists and fast-paced plots aimed to mesmerize the reader."

~Susan Schjelderup, Founder, Backyard Book Club and contributor to the *I Matter: Finding Meaning in Your Life at Any Age trilogy.*

White Noise Whispers

by

T. S. Tripp
with
Edward Mickolus

White Noise Whispers

Cover Art by *Kim Mendoza*

The Wild Rose Press, Inc.
PO Box 708
Adams Basin, NY 14410-0708
Visit us at www.thewildrosepress.com

Publishing History
First Edition, 2023
Trade Paperback ISBN 978-1-5092-4847-6
Digital ISBN 978-1-5092-4848-3

Published in the United States of America

Dedication

To the men and women of law enforcement, defense, and intelligence communities who risk their lives to protect us.

To our families: Steve, Nick, Madison, and Emily Tripp, as well as Susan Schjelderup, Ciana Mickolus, and Kaia Davis. Thank you for your unending support.

Acknowledgments

Our thanks go to numerous colleagues who provided their expertise and counsel during the writing of *White Noise Whispers*. They include:

Lt. Gen. Richard Tryon, USMC (ret.), who previously served as commander of United States Marine Corps Forces Command, 2nd Marine Division and the 24th MEU.

AyoLane Halusky, county naturalist, Parks and Recreation, St. Johns County Board of County Commissioners, St. Augustine, Florida, on what trackers look for in the wild.

Jim Hunt, who served in Iraq during Desert Storm.

Richard Willits, Esq., longtime Florida attorney.

Dr. Ciana Mickolus, licensed psychologist, Davie, Florida.

Allyssa Reddington, patrol officer, Flagler County, Florida.

Dr. Robert Creal and Nancy Creal, clinical psychologists, Ponte Vedra, Florida.

Dr. Mary Waters, psychologist, Ponte Vedra, Florida.

Dr. Glenn Goldberg, U.S. Navy Psychology Specialty Leader (ret.). All five of our psychologists provided invaluable counsel on various disorders affecting Patient 541.

Roseann DeTommaso, former Police Lieutenant, Charlotte-Mecklenberg Police Department, North Carolina, on how police departments are organized and run.

David Boyd, retired patrolman, Jacksonville Sheriff's Office, on the sociology of Jacksonville-area police officers. David's duties included tracking down bank robbers and at-large emus.

Stephen Curran, correctional senior probation officer, Florida Department of Corrections.

Don Roscoe, combat veteran who offered invaluable advice on the title.

Dr. Jay Grusin, retired CIA senior analyst and educator, whose *Intelligent Analysis: How to Defeat Uncertainty in High-Stakes Decisions* provided an excellent overview of structured analytic techniques, including Analysis of Competing Hypotheses.

Dan Rigsby, Indiana State Police Motor Carrier Officer, retired.

Michael Reddington, Detective, Putnam County Sheriff's Office.

Also, many thanks to the Beta Readers. Their input as first readers is invaluable: David Weisblatt, Judy Deon, Danielle Gardephe, Michael Gardephe, Susan Schjelderup, and Steve Tripp.

Chapter 1

Present Day
Patient 541

The doctor taps his foot impatiently. As his eyes bore into me over the rim of his glasses, my chest tightens. He's older than me by maybe a decade and a half. Not quite old enough to be my father. The desk he sits behind is barren and lifeless. No evidence of a family anywhere in his office. Yet, his impatient, judgmental expression is one well-practiced by a parent. He clears his throat. Does he expect my secrets to spill out for his inspection that easily? My jaw clenches so tightly the tension must be visible.

The doctor taps his pencil. *Tap, tap, tap.* The sound is maddening. Behind his desk is a large window. The window is closed so only my eyes can breathe in the view. The blue sky and vegetation become life-sustaining oxygen. My gaze drifts above the treetops where a bird floats in the air currents, and I travel on its wings for a moment.

My survival depends on these distractions, yet staying focused on them proves to be impossible. Voices of the past haunt me in both my waking and sleeping hours. My mind conjures the sounds of past torment— Humvee engines, gunfire, seniors screaming, "You're weak. You'll get us all killed. You're never making it home alive." The sounds combine to create a white noise that blankets my consciousness.

The incessant tapping continues to assault my mind. *Let me in. Let me see what is buried within.* My eyes drift shut.

The tapping stops. Finally. I open my eyes. The doctor stares at me. His white shirt is creased with wrinkles, and a gray five o'clock shadow accentuates his jaw. I suppose he'll be going home soon. He gets to leave it all at the office.

"Our time is almost over. Do you have anything you would like to share?"

I stare back at the man paid to evaluate my competence. I have nothing to add, not because I'm refusing to be helpful, but because I cannot pull anything sensible from my scrambled mind. The doctor scribbles on his paper. The words are not visible to me, but the air is thick with the truth.

****

Only days pass before I am declared NGI or not guilty by reason of insanity. I am being relocated and forgotten. But then there are worse things than being forgotten. I sit in the back of a van. Two men mumble back and forth words I cannot hear. My attention turns to the world outside my window. The palm trees wave at me, and as they do, they transform to scenery from another life. The strip malls fade away, and I see the desert of Iraq. I stare at the world, wondering when and if I will ever see it again. I am numb as the van comes to a stop. The door opens, and without a word, I am led into the Jacksonville Psychiatric Facility.

I walk between two men. They don't speak and neither do I. I'm floating like a ghost down the barren hallways until we stop in front of a door. My door. I step inside and hear the lock click behind me. The room is cold and made of concrete walls. One small window gives a view of a hallway leading to more rooms like my own. I'm not allowed to wander. Not yet, anyway.

I sit on the edge of the bed and take in my surroundings; a toilet in one corner, a nightstand with a Bible set upon it, a metal bed frame. My eyelids are heavy, my body drained. I lie down and drift into sleep. I wake, I eat, I sleep. Hours turn to days, days to weeks. I open my eyes and stare at the camera in the corner of the room. The device serves as an eye into my room. I've become accustomed to its presence, which is an improvement from past feelings concerning the device.

Weeks have flown by, leaving a trail of months in their path. I am a number, not a name. Rituals form and become a safety net of sorts. When I close my eyes each night, I hope the demons of my past leave me to walk through tonight's nightmare without revisiting yesterday's.

I'm told I did some very bad things. If that's the truth, then I deserve to be right where I am. But sometimes, I don't believe the outsiders' truths. Reality can be manipulated in so many ways.

The nurse enters and tells me that I have a visitor. The same person has attempted to visit me in the past. The only outsider who has considered doing so. I shake my head, and the nurse leaves the room. I've seen enough of this person in my nightmares.

The only other person who comes to visit is Chaplain Gregory. The chaplain visits regularly despite my attempts to ignore his presence. Many would say he's attractive with his thick dark hair and blue eyes. He always wears dark-rimmed glasses creating a serious yet friendly demeanor. When he speaks, his words are soft-spoken, drawing me dangerously close to trusting him, but my mind creates a shell around itself, blocking out his words.

He reaches inside a bag that he carries with him. He pulls out a brown, leather-covered journal and sets it on the chair next to him.

"I want to help," he says.

The seconds tick by as he waits for a response. I glance at the journal, uninterested. The gift is yet another attempt to destroy me. *Tell me your secrets,* the pages whisper.

"It's yours. No one will read it unless you want them to," he adds.

I look away. Hoping he takes the hint and leaves, I lie down on my bed.

"If you want a change of scenery, we could meet in the office they let me use." He's trying to make me feel comfortable like he's not one of them. I close my eyes. "I hope you'll consider meeting with me. You don't even have to speak if you choose not to. Use your journal."

After a moment more, Chaplain Gregory stands to leave.

"Have a blessed day," he says over his shoulder.

A laugh escapes me. The sound appears to startle the chaplain. He pauses for a moment and then walks out the door.

Hours pass. I eat. I use the restroom. I take pills. I lie on the bed. And then, to my surprise, I walk over to the chair and pick up the journal and then stick it under my mattress. I own so few items that the gift is special even if I never dare to write a word within its pages.

****

2018
Jim

From the other side of the yellow tape, a crowd of people studied the scene from beneath their umbrellas. The park was a popular area to hike, and the benches surrounding the pond were often frequented by businessmen and women escaping for a quiet lunch. Today, one of those unlucky souls discovered more than he had bargained for on his visit.

The misty rain was not enough to wash away any evidence, but Jim still found it annoying. He took a sip of his convenience store coffee, scoffed at the bitterness, and tossed it in the nearby trashcan.

The victim's body was strewn across the walkway like discarded litter. One of the investigators had failed to cover him completely, leaving a hand sticking out from beneath the blanket. Expressions of shock, horror, and sadness played across the onlookers' faces. One woman openly bawled, yet she knew nothing about the victim besides the fact that he was dead. There was always one who reacted in such a manner. The overreaction bothered Jim. As did other behaviors. Some people in the crowd pulled out cell phones, hoping to document the death, before being shooed away by officers. One by one, once they had their fill of what the tragedy offered, the on-lookers backed away.

Death fascinated Jim—the finality of a moment that no one could escape. Perhaps fear was his fascination. Or maybe it was something else entirely? Nevertheless, the fascination was a vital part of being a good investigator. Unlike the other officers, he understood the onlookers despite his annoyance with them. After all, who didn't want a sneak peek at the last chapter of life? Just a glimpse, not the entire story. Knowing too much would make the journey unremarkable or, as the details unfolded, terrifying.

Crowds rarely distracted Jim, but today, in the mass of people, one person's face caught his attention—boyish yet not a boy. The man stared blankly at the corpse sprawled on the sidewalk. To Jim, this one man seemed to stand frozen in the horrific frame of a movie while everything else continued as it should.

"You have time to work on our project tonight?" Jim's colleague, Gabe, asked as if the corpse was nothing more than another stack of papers thrown upon their desks.

Jim glanced his way. Their project was drinking beer and staring at the old military vehicle they purchased with the intention of restoring the relic. Little ever got completed. "Sure. Gwen's working late again." Gabe shot Jim a look that made him far more uneasy than the dead man lying ten feet from where he stood. He shrugged off his unease.

"Thanks again for storing our little project at your place," Gabe said. "Susan insists on using the garage for her car, and you know who wins the battles in our house."

Gabe approached the corpse and lifted the blanket to study the body further. His solid build was hidden beneath the extra pounds gained from eating years of fast food and sitting in office chairs. His reddish beard drew attention away from his receding hairline. "I only see one entry wound."

Jim glanced back at the crowd. The mysterious man

had disappeared. "Did you…?"

"Did I what?" Gabe asked, still crouched over the body.

"Nothing. Never mind." Deciding to keep his suspicion to himself, Jim bit back his words. A week of listening to Lieutenant Ginny Larsen sing Gabe's praises for past cases had left an acidic taste in Jim's mouth. Outside of work, his and Jim's friendship was good, but on the job, the competitiveness was undeniable. Recently, Lieutenant Larsen had given Gabe credit for many of the leads. At first, Jim had brushed it off, thinking the incidents were rare. But recently, he'd begun to wonder if he would ever be taken seriously as a detective.

"We have an ID." A detective walked toward them, holding a wallet, presumably belonging to the dead man, in a sealed plastic bag. "Someone tossed the wallet in a bush a hundred yards away."

"Classic robbery. The guy should have just handed over whatever the punk asked for," Gabe said as he studied the evidence. "Damn shame. Now we have to inform a family that Dad won't be home for dinner." Gabe shook his head. "And for what? Some cash and a credit card? The bank will cancel the card before the perp has a chance to purchase much of anything."

****

Gabe rang the doorbell of a one-story stucco home. With a few words, the two officers destroyed the life of a woman who had been busy in the kitchen, cooking what smelled homey and inviting. Beef stew, possibly. Was the table already set for two? Notifying families was by far the worst part of Jim's job. He would be more comfortable staring down the barrel of a gun than into the eyes of a grieving wife.

Without a word between them, Gabe and Jim walked back to the car. They drove to the station, spent several hours doing paperwork, and then briefed the lieutenant on the crime scene.

Before long, tips started pouring in, and by the following day, a sketch artist had created an image that was soon released to the public. With a possible suspect and evidence to build a strong case, the investigation should have been moved off Jim's desk and onto someone else's. Jim should have been focusing on the next crime, the next victim. But something about this case wouldn't let him go. A detail haunted him when he closed his eyes—the face in the crowd, the boyish face on a man far beyond the years of being a boy. Those hollow eyes stared at the corpse. What was he thinking? Why was he there? The questions echoed in Jim's mind, and he knew, for unexplainable reasons, that he would look into those haunting eyes again.

Chapter 2

Present Day
Patient 541

Days later, I enter the sterile room where Chaplain Gregory sits behind a desk. Perhaps it was out of boredom or the offer of a change of scenery. Either way, I decided to give the chaplain a chance.

As before, his demeanor is calm and welcoming, but I sense tension as well. Whether it stems from fear of me or fear of messing up his first chance with me, I cannot say. But the fear pleases me for reasons I cannot explain.

I take a seat in the chair facing his desk. Outside the window is a large tree. Spanish moss drips from the branches. At first, the sight of the gray moss sends an eerie feeling through my body, and then something else catches my attention: A squirrel. He stares back at me as if he's surprised at discovering me as well. A memory flashes before me of another squirrel I saw in another life. I push the vision back into the recesses of my mind.

"I'm really glad you chose to come see me."

The chaplain's voice breaks my trance, but I continue to stare at the tree. The squirrel jumps to another branch before scrambling onto the roof. My eyes drift shut, and I follow the squirrel in my mind.

"I keep telling the staff they should put a bird feeder out there, but they argue the squirrels would eat all the food. They're probably right," the chaplain says.

I open my eyes. The squirrel is back. His tail twitches, and we lock gazes. The blankness I feel when I stare into the squirrel's beady eyes comforts me. The creature thinks nothing of freedom while he dances among the leaves. Squirrels don't suffer like humans do. They don't contemplate the consequences of their actions. They take their freedom for granted. My mind will always be imprisoned in one way or another. I shake away the frustrating thoughts.

For a moment, I want to talk just to end the uncomfortable silence. But words won't come. My story is too hard, and the chaplain's quest to save my soul will not be that easy.

I cannot understand how sharing the horrific details of my past will reshape the details enough to make them bearable. Trapped pain does not disappear once released. Pain, the protagonist in many great stories, never allows the author to write The End. Pain flows like a river searching for an untarnished landscape to tear apart. As the water accelerates, gaining strength and never weakening, the debris destroys another landscape and another and another.

The clock ticks. The thirty minutes of allotted time ends.

"Well, I guess that's all the time we have for today, but I hope you'll come back—even if it's just to get a glimpse of that big old tree."

The chaplain stands. There's an awkward pause as he waits for me to follow suit. For several seconds, I do not move as I stare into the chaplain's eyes. Does he feel fear as he looks into the eyes of a killer? I want him to be afraid. I want him to be terrified. I need him to know what he is up against because if he doesn't understand the enemy, then the enemy cannot be defeated.

Without breaking eye contact, I stand. He doesn't flinch until the last moment. His Adam's apple bobs up and down in that telltale way when fear catches in one's throat. The corners of my lips lift slightly, and for reasons I don't really understand, the first memories begin to bubble to the surface.

****

When I return to my room, an overwhelming urge to do something overtakes me. At first, I pace. I want to strike someone, anything. I need to release the tension building inside of me. I need to run until my legs become weak from exhaustion, but the doors to the world are locked. As I search the room, my gaze falls upon the journal I had tossed onto the bed before going to the chaplain's.

Months have passed with me trapped in the solitude of my mind. The chaplain told me that no one would read my words unless I want them to. I walk over and pick up the book with its clean white pages. Any story could emerge between the leather cover—a story of hope, heroism, love—but that wasn't going to be the case. These pages would be filled with something far darker.

I open the journal to the first page. I pick up the blue pen the chaplain had left tucked within the pages. At first, the words appear slowly, and then the action of writing overtakes me. The story unleashes, and I become an observer, fearful of what will be exposed as simple letters form words, words form sentences, sentences reveal truths: Truths that may destroy the author.

Where should I start? Where does the horror story begin? When a bridge collapses, is it the final car that takes all the blame, or should the millions of vehicles that traveled over it through the years be responsible as well? Perhaps the responsibility can be placed on a faulty foundation, how my DNA, the ingredients of my chemical makeup, morphed into a subhuman creature. Perhaps I am evil by nature, incapable of allowing any life experience to have a positive impact. I have nothing to lose that I haven't already lost. Rip me apart. Decide for yourself. Why did my foundation crumble?

I was raised in a home of impossibilities. Impossible to be good enough, to please, or even breathe, without disappointing someone. That someone would be my father. What would he say about me now?

I'm not placing the blame on the man who held me to strict standards—warning me repeatedly that each sin, no matter how trivial, tarnished my soul. Perhaps he sensed something about me. I wonder now, as I analyze myself in the quiet of my room, did he always know? After all, I often lied about sweeping under the kitchen table. I put clean clothes in the hamper instead of in my drawers. The lies came easily, even at a young age. I enjoyed deceiving him. The act empowered me after he made me feel so powerless. I cared nothing about the darkening of my soul.

During my teenage years, hormones possessed me— those were my father's words. Our relationship became more volatile as I struggled against him. I became a demon living in my parents' home. As my soul blackened with each misdeed, I avoided the people who pointed out wrongdoings and found the places where my abnormalities were accepted, even embraced. I tried out for football, where all my anger and frustration allowed me to excel.

My father was a preacher without a pulpit. He was a Catholic monk with a classroom of one: Me. When I was younger, he kept me in line with a belt. In his mind, he was saving me from the devil himself, and for that, he needed to be strong. Harsh even. I would thank him someday. At least, that's what he told me.

As I aged, my actions—coming home late, the smell of beer on my breath—infuriated him even more, and the belt gave way to fists. The belt may have hurt worse, but the punishment...Well, I guess when flesh hits flesh, it seems more personal. You feel it differently.

My father knew how to give the final blow, though, and in a way I never predicted. He was good like that. Strangely, his final revenge didn't involve him touching me at all.

****

2018
Bethany

As was her habit, Bethany Williams found the dry-erase marker and prepared to scribble a note on the whiteboard hanging by her dorm room door.

Going for a run. Usual route.

Seeing that the same message from the day before had been left untouched, she put the cap back on the marker and returned it to its resting place. The sun was peeking up over the horizon. This was Bethany's favorite time to run—alone in a still world that would soon give way to chaos. She coveted the silence, for in the quiet, she envisioned a future self, a young woman with self-restraint and dignity. That person was somewhere inside her, but memories of the night before, of her hovering between heavily buzzed and completely inebriated and dancing late into the night with some stranger, made her doubt herself. She wondered how long it would be before that better version of herself took hold.

As much as those memories disappointed her, they were not what troubled her. Remembering the conversation with her father caused a wave of nausea to slam into her, and for a moment, she wondered if she could run without getting sick.

Had she hung up on him last night? She prayed the conversation had been nothing but a drunken nightmare but knew that was not true. As a test, her father had made a midnight call that had ended with her shouting words she hadn't meant. It hadn't even been a weekend, for Pete's sake. But then, sometimes Thursdays seemed so close to being Fridays that they too deserved celebrating. Her father would be calling back, and Bethany prayed he took the time to cool down before he dialed.

In her freshman year at the University of North Florida, Bethany had developed a reputation as the party girl—a reputation she hated until about the second drink of the following weekend. It only took one, sometimes two drinks, for her self-control to begin feeling like self-induced shackles, and she started seeing the thrill of freedom at the bottom of the bottle.

Not this year. Despite suffering from a hangover, Bethany promised herself that things would be different this year. This semester, she would buckle down and concentrate on her classes and a future career that would make both her and her parents proud.

Bethany was well-aware of the tension she'd created between her parents and who would take the brunt of it. She couldn't keep doing that to her mother. Throughout her life, Bethany's mother timidly stood up for her despite the fights it would cause. Her father would never change, and unless Bethany got serious, her mother would be listening to his rants for years to come.

Why did she want to push his buttons? After all, Bethany wanted the same things as her parents—for the world to take her seriously. How was she ever going to become a detective if all anyone saw was a flighty, impulsive, blonde-haired, blue-eyed beauty? Bethany just needed some time to breathe, to have a taste of freedom after being bound so tightly by her father's rules. Eventually, she promised herself people would recognize her abilities.

After a few stretches, she began a slow run. Her muscles needed a moment to pass through the phase of fighting off the inevitable and surrendering to routine. Her body had long ago learned to enjoy the ritual of her morning run. To crave the endorphin rush. The route was about five miles long, and Bethany had done it so many times she could practically run it with her eyes closed.

She cut through the woods leading to Eco Road. The road was quiet, and even though her roommate, Amber, worried about the thick woods, Bethany felt safe. After all, the campus police headquarters was only a short distance from the concerning stretch of trees.

Bethany generally listened to her playlist while she ran but had decided to listen to the sounds of nature instead. Her mind needed time to drift aimlessly from last night's events. Of course, her pulsing headache also begged for silence. Had the guy from the bar been good-looking, or had the alcohol merely distorted reality?

She remembered leaving the bar with him. She thought back to the moment she'd stopped rambling on nervously. He'd been quiet, too quiet. For whatever reason, maybe the walk had sobered her. She'd wanted the strange man to leave her to finish walking back to her dorm alone. Despite little hints to that effect, he'd continued to walk with her. She remembered telling him she needed to get to bed early because of her morning run. When she'd seen her dorm in the distance, she'd thanked him for bringing her home safely. The man had uttered a goodnight and kissed her on the cheek. Bethany had quickened her pace until she'd stepped inside the building. That's when her phone rang, and the stranger had become the least of her worries.

Discouraged, trying to forget that she had let herself down again, she looked forward to the day's schedule. She needed to study for a psychology test because no one would take her seriously if she got another C, not to mention her father's threats. Would he really stop paying her tuition?

The pavement moved beneath her, and her new running shoes pounded out the rhythm of her steps. The repetitive movements took charge, allowing her mind to wander. The first mile of the run was always tough, but it was especially so with new shoes. Someday, some company would develop shoes with an odometer. So many miles, so much time alone envisioning the person she wanted to be. How many pairs of shoes would it take to reach her destination?

In the distance, she saw movement. Probably a deer. So many of them were running around campus. Bethany had heard of bobcat sightings as well, but she wasn't too afraid. She believed bobcats to be small enough to scare off, but then again, she could be wrong.

The hairs on her arms rose in expectation. Her gaze searched the tree line, and she prayed the deer would make its appearance and end her doubts. Very seldom had she been spooked on her run, and she was suddenly curious as to why her mind was sending off such an unpleasant vibe. Perhaps the effects of last night's binge were messing with her brain cells.

Ahead, she saw movement again. Something large. It had to be a deer. Florida didn't have a great deal of large wildlife. Bethany's heart beat hard against her chest, too intense for her typical run. She was afraid.

Glancing behind her, she saw only the path and the trees. For the first time, she cursed the quietness of the road. Even the woods seemed to observe her with an eerie silence. Unfortunately, her path was about to dip into the trees and follow a wooden walkway. The road would still be visible through the vegetation, but losing the clear view unsettled her. Her running became louder as each footfall met with wood rather than concrete. It was generally one of her favorite parts of the path. Another few steps and she would be passing the spot where whatever creature stood, hidden by the branches.

The world was frozen and stagnant. Even the birds stopped singing. Bethany was acutely aware of her heart pounding in her chest, sweat dripping down her forehead, and the steady sound of her shoes on the bridge. Only a few more paces and she would be beyond the troubling area. Bethany counted her steps, hoping that by distracting her over-imaginative mind, the fear would dwindle to nothingness, and her heart rate would calm. Ten, nine, eight…she entered the area…seven, six, five…almost behind her…four, three, two…

A twig snapped. Then another. She heard the heavy footsteps running toward her. As she turned toward the sound, the sun was blocked out by a person's frame. A small gasp escaped her lips before a hand covered her mouth. The man was dragging her into the woods. She pried at his hands, and in hopes the knowledge would matter later, she tried to see his face. The glare of the sun blurred the image.

Sweat dripped into Bethany's eyes. The world around her—the smell of sweat, firm hands tightening around her, the sensation of branches tearing at her skin—was foreign and terrifying. Images flashed before her, but she couldn't focus on any of them. Again, Bethany tried to scream, but the hand tightened on her mouth. She tried to bite the flesh, but the hold was too firm. The arm was twice the size of hers and pure muscle. Even though Bethany fought, she knew she had no chance. A fence stood between them and the woods, and Bethany clawed at it as her attacker lifted her over it. Her shirt tore as it caught on the wire.

People say their lives flash before their eyes in near-death experiences, but that wasn't the case for Bethany. Her fear was a wall that blocked all images. All thoughts. She managed to grab the wire fence with both hands, but with what seemed to be little effort from her attacker, she felt her fingers painfully extend, and a fear unlike any she had ever known filled her. The feel of metal slipped away from her fingers, leaving her with nothing in this world to grasp.

Chapter 3

Present Day
Patient 541

A week later, I walk into the chaplain's office once again. He is reviewing some papers on his desk, and I wonder what information a chaplain was privy to in his position.

When he sees me, he stands and greets me like an old friend. A smile lights his face, and he welcomes me to have a seat. The reaction sends a mix of emotions through me and puts me on guard.

As I sit, I try to get a look at the papers on his desk, but they have been neatly tucked away in the folder. In my hands, I hold the journal, although I cannot explain why I felt it necessary to bring it with me.

A light rain falls outside the window. I search the tree for my squirrel friend but don't see him. Only the Spanish moss is visible, making the scene dismal.

"I see you brought the journal. Have you been able to add anything to it yet?"

"Some."

The chaplain's eyebrow lifts in surprise. I hadn't uttered a word in months. Perhaps I should be surprised as well, but I'm not. In fact, I'm a bit curious to hear my own voice again. It sounds gravelly and unrecognizable to me.

"That's wonderful." He waits. "As I told you, you do not have to share anything that you wrote, but I'm here to listen. Of course, our conversations are confidential as well."

I glance down at the journal and notice how tightly I'm gripping the leather.

"I wrote about my upbringing." My attention drifts to the folder on his desk, and I notice his glance follows mine.

"Are you wondering what I already know?"

I don't answer.

"It's a fair question."

Again, I don't answer.

"I know you were an only child. And I know about your father."

I nod, yet I am a bit surprised by this revelation.

"Did you want to talk about him?"

"My father would be a convenient beginning, I would say." I make no eye contact. Instead, I focus on the tree. Several moments tick by, and silence settles over the room. Finally, I clear my throat. "My father taught by instilling guilt. I was the reason my mother cried. I forced him to punish me, creating an unhappy home."

I fall silent. Speaking about him is harder than I expected, yet something about the chaplain makes the words flow from me.

"I guess it makes sense that his final punishment would be the ultimate act of placing blame on me."

The chaplain lets the silence pass uninterrupted as I wrestle with the correct words and the courage to say them.

"My father had flipped out during dinner. My

mother had passed him the deficiency report the school had sent in the mail. It was one class. Chemistry, if I remember right. After tossing his full plate in the sink with enough force to break it in half, he disappeared into his office. I was happy he left. My mother and I started cleaning up. At first, she was silent, and then we had the closest thing to a bonding conversation we had ever had.

"My mother told me that my father was a brilliant man lost within himself. When he met my mother, she was a waitress, and he was alone, reading in a corner booth. He mesmerized her with his manners and intelligence." I chuckle at the image. "I can't imagine my father mesmerizing anyone, but that's how she described her first impression." I adjust my position in my seat. "Maybe if my mother had stopped being so open with me at that moment, all would have been all right, but she didn't.

"Her voice cracked when she told me that my father had let her down, almost tricked her. For all my father's intelligence, he'd failed to be successful. 'That's why he gets so angry at your grades,' she told me. 'He doesn't want you to be a failure like he became, living paycheck to paycheck and barely hanging on to a lower middle-class status.' It was then that we heard him behind us. I've never seen my mother look more terrified. I don't know if she even knew what she was afraid of at that moment.

"The next day, I went to football practice and put all I had into the workout. I wanted to be too tired to think. After practice, I walked home. I remember it being a cool fall day. I felt a sort of peace as if I had been able to sweat the demons out of me. When I rounded the corner to my home, I saw police cars in my driveway." I pause then, and a small laugh escapes me. "It turns out that my father's misguided ideas of religion were not enough to save him from himself and his warped mind. Shortly before I arrived, my mother had returned home from the grocery store and found him dead at his desk from a gunshot wound. He didn't even leave a letter explaining why. Maybe I should feel thankful for that."

"How did this affect your relationship with your mother?" the chaplain asks.

"Relationship. I'm not sure you can call what I had with my mother a relationship. She blamed me for my father's death. When she looked at me, her eyes held something I can best describe only as hatred. After all, I'm the one who pissed him off the night before. I'm the one who caused her to speak in such a way and betray my father." My stomach clenches at the memory. "Yes, in her mind, even her own words were my fault. And without my father in the picture, I was the reason she had to work such terrible jobs to support us until she could get rid of me somehow."

"What jobs did your mother do?"

"Waitressing. It's all my mother knew." I pause, deciding on my next words. "She cried all the time. The crying and shouting and blaming, I couldn't take it. 'You did this. You're the reason your father is dead. You destroyed everything.' I heard the mantra so many times the words echoed in my mind even when she was nowhere near me."

"What did you do when she reacted this way?" the chaplain asks.

"I usually stormed out of the house. Found a friend who didn't expect me to discuss my home life and drank whatever I could get my hands on."

"Is your relationship with your mother the reason you enlisted?"

"Hell, no. For some stupid reason, I still had bigger dreams. The NFL." I laugh at the memory, but another guttural sound cuts òff the humor. I fall silent as the clock ticks away the moments. "My coach took me under his wing. He made me believe I could get a scholarship and get in a college where I would get noticed." I stare out the window as I speak. I had been transported back to a time before life had transformed me into this broken man.

"My mother never attended my games. She would have enjoyed watching my last one, though." I shake my head. "Damn, it was a great day up until the end.

"I remember every detail. The sun was beaming down on us, and the temperature was in the mid-sixties. We were playing our rivals that day." A smile plays at my lips as the story unfolds. "We went into half-time with a two-touchdown lead. The energy in the locker room was contagious." My eyes shut momentarily, and I breathe in deeply. I feel possessed by a younger version of myself. "I could almost taste the cold beer we would be drinking after the game to celebrate.

"The second half was tougher than we predicted. We battled back and forth—touchdown for us, touchdown for them. The incident that changed my life happened in the game's last five minutes. The last damn five minutes. Gets me every time I think of it. The quarterback called through the air, 'Blue 22, Blue 22.'"

I cup a hand at my mouth, imitating the call, losing myself in the memory. "I darted to the right. The linebacker's breath was hot on my neck. The ball spiraled through the air."

My hands prepare to catch the imaginary ball. "And the leather pressed against my fingers as I pulled the football snugly to my chest." I stop there, holding my hands against my heart. "I breathed in the crisp air while the sun shone down upon me. I could do this. I could rise above my situation." My hands fall to my lap. "One moment was all I got before the linebacker slammed into me like a freight train. I felt my knee pop. I hit the ground hard. I remember watching the ball roll out of my reach.

"I still feel pain shoot through my knee joint at times. My mother came to the hospital room. She never consoled me about losing my dream. She spoke of God's will, of humbling me, of trials making me stronger. I knew nothing of these transformative occurrences. All I knew was that I was adrift in a world that had lost meaning."

"Is this when you enlisted?" the chaplain asks.

"For a year, I hung out in college bars drinking away any chance of earning a scholarship once my knee healed. The injury just wrecked the dream for me, I guess. Even if I could afford tuition, I wasn't ready to commit to four more years of schooling without the thrill of football. I had no clue what I wanted to be at that point in my life. I was as lost as I had ever been up to that point."

"What did make you decide to enlist then?"

I laugh. "I found direction in the strangest of places. I had stumbled into a dorm room with a headstrong college girl. She smiled at me in a sheepish drunken way as she unbuttoned her shirt. Somehow, she made me feel like she was doing me a favor by sleeping with me. The feeling didn't stop me from crawling into bed with her and enjoying myself, but my mind was a million miles away. When we finished, she climbed out of bed without a word and walked to the bathroom. I shouldn't have cared if she'd used me. After all, I was using her, too. But the way she just walked away… Well, she took my man card, I guess you could say. Even the college women were above me. The following day, I enlisted."

The room was silent for several moments.

"What?" I say gruffly. "You expected something more sinister? A strict, suicidal father isn't enough to gain your understanding and forgiveness?" I sit back in the chair and look the chaplain straight in the eye. "Maybe I could have been normal despite my upbringing. There's always that chance. But life had more in store for me." My gaze drifts to the window once more. "My story had just begun."

****

2018
Amber

Amber walked past the woods that held ugly secrets. She had several classes to attend before meeting her study group at the library. After class, she stopped by the room to grab a book she'd forgotten. The only thought she gave to Bethany was frustration that her running shoes were thrown in the middle of the floor again. The typical behavior failed to raise any alarms. As for not seeing Bethany? There were many days that they didn't see each other until late afternoon.

The two of them were so different some people questioned how they could be friends. But the friendship worked. Amber always knew her looks paled in comparison to Bethany's, and she was okay with that. Growing up in Oklahoma and being known for officially becoming a champion at calf-roping at the local rodeos gave her confidence without needing mascara and French manicured nails. She was neither envious nor put off by others' needs for those things. "To each, his own" was her opinion.

Amber's vision of her future after graduating from UNF involved veterinary school. All the other frivolous ways of the world were entertainment, mere distractions, which temporarily caught her attention. Bethany's adventurous nature reminded her to have fun. At the same time, Amber liked to believe her more reserved nature benefited Bethany. Experience youth, she told herself, and then settle into the life she desired.

In the late afternoon, Amber returned from class and crawled into bed, grateful to snag a half-hour nap before dinner. Moments after her head hit the pillow, she settled into a deep sleep. Just before Amber slipped into a complete abyss of REM, something jolted her awake. At first, she couldn't place the feeling, yet the sensation continued to pull at her. Sitting up, she looked across the room. Finally, her gaze settled on the Adidas box resting on the floor near Bethany's shoes. The container was empty, which meant Bethany had not changed into her usual sandals—her preferred footwear for class. Amber's brain tried to put the puzzle together. Perhaps she'd gone to the gym in her new sneakers. Bethany was known for having fits of exercise after a bender.

Amber replayed the night before in her mind. She had begged Bethany to go out and then she'd decided to come home early from the bar, leaving Bethany dancing on the dance floor. Amber had heard her stumble into the room sometime after midnight. She'd been on the phone, fighting with her father. Amber had been tired and had chosen to find out more about the ordeal later. She glanced around the room for more clues. Where was she?

Grabbing her phone off the nightstand, she texted Bethany:

—*Hey girl, where are you?*—

Amber watched the phone for several minutes as if she could force it to reply. Nothing. She texted again:

—*Please text me immediately. I'm a bit worried about you.*—

No response. Amber sat cross-legged on her bed, drifting between unsettled waves and feelings of foolishness. Bethany would text back any moment, she was sure. She expected Bethany to reply, slightly charmed by Amber's worrying. Still nothing.

At five thirty, Amber decided to go to dinner. Maybe Bethany would show up there before going back to the room. Sometimes, this was the case. Instead, Amber sat alone, watching the crowds.

She began texting friends who had classes with her. After a few anxious moments, the responses started to light up her phone. No one had seen Bethany.

Chapter 4

Present Day
Patient 541

Days pass before I meet with the chaplain again. The conversation begins slowly. He tries to jostle the memory of our last visit from me. The months of silence have exhausted me, so I cave to his prodding.

"On your last visit with me, you told me why you enlisted. How did your mother react to this decision?"

"When I told her, she stared at me stone-faced." I laugh. "For a moment, I believed she might be upset that I was leaving her."

"What makes you think otherwise?"

I contemplate my response. "The precise moment she called me a murderer was when I realized she wasn't afraid of losing me. She was only afraid of what I would become through the process of transforming my life."

"I'm sure those were hard words to hear."

"Hard? She made me feel like shit, just like she always did. I remember how she turned away from me and started washing the dishes. I began to leave the room, and something made me try one more time. The woman with her back to me was my mother, for God's sake. I still hoped for something from her, some mother-son bond."

My demeanor softens, and for a moment, I am the

young man crushed by his mother once again.

"I was scared—lost. I didn't know what the military held for me. I only knew I needed direction." My voice is quiet, even to me. "I walked up behind my mother and wrapped my arms around her. 'I'm sorry for everything. I'm sorry I couldn't have been a better son.' There it was. I said it. And then I waited. Her body remained rigid, and the moment went from hopeful to awkward fast. My arms realized the mood before my mind could admit to it. They slid off her and hung at my sides like they didn't even belong to me. After a moment, I walked away. I'm sure we talked after that incident, at some point before I left, but for the life of me, I don't remember a damn thing we said."

"Thank you for sharing. I can see that it was difficult."

I ignore his remark and sit upright in my chair. My voice becomes business-like, and the young man who had appeared earlier disappears behind a curtain.

"In a blink of an eye, I was at the Recruit Training Depot at Parris Island, South Carolina. I spent seventy days there. For over two months, I experienced the most brutal physical and emotional training I had ever dreamed of incurring: crawling through mud, doing push-ups, running, and climbing. Every moment ripped a piece of the individual out of me, replacing it with a new self that existed within a larger body of selves.

The training made me a new man, and for a while, I envisioned the experiences I stored away would fuel my future. I would share the stories of my military life with my children and grandchildren. For a while, I thought fighting beside my fellow man would erase all the brutality I had endured. I thought war could make me believe in humanity again. But sometimes, humanity gets lost in the battles fought to protect it." I become quiet. The chaplain's gaze follows mine to the scene on the other side of the window. A squirrel scurries along on a bush. We watch him together for a short time.

The chaplain glances at the clock. "Take your time. There's no rush."

I laugh.

"Why did you laugh when I said that?"

I glare at him. "Because you know there isn't any rush. Because you know this is all pointless. The only difference between now and ten years from now is that I will have shared my story, and you will have fulfilled your curiosity, the world's curiosity. I won't be cured or forgiven. My life, my secrets, they will just be exposed. Nothing more."

The clock ticks loudly, making the room feel uncomfortable and empty.

"Is that what you think our sessions are about? Fulfilling my curiosity?"

"Why else are you here?"

"Because I believe in hope and forgiveness."

At this, I laugh openly. "There are some things no one should be forgiven for, and you are a fool for believing in the impossible."

Many minutes pass in silence. I slap my legs with my hands. The chaplain jolts slightly.

"Your silence is an acknowledgment of the truth, I'm guessing?"

"It's an acknowledgment that you're not ready to accept any other truth."

"We can agree on that." I look at the clock. "I'm done for today."

"Okay."

We both stand, and he walks me to the door where someone will escort me back to my room.

Hours pass with me staring at the ceiling, replaying our conversation in my mind. The truth, begging to be freed, scratches at my mind. I grab the pen and journal and begin to write.

People talk about basic training as if it dehumanizes a person. Well, I suppose for some, that would be true. To me, basic training was the great equalizer. We were all scum, not worthy of praise. We crawled through the mud, rifles in our hands, pretending a battle loomed before us. The earthy smell filled my nostrils. I could barely make out the other men's skin color beneath the layers of mud that dried and cracked before peeling off. There were differences, though—differences that would become more apparent later.

I guess, if you listened and watched closely, the differences were already apparent. Some men, as they scrambled under the wires, set their jaws as if they were born to withstand brutality. Others whimpered quietly with sounds they attempted to disguise as grunts. What did people predict of me when they observed me? Could they hear my heart pounding? They could not have heard the voice of my father screaming at me from a place that seemed so close. The sound reverberating in my mind was as authentic as the drill instructor's voice being shouted from above us. I half-expected my father to climb from the mud as if escaping from his grave.

I dug harder into the earth, desperate to get as far away from my past as possible. When I scrambled out of the obstacle course at the other end, I realized I had beaten all the other recruits by quite a distance. Later, in the shower, I scraped away the black mud that covered my body, leaving my skin raw.

I set down my pen. The memory of me covered in mud replays in my mind. The image of me is like my father described me, stained with sin. I think of the chaplain and wonder about his mission. Had he not learned that stains cannot be washed away?

The evil deeds of my past had blackened my soul. If he didn't understand that truth, how could he understand me at all?

****

2018
Jim

The sun beat down on the crowd of what appeared to be a hundred people bustling around the flea market. Jim could think of a million other places he would rather be on what felt like the hottest day of the year. Yet here he was with Gwen. Hell, being at work would be more invigorating.

Jim trapped a yawn with his hand—the third in under five minutes. Last night, he'd woken several times in cold sweats because he had dreamed of the man's face in the crowd. Sometimes, the guy wore a hoodie. He would slowly lift his face toward Jim, and his eye sockets would be hollow. Other times, the man's skin appeared melted. Although Jim thought the man in the crowd wore an old military uniform, he couldn't be sure.

"Jim, are you listening?" his wife asked.

"I'm sorry. What did you say?"

With an indulgent smile, Gwen shook her head. Jim liked these days, the ones when he was allowed to touch the lion's mane, feel its softness. Today was one of those days, a day where Gwen didn't belittle him with her disapproving eyes.

Gwen Castille had been born determined to oversee something, making her job as an air traffic controller the perfect fit. It also helped that she was obsessed with airplanes. According to her, this trait manifested from being the only girl in a family of four children. To fit in with her brothers, she at first faked interest. Soon, her interest became genuine. Two of her brothers became pilots. The other one went into the corporate world.

Gwen's quest of the day was to find the coveted British Airways Concorde model for her collection. Watching his wife, determined and passionate, unfazed by the heat, reminded him of what had drawn him to her in the first place—her will to be in control. For whatever reason, Jim needed this from her. This quality also drove him half-crazy at times and led to numerous disagreements. Or at least, Jim disagreed with her in his mind.

Despite knowing there was no use complaining, the heat made comments seep out of him without permission.

Gwen pulled on his hand. "Come on."

Jim studied her eyes, glistening with excitement, and he knew that he would, as always, succumb to her wishes.

The thick Saint Augustine air clung to Jim's skin and melded with the perspiration from his body. Gwen's hand grasped his firmly as sweat pooled in their palms.

"What is it, like ninety-five degrees out today?" Jim asked while swatting a fly away from his face. Florida flies crept out of the secret places they inhabited whenever vendor food and humidity were present.

"It's always ninety-five in August. Don't be such a wimp," Gwen said while in full stride, her loose ponytail bouncing behind her as if she were a toddler determined to have her way.

Jim decided to embrace the day and look for parts for Gabe's military vehicle still sitting dismantled in the garage for what he could not deny had become an excessive amount of time. From what he could tell, Gwen didn't mind their project. Despite her dislike of Gabe, she encouraged the work connection, and Jim sensed she wanted him to have his own interests.

Occasionally, when he and Gabe were supposed to be out working on their project, Gwen would open the garage door, roll her eyes, and announce dinner was ready. "Do you two do anything but drink beer out here?" she would say and then shut the door before they could give their lame response. After leaving her remark hanging in the air, she would spend her evening in the house where life was tidy and organized to her liking. Gwen didn't complain much beyond that. After all, her hobby is what had brought them to yet another glorified yard sale.

A screaming child brought Jim back to his sweltering surroundings, yet his mind remained half in a haze of his dreams. Passing the men and women with forced smiles selling their wares and waving makeshift fans, Jim reminded himself that things weren't that bad. Although he remained a lowest-rung detective, his job beat sitting behind one of these tables every weekend. He smiled back at the vendors without pausing, letting them know he wasn't interested.

The various relics reminded Jim of the contents of a hoarder's garage. Old records, boots, and so many useless items were laid out with only an occasional gem sprinkled in amongst them. Today, Jim joined the rodents that pawed through the debris, trying to find a magical artifact that could ignite a momentary spark of excitement.

Mid-70s Shaun Cassidy smiled up at him from a stack of records. His white shirt and slacks were separated by yet another white garment, a sweater with black stripes. The words *Born Late* were written across the front of the album cover. Jim picked it up and studied the back cover, reminiscing as he read each song title.

Setting the record back in its place, Jim scanned the area. He couldn't shake the feeling that someone was watching him, but he didn't see anyone paying any particular attention to him. He drew in a deep breath and let it out slowly. After repeating the action, his heartrate calmed.

Working as an investigator, seeing the craziness that lurked on the streets, instigated his imagined scenarios. But investigators didn't share their fears. They didn't tell their wives and coworkers that sometimes they woke up shaking from nightmares. No. Investigators learned to breathe deeply and bring themselves back without ever alerting the ones around them that they had momentarily disappeared to dark places.

"Jim, come. I think I might have found it."

Jim felt Gwen's hand, small yet demanding, slide into his. Suddenly, he was being pulled through the ambling crowd toward a distant table. Gwen slowed as they approached, showing no excitement to the seller.

For her, haggling was like working a free drink at a college bar. For every dollar she shaved off the price, Gwen found power, and Jim had witnessed her excel at her sport like an Olympian time and time again. Jim smiled as he watched his wife play her game. After all, she could probably find every model she ever desired by typing its name into the search bar on Amazon. A couple more clicks, and her item would appear in the shopping basket, but then, what would be the fun in that?

She picked up the Concorde, studying the pointed nose and sleek design as she nonchalantly turned it around in her hand.

"How much for this little thing?"

The man placed his hands on the sides of his lawn chair and, with effort, got himself to a standing position. Beneath the shadow of his gray beard, his jowls drooped, and Jim guessed him to be in his sixties. Then again, the man's red bulbous nose could be a sign that he had chosen to speed the aging process with his alcohol of choice. Jim's bet was whisky.

After clearing his throat, the man answered: "I'll take five for it, dear."

Pretending to contemplate, Gwen turned the model over in her hand. "How about three?"

"Four, and you have yourself an airplane."

"Deal." She rifled through her wallet for some singles.

Jim noticed a sprawling assortment of electronic devices a few tables down.

"I'll be right back," he said to Gwen as he lightly laid his hand on the small of her back.

Gwen looked up just long enough to see the general direction in which he walked.

Jim approached the table and scanned the remnants of past technological advances that were now nothing more than 3D puzzles for tinkering minds. A gruff voice interrupted Jim's thought.

"Can I interest you in something?"

Jim eyed the tall, lanky man. An eagle tattoo with one word, *Marines*, above it and *Operation Iraqi Freedom* below it were sketched onto his forearm.

"You have quite the collection here," Jim said.

"You don't have to bullshit me. These relics are a bunch of junk to most people."

Jim's hand shook as he reached for a walkie-talkie handset lying in front of him. The unsettled feeling would not leave him.

"Got this from a Marine that, I guess, served in Iraq. Knew I sold trinkets and just handed it over. I think I've got the other one here somewhere." The vendor bent down and began rummaging through a box.

"How much you asking for it?"

The man looked Jim up and down before responding. "Ten dollars."

The man's words were curt. Jim was nearly forty and still had a thick head of wavy, brown hair. His good looks sometimes brought out a level of animosity from the older generation, but he sensed this was not the case in this situation.

Slightly curious as to what had triggered the man's dislike, Jim smiled behind his sunglasses.

"I'll give the walkie-talkies to you for five, though."

Was the stranger that desperate for a sale, or was there another motive? Jim glanced back at the walkie-talkie, intrigued for unknown reasons.

"Here it is."

The man set the other handset on the table and Jim reached in his back pocket for his wallet. He scanned the crowd for Gwen. She was still gabbing with the more cordial older man at the nearby table, probably describing her collection now that it wasn't affecting the deal. Jim handed the man a five without making eye contact, stuffed his wallet into his pocket, and headed back to his wife.

When Gwen saw him coming her way, she wrapped up her conversation. "Thanks again. Have a wonderful day." Sweetness dripped from her words, and for a moment, Jim had a hard time envisioning the driven, unstoppable woman behind her smile. She looked down at his hand, holding what very well could have been pieces of junk. "What do you have there?"

"Walkie-talkies."

She smiled. "So, Detective Castille, what exactly are your plans for two old walkie-talkies? Whom do you think you're going to talk to with them?"

"You'd be surprised at the number of characters out there that I can communicate with." Jim smiled back. "I can intercept neighborhood kids out doing pranks. That would surely get me a raise and more opportunities."

Gwen laughed. "Have you heard of smartphones? No kid alive is running around with a walkie-talkie and announcing his toilet papering schemes to a bunch of other buddies that for some reason don't have smartphones, either."

"Truckers. Maybe I'll intercept some of their conversations. Who knows, maybe I'll be able to track down an eighteen-wheeler full of cocaine."

"Don't they operate on different frequencies?" Gwen asked, still apparently amused with her husband's purchase.

"Sometimes things get twisted, and people overhear their conversations."

"Really?"

"Sure," Jim said, not sure of any of it. "And did you think of the possibilities with baby monitors? Do you know how many corrupt housewives there are out there? It's just a matter of time before one of them plans to take down her husband."

Again, Gwen laughed. "Well, who can blame them?" She reached up and kissed his cheek.

"Do I need to start sleeping with one eye open?" Together they dodged two young boys chasing each other.

"Why don't you just finish the project taking up our garage?"

"That's a long-term project to be savored for many years to come." Jim pulled Gwen in to kiss her on the forehead. "Don't you worry about it, dear; I have a feeling these walkie-talkies will bring great things my way."

"I don't know about that, but if it makes you happy, then I'm glad you have them."

Gwen wrapped her arm around Jim's waist as they walked toward the exit.

An impulse overtook Jim, and he glanced back at the gangly man who had sold him the walkie-talkie. The stranger stood, hands behind his back, staring in Jim's direction. Despite knowing the man was not the one in the crowd from weeks before, a chill ran up Jim's spine, followed by a distinct feeling: Something, or someone, was drawing closer.

Chapter 5

Present Day
Patient 541

The nurse enters my room to ask if I want my weekly visit with the chaplain. I want to say no. With each visit, with each journal entry, anger wells up inside of me like lava inside a volcano. I don't want to rehash my memories, but I can't stop now. The recollections haunt me day and night. Even though the chaplain's journal is the cause of it all, when asked if I want to meet with him, I agree to it.

I sit silently for some time. Chaplain Gregory begins the conversation. "Did you add anything to your journal this week?" The chaplain gives me a moment to respond. I don't.

"During my years visiting this facility, I've spoken to many veterans. You might be surprised by my ability to understand your situation."

"You've never been in the military, have you?" I eye him with disgust. "No need to answer." I swallow my anger and contemplate whether he's worthy of hearing my story. Then I take in a deep breath and let my words drift out into the air. "Before I begin, let's get one thing clear. If you've never served, you can't understand."

"My apologies. You're correct. I can't claim to understand experiences like yours without having been there myself."

Giving his apology time to soften my anger, I stare at the chaplain. He doesn't flinch while awkward moments pass. He just waits. His courage is respectable as well as ignorant. Perhaps when he hears my whole story, he will not be so brave around me.

"I wrote a good amount."

"That's wonderful. Do you find writing to be helpful?"

"I can't answer that yet." I glance at the journal. "Maybe someday, but today...today, it doesn't seem helpful at all."

He nods. The clock ticks away several minutes. I don't know how to move forward. I don't know where to start. I look at the journal again.

"I guess I can read part of it."

The chaplain sits still as if any move would wreck the moment.

I open the journal and begin to read aloud.

"I finished basic training and went on to MCT or Marine Combat Training. Then I completed MOS, Military Occupational Specialty, training. When I was in MOS training, the first Battle of Fallujah was underway. You might know it as Operation Vigilant Resolve. Then again, most people, safe in their beds, don't know the difference between Afghanistan and Iraq.

I envision myself on the frontlines with the men already in Iraq. The Marines were scouring the buildings, searching for extremists and insurgents, hunting for the ones responsible for killing the four American military contractors."

My hands grip the journal, and my jaw clenches as I speak. Again, I find myself furious with the world and how little people truly understand. But wasn't I one of them at one point?

"Were you one of those people? The uninterested ones?" I ask.

"I work with veterans. It's my job to stay abreast of world events."

"I'll refresh your memory anyway."

I looked back to my journal and began to read again.

"The first battle of Fallujah began on April 4 and was nearly a month in as I climbed ropes to nowhere and hurdled myself over walls. Each of us found ourselves lost in private thoughts as we morphed into superhumans capable of completing unimaginable, necessary tasks.

"On May 4, 2004, the battle officially ended in the way ongoing wars often do—messy. Muslim extremists and resistance fighters still controlled the city. On May 15, a 2,000-pound JDAM GPS-guided bomb found its target—the northern district of Fallujah. Even as the dust settled onto the rubble, the next battle seemed inevitable despite a momentary ceasefire giving time to plan the consolidation of US and Iraqi soldiers who would patrol the city.

"My training ended in June. Tensions in the Middle East were still running high. I was deployed overseas into a world impossible to train for properly. Overseas is a different world. I'd been told my survival would depend on factors as simple as which door one Marine burst through versus another."

I laugh softly and pause for the space of several heartbeats.

"You would think we would be paralyzed with fear, but that wasn't entirely true. Yes, there was fear, but also excitement. The two emotions blended into an intense

feeling I can't explain. Still, the adrenaline from these feelings was the fuel I needed to carry me across the ocean into the unknown.

"Every aspect of my life was out of my control, and the idea was freeing and exhilarating. The next time I set foot on US soil, if I was lucky enough to do so, I would be a new man, and that had to be a good thing."

I look at the chaplain. "Wouldn't you think, chaplain? The new me had to be a better man than the kid who destroyed his family."

"Why do you feel you destroyed your family?" the chaplain asks.

I take a deep breath, exasperated by trying to make him understand. I shake my anger away and continue reading.

"The powers that be sent me to Camp Matilda in Kuwait. We awaited orders to leave there and make our way into Iraq, but for some time, we waited and passed the time doing drills and preparing in the way Marines do.

"Shane was the first person who I remember meeting when I arrived. In truth, he most likely wasn't the first Marine I met, but the moment I saw him remains a vivid memory. He entered the chow hall, high-fiving everyone, slapping their backsides, and wearing this grin. God, I hated that smug-ass smile.

"Shane was an arrogant son-of-a-bitch right from the get-go. He was the type of guy who got the girls' attention—tall, broad-shouldered. His hair was light brown and cropped like the rest of ours. A decent-sized tattoo peeked out of the sleeve of his T-shirt. I could make out the bottom of a globe with an anchor wrapped around it. I would later see it well enough to know an

eagle sat at the top of the image. Men wearing camo pants and green T-shirts filled the room, but Shane was the guy the room seemed to orbit around."

I pause, trapped in my memories until I become aware of the quiet. The chaplain waits without a word.

"I guess in some ways, I was always torn between two realities of myself. On the football field, I was feared. Damn, I loved that feeling."

I look the chaplain up and down.

"You've never felt that kind of power. To walk amid people and have them look up to you. To have them move out of your way without realizing they even did it." I inhale deeply and let out a long slow breath. "Then I came home where I was slammed against a wall before I had the chance to throw my backpack down in the hallway. The perfect upbringing for a Marine when I think of it. Prepare to be abused so that you could later be feared." I chuckle and look to the ceiling. "Thanks, Dad, for the awesome preparation."

I lock gazes with the chaplain. He nods, encouraging me to continue. I look back to the pages.

"Shane didn't fear me, and somehow, something about him made that abused kid inside of me shine through. He sensed the weakness, and he came at it. His energy was drawn to mine like opposite magnetic fields.

"Shane slapped his tray down on the table where I was sitting. Nameless men sat on either side of me, and as much as I would try to remember who they were, I can only recall blurred faces.

"Shane looked around the table and said, 'Who's the new guy?' No one answered, so I told him my name. The left side of Shane's lip curled into a half-grin. 'What a pleasure it is to meet you, Private.' The sarcasm

at the same time."

Jim smiled over at her occasionally, displaying the expected reaction but not sharing his wife's enthusiasm.

"When I die, will you keep coming to flea markets just to honor my memory?" she asked.

"Do you want me to be miserable for the rest of my life?"

"You're so not a romantic." She rolled her eyes but didn't seem genuinely agitated.

The ride home took only fifteen minutes traveling north on I-95. The wooded roadside blurred past uneventfully, with only the tractor-trailers whizzing by, occasionally returning him to reality. Jim's stagnant mood threatened to suck him in like quicksand. His mind was far away, visiting a place where he was frequently finding himself, a place that lingered between the blues and depression.

Years had passed since he had celebrated earning the title of detective. He and Gwen had gone out to the Town Center to celebrate; visions of future cases had lit the night on fire. Jim had felt like he was standing on the springboard to his career. Yet, years later, he found himself still standing on the same ledge, watching as others received the opportunities and earned accolades from their lieutenants. He hoped that working toward his degree in criminal justice would earn him a promotion, but it wasn't guaranteed.

In the beginning, Gwen was constantly reminding him how capable he was and how he would have solved the case in half the time. The inspirational speeches were transitioning to something a bit less patient. Jim couldn't deny a slight animosity building whenever he heard what he privately referred to as "the tone."

Jim turned off at their exit and, within minutes, pulled into the driveway of their one-story home with white siding. Gwen preferred it to the stucco; she insisted it was homier and trendier. Jim wasn't sure of any of that, but the house stood before him, pristine with well-manicured shrubs and flourishing vinca giving it color. Gwen was unsurprisingly meticulous in her upkeep.

Jim unlocked the door, and the bright kitchen with tall white cabinets, many with glass doors exhibiting the matching serving bowls and wine glasses, greeted him. Since there weren't children and may never be any, he and Gwen had each claimed an area of their house and designated each spot as their personal she shed or man cave. Gwen's was the office. The wall unit cabinets with several glass doors made it possible to showcase her collection.

"I'm gonna go find the perfect place for my latest find," Gwen said, laying a soft kiss on Jim's cheek. Over her shoulder, she added, "And stop thinking about it."

"What are you talking about?" Jim asked, even though he didn't need an explanation.

"You're getting that depressed look on your face again. That's no way to make things happen for yourself," she said. "You know it's the truth."

Jim's jaw clenched as he bit back the words he wanted to say. "Since when did you become a mind reader?" He smiled if only to appease her so she would stop talking.

"I know everything," she said as she disappeared around the corner.

"Sometimes, I wonder." Jim eyed the walkie-talkies on the counter. "I'll be in the garage if you're looking for me. Gabe's coming over to work on the project again."

Jim let the garage door shut behind him, and some of the tension within him immediately eased as he distanced himself from his wife's judgment. Gabe wouldn't stop by for another half an hour, and Jim savored the time alone. Something else was bothering him, something about the case of the murdered man in the park. He wouldn't share that the event triggered darker emotions because he couldn't explain why a face in the crowd kept him awake at night. Not the corpse— the dead husband—but instead, the face that was there one minute and gone the next.

Jim turned the dials on one of the walkie-talkies. Nothing. He opened it up and examined the insides. He knew nothing about the internal parts of his new toy, but tinkering took his mind off his troubles. The act of taking objects apart to see how they worked was as cathartic as meditation was for some. His thoughts wandered while his hands worked independently of his mind.

The door to the garage opened, and Gabe entered with a robust, "What you got there?"

"I got us a little something at the flea market." Jim showed the purchase with a wave of his hand.

Gabe came closer and studied the handset. At first, he said nothing. Then, with a nod, he said, "I think we could have some fun with these." Gabe's smile grew. "Oh yes, we can have some fun with these."

"That's what I told Gwen," Jim responded.

"What did you tell me?" Gwen had slipped into the garage behind Gabe.

Jim looked from his wife to Gabe. "Gwen didn't appreciate my purchase as much as I did."

Gabe made a small grunt, and once again, Jim sensed the tension between them. He knew nothing had happened between them—no serious arguments or even apparent disagreements. Their personalities melded like oil and water, and since neither of them cared to change, it would just remain awkward.

"Whatever makes you happy," she said dismissively. "I'm running to the store for dinner. Do you need anything?"

"No. I'm happy with whatever you want to make," Jim answered.

"Good answer. You two can go back to—" Gwen rolled her eyes, "—whatever it is you do." She gave the garage and its contents a once over with her gaze before turning to leave.

"Brr," Gabe said as she closed the door.

"What's that supposed to mean?"

"Oh, nothing. Just didn't feel the warmth radiating from her." Gabe went to the fridge and grabbed two beers. He took a large swig of his own as he handed Jim his. "In case you need one as well."

Jim shook off his response. After all, Gabe remained Jim's closest colleague. He had worked as an investigator for two years before Jim took the job. They immediately bonded by sharing cop anecdotes—laughing over the amusing ones and playing judge and jury over the ones they suspected to be urban legends. Hours passed as they performed stakeouts while sipping coffee so that the caffeine would kick in when the stories ran out. Jim couldn't deny that their relationship was becoming more strained in the office. Their project was now essential to the survival of their friendship.

There were other detectives, but their successes didn't sting quite the same way. The others were more than a decade older and had been with the department far longer than either Jim or Gabe. Taking orders from Gabe, a man who should have been Jim's equal, created awkwardness between them, but being sensitive was not how one climbed the corporate ladder.

Jim studied the back of the Cobra CX398A walkie-talkie. Would the secrets to the device reveal themselves when he opened the back? Even if he got it to work, what would they do with the walkie-talkies? Gabe, bored of the new devices, examined the vehicle.

Gwen was right. No wife would expose her plan to kill her husband. No kid was running around with a walkie-talkie devising pranks, especially on a walkie-talkie of this design. Even if Jim got them to work, no trucker with a load of drugs would incriminate himself.

An hour later, after accomplishing little to nothing on their project, Gabe headed home. Jim went back to the table. Gabe had taken one of the useless handsets with him.

It was doubtful his colleague would have any luck getting the old gadget to work. More likely, Gabe wouldn't even try. A rush of embarrassment filled him. Gwen was right, which made this most likely the first time Gabe had ever agreed with his wife. Jim figured he had seen the last of the walkie-talkie.

Chapter 6

Present Day
Patient 541

The journal sits untouched beneath my mattress. The last time I tried to write in it, a crippling migraine forced me to close the pages. Remembering is too difficult, and I cannot see any benefit to recalling the images I had successfully tucked away.

What made me agree to meet with the chaplain on this day, I cannot say. Perhaps it was defeat. Before heading to his borrowed office space, I catch a glimpse of myself in the mirror. My skin is ashen; my eyelids are heavy. I'm surprised the chaplain notices my condition as well.

"You look tired," he says.

I take a seat in front of him and rest my elbows on my knees. Instinctively, I rub my hands through my hair.

"How are you sleeping?" the chaplain asks. I eye him with something close to anger, but he cautiously continues. "Maybe we could see about a prescription that would help you sleep."

I huff out a laugh. "Yeah, chaplain, just a good night's sleep should solve all of my problems."

"Sleep never hurts."

"I take medicine. It doesn't help."

I curse him under my breath and rest my head in my

hands once more. He waits. A dark mood overpowers me, and I clench my jaw so tightly my head aches. Fierce and angry, I gaze at him.

"What are we really doing here?" I ask.

"What do you mean?"

"How can you help me when you haven't seen what I have seen, felt what I've felt? Done what I've done? You can't help. I can rattle on all day about the life of a Marine, but you won't get it."

"You misunderstand my purpose."

"What's your purpose then?"

"My help doesn't come from me understanding you but from you understanding yourself. How did you get where you are today?" The chaplain's voice eases my tension slightly. "When you understand that, sometimes your situation begins to make sense. It's like shining a light in a darkened maze. Without the light, you feel surrounded by darkness. When you illuminate the pain and suffering that created the walls around your inner self, you can better see how to navigate your way out of the maze."

I laugh out loud. "My path to normalcy is that easy."

"I never said it would be easy. The path to self-discovery and forgiveness will be long and difficult, but I believe it is possible."

"You believe?"

"As should you."

I lean back in my chair and study the tree. Moments tick by in silence.

I open the journal and take a deep breath. As I exhale slowly, the words escape into the air.

"Some men join the Marines ready to fight. They look forward to battle like the whole damned war is a 3D

video game. Shane was that kind of person."

I breathe in deep again. As hard as it is, I need to be heard, and the chaplain seems as good a listener as any.

"I think the world would be quite surprised if people knew how easily it came to most of the men. In the moment, anyway. And as much as the world may not agree, where would we be without young men, capable men, willing to fight? Where would we be?"

"Did you want to object? I'm sure everything I say here goes against your teachings."

"We were never promised a world without conflict. In fact, we were promised quite the opposite in this life."

"Why?" I shake my head. "That's bullshit. The whole concept. Why do you devote your life to teaching about a book that pretty much says, 'I created you. Now prepare to suffer'?"

"Would the Bible be more believable to you if it told you your life on Earth would be pain free?"

"It would make more sense if we weren't born to suffer."

"We are born to be joyful, but the darkness in our world makes us forget that. The Bible helps us see through the darkness. It gives us hope."

"Well, I don't have an ounce of hope."

"There is always…"

"Stop." My voice is forceful, and the chaplain straightens in his chair. I close my eyes and breathe in deep, hold the air, and let it out slowly. My heart rate calms and the tension in my body eases. "Let's move on with the story. I'm not sure what I expected when I enlisted. Maybe respect. I could go home and tell people I had become something. I was now a Marine." I push out my chest as I say the words with mock pride. "People respect that, don't they?" I adjust myself in the seat. "I never imagined killing anyone. That sounds crazy, doesn't it? I didn't put two and two together. Marines going to war meant killing people. Any rational human being would understand that death in some way was inevitable in combat. I thought being a Marine equaled being respected, and I needed that. Damn, I needed that so badly I could taste it." I shake my head. "Life showed me how irrational my logic was, didn't it? Who respects me now?"

The chaplain doesn't try to answer my rhetorical questions. He sits back in his seat. His hands are folded in his lap.

I glanced back at the journal pages. For some reason, they make me feel safe. I wouldn't slip. My words were almost rehearsed. Not lies but thought out beforehand. I controlled the conversation this way.

"Kuwait was a dry, lifeless desert. We went to Kuwait for our in-theater processing before heading to Iraq. Despite being lifeless, the environment buzzed with energy as if static bounced in the air we breathed."

I laugh. "Potential energy. Remember learning about that shit in science class. The ball, just sitting there at the top of the hill, has the greatest amount of potential energy. The ball appears lifeless, but it's not, and the environment in Kuwait wasn't a ball. It was more like a bomb waiting to go off. I've never felt such..." I pause and shake my head. "Such a crazy mix of energy."

The chaplain's silence is comforting, like my words get the freedom to leave me without judgment.

"The looming death that awaited us and the silence that comes with waiting combined to form an explosive feeling. We waited. There was so much waiting in the

beginning—cleaning weapons, going through drills, routine jobs.

"I can't deny the similarities between Camp Matilda and a football locker room. So much testosterone and anticipation. Marines talked about shooting Hajis the same way we trash-talked the other team before a game. Parts of it felt...right. My battalion replaced my football team. And sometimes, when I watched my fellow Marines lift weights or toss a football around to pass the time, I believed that only good things would come from my decision to enlist.

"Nighttime was different. I would lie on my cot, stare at the tent walls, and listen to the wind whip against the canvas. Occasionally, I could hear one of the men snore or mumble in his sleep, but mostly all I heard was the constant wind. The sound was eerie as shit. Home was so far away that it felt like it was on a different planet."

A somberness came over me as I remembered those nights.

"Sometimes, I even wondered why I left home. At times, I missed my mother, even though I'm pretty sure we hated each other by the time I walked out her door."

My hands grip the journal so tightly that my knuckles turn white. I force myself to relax and take a deep breath. As I breathe out, my body relaxes, and I return to my story.

"Sometimes, a massive gust would lift the sides of the tent, and the sand would blast in on us. We all ran outside and hammered in the tent posts that had pulled out of the dry ground. We couldn't see a thing in the dark, not to mention the cloud of dust caused by the wind. Our mouths filled with sand until we gagged. I was so

sick of sand, and I hadn't even seen a battle."

Again, I pause, remembering too clearly.

"You could barely find a blade of grass. The whole damn place seemed lifeless...except for the camel spiders. Rumor had it they were a foot long and could run twenty-five miles an hour. I never actually saw one. Come to think of it, I never met anyone who claimed to have seen one, but the rumor spread through the crowd like ghost stories at summer camp. Most likely, that's all they were, just tall tales. Stressed minds were prone to exaggeration."

I stall a moment, letting the memory replay in my mind.

"Still, I didn't care to encounter one. All those threats of giant camel spiders crawling into my blankets, and now I hear they're no more harmful than scorpions."

I shake my head.

"Like we didn't have enough shit to worry about, someone had to make up alien-like arachnid stories."

My mind shifts from my own story as I suddenly become curious about the man listening to my every word. "Have you ever been hated, chaplain? I mean, really hated, to the point that someone would celebrate putting a bullet through your skull. Now that can really keep a man up at night. That much hatred makes a place seem desolate."

The chaplain locked gazes with me but did not answer.

"Being hunted by not so much a man, but an emotion, is a terrifying thing, chaplain. And in the places where I traveled, the hatred was thicker than dust clouds. All that hatred, well, it was going to change us no matter how much we tried to deny it to ourselves."

****

2018
Jim

Gwen entered the kitchen and tossed the mail onto the counter. "We forgot to get this yesterday. There's something in there for you." Jim half listened. How flushed her face appeared. She looked as if she had run home.

A playful grin lifted his lips. "How heavy is one grocery bag?" Jim asked.

"Nothing I can't handle, my dear."

"Are you okay? You were gone awhile for one bag of groceries."

"My mom called. I know how you hate to hear us ramble on about family crises, so I decided to finish the call before coming home."

"I don't recall complaining about you talking to your mother."

"Come on, Jim. Your eye rolls say it all."

Gwen started pulling groceries out of the canvas tote. Shrimp and cauliflower rice, along with a big bag of cheese. She would be burying his vegetables with dairy again, trying to get him to eat healthier.

Jim eyed his wife suspiciously while she pulled out a pan and plopped the bag of frozen vegetables into the microwave.

"You're probably right. No need to get your husband involved with all that drama."

Gwen smiled over her shoulder. "You're asking for it with your sarcastic remarks. Next time, I'm going to wait and speak to her when you're watching whatever sport you're favoring at the moment."

Jim let out a small laugh. "Touché." And then added, "Can I open some wine?"

"Chardonnay. Heavy pour, please."

"On it." Jim went to the wine fridge and pulled out a random bottle of her choosing. He never knew good wine from bad but figured if she had bought it, she would like it.

"Did you have a nice time with Gabe?"

"Fine. Nothing as interesting as family issues and grocery shopping."

"What a shame. And Gabe always seems like such a treat to be around."

"What do you two have against each other?"

"I can't quite say, honestly, besides the fact he makes me feel, I don't know, judged maybe."

"What would he have to judge you for?" Jim poured the wine and handed his wife the glass. "Why would you care what he thinks anyway?"

"Exactly. Why would I care what he thinks of me?" She took the wine and kissed Jim on the cheek before returning to putting groceries away.

Dinner conversation dragged painfully. What detail of Jim and Gwen's lives could they rehash if only to rid them of the silence that lingered between them? Shouldn't life give them enough fresh material to carry them through a measly meal?

"So, did the walkie-talkies work?"

Jim appreciated the effort.

"Not yet. We were busy on our project today." Even Jim knew how ridiculous he sounded. Same story every day. He cleared his throat and winked at his wife. "How about we have some me-and-you time after dinner?"

"Okay." Gwen ate another shrimp while glancing down at a text.

Jim emptied his wine glass. When did casual conversation get to be so much work?

Together they cleared the dishes. The clanking of the ceramic plates broke the silence.

"Do you know what sounds great? A bath. Would you mind if I...?"

"Does that mean you're not up for some you-and-me time?"

"Of course I am. Meet me in the bedroom in five. I'll take a bath after, and you can catch up on your sports."

"Sounds good." Jim glanced at the clock. "Five minutes starts now. I'll finish the dishes."

"Okay." Gwen set the drying towel on the counter and headed for their bedroom. Jim watched her leave and rubbed his forehead in exasperation.

After putting the last pan away, he headed to the room. Perhaps Gwen had wanted the five minutes to slip into some lingerie. How long had it been since she wore something besides an old T-shirt to bed? The thought of seeing her wearing the silky garment excited him. Yes. Gwen could very well be thinking they needed a special evening. But when he entered the bedroom, Gwen was seated on the side of their bed, typing on her phone.

"You ready for this?" Jim asked.

"Yes. Just finishing up a work text." She tossed her phone on the nightstand and lay back on the bed. "I'm all yours."

Something told Jim that was anything but the truth, but he smiled anyway. He kicked off his shoes, threw his shirt to the side, and unbuckled his pants. Gwen's phone vibrated. Her gaze didn't shift in that direction, but her expression changed.

"You want to look?"

"Just quickly."

By the time she glanced his way again, she was wearing a smile, and he wasn't wearing anything. He crawled in bed beside her and began kissing her neck. Slowly, their bodies came to life. He touched the spots he had learned she liked, and she did the same. Sex was much like their dinner conversation, uneventful and mundane.

When they had finished, she crawled out of bed and ran the tub water.

"Oh, by the way, my mom wants to have some girl time this next weekend. Mind if I stay at her house? You know, girl time with my mom will involve wine."

Jim threw on some pajama bottoms and a T-shirt.

"You just had girls' night with her Thursday, too."

"That doesn't count. You were at class and wouldn't have seen me anyway." She stepped into the tub and slid into the bubbles. "Plus, that night wasn't wine night. I was giving decorating advice."

"Whatever. Have fun. Maybe I'll do something with your buddy Gabe or catch up on some classwork."

"How's your class going, by the way?"

He knew she didn't care, and he had no desire to waste his time pretending.

"Fine."

Jim headed back downstairs.

Hours later, he crawled into bed beside his wife. He studied Gwen's sleeping profile and listened to her rhythmic, deep breaths until he admitted to himself sleep would not happen yet.

Jim slipped out from between the sheets. He gave Gwen a look over his shoulder. She was sound asleep. He tiptoed down the hallway and headed to the garage. Closing the door behind him, he felt a heavy breath leave his body.

Pulling out his pocketknife, he began carefully prying apart the two sides of the walkie-talkie. The exterior popped open without much effort. Jim half-expected a spider to crawl out of the old relic.

As he studied the device, he thought about his marriage to Gwen. The union and walkie-talkie shared similarities. All the parts were there, they just weren't functioning, and he had no idea how to fix any of it.

A strange air filled the room, and the hairs on his arms rose. Why did he feel like something or someone else was in the room with him? He stared at the dismantled device. Silence penetrated his ears until the nothingness became deafening.

Gwen opened the garage door. Startled, he dropped the pocketknife. He left it at his feet and stared at his wife. She had brought him back to a world where walkie-talkies couldn't grab hold of his mind and drag him to dark places. He should be thankful, but he only felt frustration when he locked gazes with her.

"Jim, what are you doing?"

Jim shook his head as an animal might shoo off buzzing insects.

"You okay? Why did you get out of bed?" she asked.

"Sorry. I couldn't sleep."

As Jim turned from the walkie-talkie, something caught his eye. He glanced back at the instrument, studying the little red light that he could swear was fading. He switched the walkie-talkie back on. Nothing.

Gwen called again. He stared at the light. There was some life to it, he was sure.

"Jim." Irritation replaced the sleepiness in her voice.

"Coming," he called back, hiding his annoyance.

He walked by her, his body brushing against hers as she stood in the doorframe. "Didn't realize you would miss me." She followed him silently back to the room. He figured Gwen wanted to keep a close watch on the one she feared she had reason to lose.

Chapter 7

Present Day
Patient 541

Back in my room, I stare at the ceiling and replay the parts of my life that I had shared with the chaplain. I wouldn't see him again until the following week, but the story had already begun to force its way from my mind. I crawl from my bed and search under my mattress until my fingers touch the leather cover of the journal.

The chaplain has scraped away at the shallow grave hiding my memories. Images in my mind explode like minefields now, and the shrapnel needs a target. I'm forced to relive my memories, knowing that I walk through them with the ghosts of the men who didn't see the other side of the war. Are they happier now? They are certainly better off than I am. If only I could trade places with them. I'm sure many of the men who lost their lives would have transitioned back to being a civilian far better than I.

The faces of the men flash before me again: Shane, the man I hated in the chow hall and needed near me in the battle; Toby, the one I sought out in the chow hall and wanted to run from when the first shots were fired. It's Toby I envision as my pen touches the clean white surface of the paper, and I watch as ink words formed by the movement of my fingers fill the next pages.

Toby had light-brown hair and features that had yet to transform from childhood cuteness to masculine toughness. When I looked at him, I could envision his mother's hand wiping melted chocolate from his lips. This child-like characteristic triggered different emotions from different people. Did I want to protect him or kick him for being so damn vulnerable? My feelings wavered from day to day.

Feelings of my own inadequacy undoubtedly fueled the swing of my emotional pendulum. Befriending Toby could be as suicidal to my rank as attaching myself to an anchor before jumping overboard. In the beginning, I needed him. We found a true friendship in the chaos. He became the place where I could expose my fears, where a gentle nod in agreement created what felt like a life-long bond.

For a moment, I was back in the chow hall, eavesdropping on the conversations that took place at Shane's table. Sometimes, after the conversation slipped to inaudible decibels, a few of the Marines would glance our way. Toby and I shared uncomfortable silences before letting the moment disappear.

I would learn that Toby, as I'd suspected, was a momma's boy. His father had run off before Toby was even born. His mother put him into karate classes when she learned he was being bullied, and when he told me his story, I wondered if the ones doing the bullying would have been my friends once I began hiding my own weaknesses behind a football team. I looked across the table and sometimes hated the man who reminded me too much of the person I was trying to hide, the one who cowered in the corner when his father's fists found their target.

Toby asked me one time if anyone had ever bullied me.

I laughed. "Only one person."

"What did you do?"

"I killed him."

Toby laughed. I smiled as I took a forkful of food.

"No, really, how did you handle it?"

Some parts of my life were mine and mine alone. I refused to share, at that time, even with Toby, the one person who would understand.

"He moved away," I lied.

"Lucky you."

"Very lucky." I glanced across the chow hall at the other Marines, laughing at some joke I would never hear. "Your days of being bullied are over now."

Toby looked toward Shane. "Do we ever really get over being bullied?"

"I guess that's up to you, Toby. Stop taking people's shit."

He raised his arm, and we bumped milk cartons. "Here's to not taking shit."

****

Our Master Sergeant, Joel Brady, entered the chow hall with a woman at his side. In my memory, time went into slow motion, and the light illuminated her, creating a halo, but the actual moment wasn't like that at all. Time rushed over it the way it speeds past most moments, making it slip through my fingers, impossible to capture. Her hair was pinned back tight on her head, but I envisioned what the golden locks would look like if they were allowed to flow freely, cascading down her back like a waterfall. I found myself enamored by her high cheekbones and distinctive eyebrows. She was certainly the most beautiful woman I'd seen in months. Perhaps she was the most beautiful woman I had ever seen.

"Men, this is Dee Winters," MSgt Brady announced. "She's an embedded reporter, which means she's going to be the fly on the wall recording all the shit that happens in our battalion." He surveyed the room. "I don't need to spell out what I expect from each of you while she is with us."

I didn't realize I was staring at her until we locked gazes. My gaze darted down to my plate, and when I looked up again, she was smiling at me in a way that said, I saw you.

As I headed to Toby's table the next day, I heard her voice, like chimes dancing in the air.

"There's an open seat here."

Shane stopped speaking to the Marine next to him, and I felt his eyes boring into me. He had the will and ability to make a fool out of me in front of the only female I'd seen in weeks. A trickle of perspiration dripped down my neck, and heat rose from my face. I hoped the redness wasn't apparent, as I focused my gaze on her. I sat, and she introduced herself. I did the same.

"What exactly are you looking to report?" I asked.

"Anything. Everything. The world wants to know the goings-on in the war."

Her words should have triggered cautiousness, but my fellow Marines and I were charmed like snakes lifting their ugly heads out of their baskets, not realizing how, with one blow, those very heads could be chopped off.

Slowly, the conversation between the other Marines began again, and for a while, they forgot about me or acted as if they had. I tried to ingest the powdered mashed potatoes while stealing glimpses at Dee. She picked at her food, laughing when appropriate and giving a verbal jab when necessary.

I forked up another bite—green beans, which had grown cold. Somehow, I had perceived myself as being in a bubble, only wanting to exist as an outsider to their conversation. That was until Dee's laughter softened to a warm smile, and she turned her gaze toward me once again. The two of us existed alone in my bubble until a shift in the air alerted me that something had changed. My gaze drifted toward Shane.

Shane clenched his fist around his fork as if it were a shovel and loaded his mouth with meatloaf. His gaze, demanding attention, bored into mine until his lips lifted into a smirk, arrogant and faint. When I turned my attention back to Dee, she was engaged in a conversation with another Marine.

"Are you ready to see your first battle?" Marshall asked. Marshall was what I envisioned a Marine to be: confident, strong, and loyal. Someone you want on your side when going into battle. Someone you want to emulate. For those reasons, I forgave him for his seeming allegiance to Shane.

His question brought me back to reality, and I slowly turned my attention away from Dee. "Think this battle is going to happen?" I asked, hoping to sound more annoyed with false promises than anxious that the rumors may not be rumors at all.

"It's looking that way. Fallujah remains a beehive for insurgents, despite the last battle. Lots of hot heads getting psyched up over this one." Marshall nodded in Shane's direction. "If you ask me, some people are a bit too eager."

Shane had apparently been listening to our

exchange. "I guess that's what happens when a man trains for a year to fight and finds himself trapped in a camp in the middle of nowhere, listening to the wind blow. It's like caging a pit bull and repeatedly poking him with a stick. At some point, it's going to get ugly."

I took another bite, going through the motions of eating despite the churning anxiety in my gut.

"You're exactly right, my man. Preparing for war is like an emotional walk on a tightrope. If you lose your balance, you lose yourself." Marshall's thoughts appeared to drift to another place. "It happens way too often."

"If I were a betting man, which I am," Shane said with a condescending wink, "I'd say the orders will come through as soon as the votes get tallied. Bush gets reelected, and within days, we'll be kicking some insurgent ass. I hope the civilians are taking the warnings seriously and evacuating Fallujah, kids and all, while they can."

We all knew the orders. Boys twelve and over left in the city would be considered a threat. The last bite of mashed potato I had swallowed fought to come back up. Twelve years old—not even a teenager. And who exactly was checking proof of age in the middle of a battle? Could some nine-year-old children be mistaken for twelve? Who was worse, the father who handed his son a weapon and taught him to kill or the Marine who looked the child in the eye before shooting him? I couldn't help but envision my mother's scornful glare as she warned me once again about the black mark on my soul.

****

2018

Amber

When Amber could not locate Bethany by Saturday afternoon, she made the necessary calls to both Bethany's parents and the police. Two days later, Amber walked into the police station to retell her story as if she had not already recalled every detail during the phone conversation. Standing in the precinct made the situation too real, but given the length of time since Bethany's disappearance, Amber knew she was making the right choice.

After telling the man at the desk her name, an officer led her to a room that looked just like the ones on TV shows. He motioned for her to take a seat. After he left, she scanned the room while she waited. A camera loomed in the corner; Amber suspected each babbling sentence she offered would be recorded. A large mirror covered one wall. Was it a one-way window through which someone watched her?

The door opened, and two officers entered just as she predicted the scene would play out. They both wore slacks and dress shirts. She guessed both men to be in their forties. They were handsome for their age, and she couldn't help but think of Bethany. They would have shared a private smile if she were sitting next to her.

The one in charge introduced himself as Detective Hunter before introducing his partner as Detective Castille. Detective Hunter took a seat across from her while his counterpart leaned against the wall with his arms crossed.

Amber wasn't nervous about being questioned. She wasn't a suspect, after all. Yet the cold, sterile room stirred a sense of guilt that pressed like a stiletto heel in the middle of her chest. Taking a deep breath, she reminded herself the detectives just needed a record of the events as seen by the person closest to the situation.

"Thank you for coming in, Amber." Detective Hunter's voice calmed her. His persona was professional and confident. Hunter's partner was an enigma.

"I called Saturday."

"We know. And we know you went over much of what we will be asking you, but we want to be sure we cover every little detail. You understand?"

"Of course. I'll do whatever I can to find Bethany." Amber's voice cracked, and Detective Castille handed her a box of tissues. Maybe he was kinder than first perceived. "I called Bethany's parents Saturday morning. I thought maybe—I don't know—I don't know all of Bethany's friends. Disappearing isn't typical behavior, but her being at a friend's place seemed as plausible as anything else."

Detective Hunter flipped through some papers in front of him. "It says here some people thought they saw her Friday."

"Yes. Brad, a mutual friend. He thought he had seen her in the back of class Friday morning. I mean, it was a large lecture hall." She wiped the tear from her cheek. "A friend of Brad's confirmed it, to the best of his memory anyway. But then others I asked said she wasn't there. I just kept hoping she would show up."

The detective flipped through the papers again and then looked Amber in the eye. "Did you know the man Bethany was dancing with at the bar?"

Amber shook her head.

"But you left her there."

"Not alone. We had other friends there as well." Her

tone had become defensive, and she tried to calm herself. "The other girls told me she left the bar glowing over the guy. The man from the dance floor walked out behind her, but with her," she added quickly. "He wasn't like stalking her or anything. Our friend Tiffany saw Bethany give her a thumbs up."

"Your friend didn't speak to her when she saw her leaving with a stranger?" Hunter asked.

"No. Tiffany just returned the gesture."

"Could you or your friend identify the man from the dance floor?"

Without looking up at the detectives, Amber shook her head. "He and Bethany were dancing in the corner of the bar. He was wearing a baseball cap. That's all I remember." Amber's hands tightened on themselves. There were more pressing issues than underage drinking, and she needed to be truthful. "We were both pretty drunk."

"Was this typical behavior? Getting drunk and going home with strangers?" asked Hunter.

Guilt overtook her, but again she reminded herself that they needed to know everything. "No, but…" She paused, swallowing hard. "Sometimes it happens. We're in college."

"She never mentioned a name to anyone?" Hunter asked while Castille listened silently.

"I don't think so, and I already told you, I barely saw the man. And I didn't get a chance to talk to her." Amber glanced up into the eyes of Detective Hunter. "Bethany was a good person. She just liked to have fun on occasion."

"We're not here to judge if she was a good person. We're here to find her, and every detail helps," Detective

Hunter said softly. He glanced at his notes. "Could you describe the man you saw to a sketch artist?"

Amber shook her head. "No. Not to be rude, but I think I've made it clear I wouldn't recognize him."

"Some people are surprised by what they remember when the artist starts to form the picture."

Detective Castille spoke again. "When was the next time you saw Bethany?"

"She walked into the room already on the phone call."

"What was her mood when you saw her?" Castille asked.

"She was talking with her father and seemed really agitated."

"Is this why you waited to call her parents?"

"Yes, but also, I didn't want to worry them." Amber glanced down at her hands. "They're having some issues."

"What kind of issues?" Castille asked.

"Her father, well, he's been frustrated with Bethany's partying. He sometimes would call late at night to ensure she was behaving herself. They were fighting on the phone that night. The last thing I heard Bethany say was, 'Then cut me off since you have no faith in me graduating anyway.' "

Amber wiped a tear. "Bethany left the room, and I never saw her again. I can't be sure if she came back to the room. As I said, I had quite a bit to drink. I can't remember." Then, she began to cry, and both detectives allowed her a few minutes. "When I called her parents Saturday, and they had no idea where she was, I knew it was time to get help." The crying turned to sobs. "What if I waited too long? What if it's too late?"

Chapter 8

Present Day
Patient 541

The headaches are coming back. The more I think about Dee, the more gut-wrenching images of my time in the Middle East rise to the surface. Cold sweats interrupt my nights of sleep. I wake to my body jerking as if a bomb has exploded nearby. The prescription for my PTSD does nothing but make matters worse. The nurses remind me that loss of appetite and sweating can be side effects of the drug, but I know from where my symptoms come—my memories.

The recollections that I am reliving that are keeping me up at night are not even the memories that I need to be concerned about according to the law. My horrific memories of war are all just a part of being a Marine. They don't make a person a criminal, but they can make him too crazy to stand trial. Isn't that what the doctor said about me—Not Guilty by Reason of Insanity, better known as NGI? They spoke of PTSD and dissociative episodes.

All stuff I don't care a thing about. My life is over. I left the war, but the war has continued in my mind. In Iraq, I was expected to kill. I thought I could transition back to civilian life. I thought I would be respected. But what I did when I came back home is what the world will never forget about me.

****

Six months have passed since I entered the Jacksonville Psychiatric Facility. Knowing I would be evaluated today has not helped my sleep or headaches. I will sit in front of people paid to declare me fit for the world or still a danger to society. I'm not ready. This fact should be evident to professionals used to dealing with insane people, but just in case, I didn't intend to make anyone contemplate releasing me into a world that should and would destroy me.

I enter a room that appears like a small cafeteria. The only furniture is a ten-foot table and three chairs. Two on one side and one on the other side for me. Two men are staring at the papers on the table. I am but a number to them. One of the men scribbles something on a pad before looking over his reading glasses at me.

"Good afternoon," he says.

A typical conversion begins with such greetings. Will I ever greet someone in such a way again? Will I ever pass someone on the street, smile, and offer a greeting? The fact that I will most likely never partake in a trivial exchange again slams into me like a sledgehammer. Was I even a part of humanity anymore, or have I been pulled out and thrown in the junkyard? I know the answer. I take my seat without responding.

"How are you sleeping?" he asked.

"Like a baby." My sarcasm was not lost on him.

He nodded in a way that said, "Okay then, be that way."

"I've been told you're keeping a journal."

"And I've been told it's none of your business."

Again, he scribbled on his notepad. My tone had

served its purpose.

"You're correct. You do not need to share what you write in the journal, but for me to properly assess whether you are ready for the outside world, you will need to speak to me to some degree."

"Sorry. Not today."

We stare at each other until he looks away and scribbles one last note on his pad.

He closes the folder and folds his arms across his chest.

"That will be all then."

I return to the room and pace until I'm dizzy. I need to escape these four walls, but there is nowhere for me to run. The journal is lying on my bed, and when I see it, I freeze. The empty pages are the only place a piece of me can be free. I open the book. I would be the one writing the story, yet I couldn't predict where the words would lead me.

Before beginning, I glance over what I had already written. Surprisingly, the writing has come easy to me. Perhaps, a piece of my father had seeped into my make-up after all. He was so often lost in literature. As a child, I had never understood, but as an adult with secrets, words flowing out of my mind, through a pen, and onto paper were an unexpected lifeline. I push the thoughts of my father out of my mind and begin to write.

Master Sergeant Brady was tense, which meant we were all tense. He knew details we were not privy to, and part of me felt thankful for that. In the weeks prior to Fallujah, an anticipation of something big always hung in the air. I remembered preparing for hurricanes back in Florida—securing any external objects that might blow through a window while my mother stocked up on water, non-perishable foods, and batteries. We would watch as the storm moved over us, our heart rates accelerating as the palm trees bent to unnatural degrees. When the winds subsided, we cleared away debris and rode around, checking out who fared better or worse than the two of us. I wondered, then and now, how something so destructive created excitement. The mind muddled some sensations, I supposed.

In Kuwait's hot, arid air, we Marines passed time working on our Humvees, cleaning weapons, and keeping in shape until we received the orders that we had been waiting for all those weeks. We would leave in the morning and start making our way through Iraq until we made it to Fallujah.

Lance Corporal Shane Martin, Private Toby Urbank, Corporal Marshall Davis, Dee Winters, and I were all in the same Humvee. Over the radio, we referred to ourselves as Victor 3. It meant the third Humvee.

Our battalion loaded into our caravan of Humvees. Marshall, working with the radio, rode in the passenger seat. He was the main man in our vehicle and was referred to as the actual in radio talk. Shane had the turret position, which I had no desire to hold. Controlling the main weapon on the roof of the vehicle, he was exposed more than any of us. Toby drove the Humvee, a job he did in near silence. He insisted he was quiet because he had to focus, but we knew the real reason: Toby was scared shitless. I sat behind Toby, and next to me sat Dee.

As I write the words, images of Dee flash through my mind. My stomach lurches and the pen drops from my hand.

****

2018
Jim

Gwen wasn't home when Jim returned from work. The sound of the keys tossed on the counter echoed through the empty house. Gwen would usually remind him to hang them on the hook. A crockpot meal sat on the counter, and the smell of pot roast wafted through the air. As hungry as he was, he would wait for Gwen. She had warned him she would be running a bit late. Jim shook off the memory of Gabe's accusatory eye rolls—his reaction when Jim had mentioned Gwen would be late.

Maybe Jim should have cared more, but for whatever reason, he didn't. Not really, anyway. Jim had his own hobbies and ambitions that kept him busy. Not to mention, he attended classes at UNF twice a week after work. Jim was slowly working toward the Criminal Justice degree, which Gwen had guilted him into, even though he told himself that advancing his education was his decision and not hers. Truth be told, Jim doubted furthering his degree would help him get noticed. The accomplishment would take a change in karma, some supernatural shift of energy far from his control.

There wasn't a class tonight, and Jim savored the quiet time because soon enough, Gwen would rush in like a gust of wind, disrupting the solitude. Opening the fridge, he found the weird health drinks that Gwen assured him were the reason for her healthy skin and youthfulness. Healthy skin was not his concern, so he closed the door and stepped into his man cave instead.

Jim's small fridge, holding the cold beer he craved, sat in the corner of his garage. Gwen never ventured into his stash but chose instead to ignore his unhealthy habit. "And this is what keeps me young," Jim said aloud as he popped off the bottle top using the opener he had screwed onto the side of his workbench. Jim let the crisp beverage slide down his throat and drown just a bit of his day. He would only have one, maybe two, but he would enjoy every sip.

He scanned the garage, and his gaze settled on the walkie-talkie. Gabe hadn't mentioned the walkie-talkie that day, but they had been busy with the Williams case and interviewing her college roommate. Pulling the stool up to the bench, he set the beer down and picked up the dismantled artifact.

Something had made him buy this ridiculous gem, but what? Jim turned it over in his hands and then noticed one wire, slightly loose. With the smallest of his screwdrivers, he tightened it, slid in new batteries, and closed the walkie-talkie. He switched it on and waited as he took another long swig. Beyond that fix, Jim knew he would need to do some research.

Jim's shoulders slouched as his body released a sigh it had held all day, and that's when the green light flickered for a moment before staying lit. Jim's eyebrows rose, and a small smile played at the corners of his lips. *Maybe I have something here.* He picked up the walkie-talkie and adjusted the dials. Static. More static. Then a voice mixed in with the confusion of white noise. "Gabe?" Jim asked into the device. Silence followed. Then he heard a whisper of a voice again. Female, he believed.

"I can hear you. Who am I speaking with?" Jim shouted into the relic, not worrying about using accurate lingo over the airwaves.

Jim believed he heard "Bett," but the reply was so choppy he couldn't be sure.

"Come again, I can't hear you." If he adjusted the dials, he could lose the voice altogether.

"Bette Williams," the female voice said faintly.

"Did you say Bett Williams?" Jim's heart raced with childish excitement. He had contacted someone, and, at that moment, he found the excitement well worth the five dollars he had thrown away at the flea market.

"E Williams," the voice said again.

"Not Bett?"

Then quite clearly, the voice said, "Bethany."

The hairs rose on his arms. "Bethany Williams?" he asked.

"You need to find me."

But how would Bethany Williams, the missing college student, be communicating with him on his walkie-talkie? How would she even know he had it? He tried to calm his racing heart while all the possibilities consumed his mind. His thoughts reverted to the man he'd bought the walkie-talkie from and the strange feelings that had overwhelmed him as he walked away from the table. Something about that guy had creeped him out. Could he be involved? The man knew Jim had the walkie-talkie. What else could he know about him?

What were the chances the flea market man was her kidnapper? Could he be forcing her to speak into the walkie-talkie? Why would he draw Jim in this way?

Jim shook his head at his paranoia. The mysterious voice had to be part of a prank. Would Gabe be that callous?

He decided to go along with the prank. He'd keep his emotions light so when the joke was over, the humiliation wouldn't sting quite as badly.

"Where are you?"

"In the woods…" The rest was lost in static.

"In what woods?"

There were words he could not hear, and then, "near the fields…"

"Why don't you just come out?" Jim shook his head in annoyance. He took a swig of beer and slammed the bottle back on the table while envisioning Gabe at the other end and perhaps his wife, Susan, laughing beside him. Jim heard only silence. But what if the voice wasn't Susan? Still silence. "Bethany, why don't you just come out of the woods?" Jim's tone was serious but not panicked.

A long silence. Just as Jim was about to give up, the voice of a young woman said, "Because he killed me."

Chapter 9

Present Day
Patient 541

After dinner, the urge to keep writing overtook me and I retrieved the pen that had rolled beneath the bed. For a moment, the tip froze against the paper, and then the words began to flow again.

For a while, the adrenaline pulsed through us, and we were entertained as we headed out on our journey. Then days passed when we saw nothing except sand. We sang, we busted on each other, and Shane shouted down comments about hunting Hajis like he was on a safari. Marshall ignored him for the most part, but occasionally, Marshall would tone him down if he found him offensive enough. Toby, on the other hand, showed his displeasure physically. From the back seat, I watched as his neck turned shades of red.

In the beginning, the situations appeared like tests. Was I tough enough to survive in Iraq? We were at war in a foreign country. Sitting in that Humvee, weighing the possibilities of survival, I put my bet on Shane returning home unscarred in both mind and body. As for his soul, only God knew that. Marshall was leaving with a medal, well-deserved by anyone's account. Toby, well, Toby should have never come, and if I prayed for anything, it was for Toby. Sometimes, when I listened to him talk, my mind drifted from his words, and I wondered how his death would happen. I envisioned him a corpse in the desert sand.

Everything came down to survival. To survive, I did what I needed to do. I gravitated toward the ones I thought could lead me out of hell in one piece. I joined the hunting safari. I searched for wild beasts lurking in the sands. They could destroy all of us if we were not able to destroy them first.

I remember the first bodies we passed, lying on the side of the road, discarded and forgotten. Even Shane went silent. Not for long, but he did go quiet. Then an internal instinct kicked in for us. We could either be sucked into a dark hole or start sputtering out enough hatred that nothing could touch us. Our words became our shields. Shane led in the efforts, and I followed suit.

Dee watched me. Me more than any of them. She was always scribbling on her damn pad. Sometimes I would stop and ask her if she got all that or needed me to repeat anything. "No. I got what I needed." Her gaze bored into mine. I wondered if she saw me hiding in there. I wondered if it's why she was so disgusted by my actions and words.

Still, I envision Dee's crystal blue eyes judging me. Writing about her is like pushing on a bruise. The sensation is painful and pleasant at the same time. Dee's judgment stung more than any other consequence, more than standing in the courtroom listening to the cries of the victims' families.

But if I searched beyond the judgment in Dee's crystal blue gaze, I swore I saw a piece of heaven. Maybe that's why I always looked away quickly. Something about her eyes burned. They never stopped staring into mine, though.

The desert passed by outside. One sand dune after another. My head bobbed against the window of the Humvee, but eventually, my mind gave way to sleep. My dreams were turning into nightmares. Images of corpses slapped my unconscious mind until it could no longer resist the urge to allow them to play like a movie reel. It seemed only a short time had passed before a bump jolted me awake. I rubbed my eyes to force out my subconscious nightmares. The sun shone in through the window, giving Dee a halo.

"Well, good morning," Dee said.

"What did I miss?"

"Sand dunes." Dee smiled at me, making something inside of me dance.

I looked out the window. "Well, lucky for me, there are a few more dunes left to see."

We drove for hours, singing, searching the sand with glazed-over eyes, dreaming of home-cooked meals served in warm kitchens. Our guard was down. The problem with letting down our guard was that no one was aware of the fact until the lead Humvee lifted off the ground in an explosion of dust and flames. Yet, we were far from Fallujah, far from the battle that was our destination.

Chaos followed. Some Marines ran to the burning vehicle. I grabbed my weapon and ran to a dune, not only for protection but to destroy any threats. Several Marines were already scanning the horizon. In the desert heat, the air danced above the surface of the sand and played tricks on our eyes. Instead of sand, I saw the flowing garments of the insurgents, but when I blinked, the images disappeared. The bomb that took out my fellow Marines had been set long before. The enemy was long gone.

I avoided the vehicle until we were told to head back to our Humvees and move. Inside my mind, I screamed not to look. I begged myself. But when we passed, I stared at the unrecognizable corpses. A piece of me stayed there in that vehicle for weeks to come. Slowly, I would recall those images, and they would become a part of me again like puzzle pieces chewed by the family dog and found under the coffee table. They were the pieces that one might hold in one's hand and wonder if they should be tossed or salvaged. I salvaged them. I put the broken pieces of myself where I thought they should go and slammed my fist into them until they fit.

****

The nurse shows up at my door while I sit staring at the ceiling, trying to erase the memory.

"Chaplain Gregory is here if you would like to visit." Strands of gray shine amongst her dark hair. She has worked the day shift since the beginning of my stay here.

"Why not?" I say as I lift myself from the bed.

"He's a good man. I think talking to him is a smart choice."

I don't respond.

"Your other visitor came by again. Are you sure you don't want to meet with him?"

"Positive."

She nods, and we walk down the hall together.

Talking about myself, my feelings, is too much today. I couldn't think about corpses and death while attempting to analyze myself. Even killers need a reprieve from the self-centered world they create for themselves. Time to discuss someone else.

"Toby was unraveling." The chaplain looks up from his notebook, most likely surprised by my curt beginning. "We all saw it, but being a little crazy…well, let's just say, sometimes I envied him."

"Forgive me for not remembering each name. Toby is…?"

I stare at the chaplain for a moment. How much had I told him, and how much had I written in my journal? I recap my story, sharing what is important. Who is who? Where did they sit? I leave out my emotions and feelings about Dee.

"When you say unravel, what do you mean?" the chaplain asks.

"His big boy armor, if he'd had any at all, shed off him. He cried at night. Bawled: I mean, literal sobs." I shake my head at the memory. "He dug his foxhole away from the group so we couldn't hear him, but we did." A sickening chill runs up my spine as if I were back in that desert, staring up at the sky from my own foxhole and holding back sobs of my own just so I could bust on him in the morning. I wouldn't share that part with the chaplain.

"What do you mean by foxhole?"

"We dug holes—we called them foxholes—to sleep in at night. They were shallow but deep enough that if a bomb went off nearby, the debris might fly over us and not through us. Some guys slept under the vehicles, but even under the camo, they were targets. Not to mention, Humvees can sink in the soft sand. You don't want to be under them when they do."

"Did Toby talk to you about his fears?"

"No. Toby wasn't talking much to anyone by this

point. I'm sure he felt I had somehow betrayed our friendship by avoiding him, but what choice did I have? Toby's weakness was dangerous."

Toby's face—I couldn't get it out of my mind. When no one was looking, he'd glance sideways at me with sad, pathetic eyes. His gaze once begged me to return to him as a friend. He wanted me to understand his fear. After a while, his hurt expression changed to one of anger, and my animosity toward him grew as well. "Our friendship officially ended when things got real out there. But we were still Marines. We still had each other's backs."

"Tell me more about Fallujah."

"Fallujah. Hell, we weren't anywhere near Fallujah yet. We were just fighting our way across the desert. Driving through cities with snipers shooting from hidden places wasn't even considered being in battle. We were just taking fire as we journeyed to our destination. The whole damn country looked like a bomb had gone off in it. Bodies lay on the side of the road, bombs lit up the night sky, buildings were exploding, and we weren't near Fallujah."

"Were you scared?" The chaplain paused, perhaps realizing his stupidity. I glared at him in case he hadn't. "Sorry. I guess the answer should be obvious."

For whatever reason, I give the man's ignorance a break. "You know, maybe your question wasn't as stupid as you think. Marines talked about the white noise." How can I explain it to this man? He waits. "When too many emotions fill your mind, it's like you feel nothing." I breathe in deeply so that I feel my lungs stretch to their limit before letting the air seep out. "At times, I felt nothing, heard nothing, thought nothing. My mind was full of white noise." I envision Toby's face again. "Maybe that was what made Toby crack. The thoughts crept into his brain, and he couldn't block them out. His mind never gave him the gift of nothingness.

"The other Marines were becoming brutal. I'm sure Toby heard some of the comments. Marshall tried to protect him. 'He's just green. Give him a chance,' he would say. 'Chance?' Shane would answer. 'His kind of weakness will get one of us killed. His father probably forced him to enlist to make a man out of him. The sad part is he'll probably make it out of this shit hole by hiding behind our corpses.'

"I didn't tell them Toby didn't have a father." When I say these words, an old pity creeps in for the person I deserted. "Shane was relentless. From his position at the turret, he saw it all. He would yell down to Toby, 'You see that Haji? His head…' I'll spare you the gory details. But Shane never missed an opportunity. Toby was driving. He could see it all without anyone pointing out a thing, but Shane was Shane, and he knew how to pour salt into the wounds."

"What did you say when Shane reacted this way?"

"Now, you sound like my mother." I can't resist laughing at the image of my mother reacting to the brutality I'd witnessed and trying to make right the impossible. "What do you think I said? I went along with Shane. I couldn't be weak. I couldn't fail like Toby."

"And what did the reporter say?"

"Dee? Oh, she didn't say much when things got rough. At least not in the beginning." I try to remember Dee in the early days. "Starting out, she handled herself pretty well when the corpses lined the roads or when the bombs went off, so close the vibrations shook our vehicle. But then again, when I was shooting at insurgents from my window, I didn't focus on her."

"Tell me more about Dee. I'm sure she didn't just sit quietly the whole time."

"Oh, no, she could give some shit back. That was in the beginning when she was trying to play her part. I think she went to Iraq believing she could be a war journalist. The façade quickly faded though, and we were left with…well, she changed, put it that way."

"It was probably tough for her being in a strange country surrounded by men."

"I'm sure, but we were on strict orders to be appropriate. There weren't many women around, for sure, and even fewer good-looking ones. I can't remember if I've mentioned it, but Dee was far above normal regarding looks. The woman was a ten. There'd be hell to pay if we were caught saying anything about her. She never complained to anyone, but she had to have heard the comments, despite our orders."

"Did you mind the fact that Dee rode in your vehicle?"

"It didn't bother me. Especially when she attempted to be one of the men." There was truth in what I said. She was one of the guys when she needed to be. But in many ways, she wasn't at all like us. She ducked when she heard gunfire. She peed in the dunes, ate out of bags with her hands, dripped sweat under her Kevlar. But death was not funny to her. Crude jokes about Iraqis made her cringe. She didn't speak out or complain, but her quietness—like Toby's—spoke volumes.

I glance at the chaplain and contemplate sharing a morsel of one story. Maybe the first one, the first time I dared to hope she cared about me, too. In the end, the memory of the night is too treasured to share with anyone.

Dee, eating from one of the little bags that contained our food, was leaning on the tire of the Humvee. I'm not sure what got into me. Maybe I acted because she looked so lonely. But I went over to her and took a seat. At first, she was silent. I was pretty sure she didn't care for me, but it didn't stop me. In fact, the idea of her not liking me encouraged me. She didn't know me. Not the real me, and I didn't feel she had the correct information to make that judgment.

Once I was sure she wasn't going to stand and leave, I spoke some cheesy words like, "You can't see stars like this back home."

She didn't respond for several moments, and I almost stood to leave. But then, she asked, "And where's home?" I told her, and we ended up sharing all sorts of details about ourselves. My mind drifted back, not just remembering our conversation, but the feel of the desert air, the smell of sweat, natural and raw, untouched by perfumes. Her shoulder rested against mine lightly enough that the contact could be considered accidental. She'd grown up in Buffalo, so naturally, I bashed the Bills. When I ripped apart her favorite team, she nudged my arm in a girlish way. The reaction was genuine and exhilarating. She had let down her guard, if only for a moment.

How could I, even if I wanted to, explain to the chaplain the transition that had taken place inside of me with each word spoken? Even if I could print out a transcript of my conversation with Dee, the mystery would remain because the magic wasn't in the words; the magic was between them. Energy circled between us, bonding us together in an invisible web.

A small smudge of frosting hung from Dee's lip. I built up the courage to brush it away with my finger. She laughed, and I heard a hint of embarrassment. As her laughter dissipated into the night air, we locked gazes. At that moment, when the moon reflected off her crystal blue eyes, I was happier than I had ever been in my life.

What started that night under the stars sparked embers that grew in intensity over the weeks. Or at least I hoped she too had noticed the tiny threads being spun as we'd sat beside each other in the back seat of the Humvee.

Sometimes, I wondered how life would have been different if Shane had been positioned beside Dee in the backseat and I had manned the turret. Would Shane have shrunk under her gaze? Would he have chosen to sit beside her that night? Because long before I decided to sit under the stars next to Dee, a feeling had emerged. I had only acted on it.

I refuse to share the moment under the stars with the chaplain despite the awkward silence in the room. I want to savor what happened, not give away the slightest piece of it by allowing someone else into the memory. Not just because of my possessiveness or that I am ashamed to admit I was in love with Dee Winters. I don't want to share the beginning because I know the ending.

* * * *

2018

Jim

The sun had set hours ago, and as was their typical routine, Jim and Gwen brushed and flossed their teeth. Gwen applied what seemed like an exorbitant number of serums while Jim splashed cold water on his face. She was rambling on about something, and all Jim could hope for was that she wouldn't quiz him later, or worse, he would fail the test by showing up tomorrow without the dry cleaning or some must-have ingredient for dinner.

"Don't you agree?" Gwen's voice broke through the mental fog.

"Sure," Jim mumbled, but in truth, the only voice he could hear was that of Bethany Williams, begging to be found.

"Sure? Are you serious?" There was the dreaded silence, and without even looking behind him, Jim knew Gwen was staring at him. One hand would be placed on her hip, and her perfect face would be set in a grimace.

Jim sighed. "To be honest, Gwen, I couldn't hear you over the water."

She turned her back toward her mirror, dabbed on one more cream, and with a huff, walked off toward their bed.

"Sometimes, I wonder if you ever listen to a thing I say. Your mind is always out in that garage, mentally tinkering with some broken-down piece of garbage. How about you try fixing this?" She waved her hands frantically, pointing at him and then her.

"I didn't realize that this"—Jim repeated the hand motion—"was so broken." The lie seemed better than the acknowledgment of the truth. The truth would lead to further discussion, which would end badly for both of them.

Gwen mumbled words Jim was happy not to hear and then crawled into bed, turning her back to him with another exaggerated huff.

Women were a mystery to Jim. He recognized the

need to pretend he understood them, yet he swore they spoke an entirely different language. He crawled into bed next to his wife and attempted to translate his language into hers. He wrapped his arms around her, whispering he was sorry into her ear. After Jim had inflated the spirit he had somehow sucked out of her, he let his hand brush her arm.

He was sure the chill bumps had formed on her skin without permission, evidence that his charm was working despite how much she resented him. Lightly, he lifted her nightshirt, and his hand drifted to all the places that fixed what was broken. Jim understood the same act was perceived quite differently by the two of them, but both would end up satisfied. What else mattered?

Jim kissed her softly and told her how beautiful she looked. "You're the sexiest woman I've ever seen," he whispered, just loudly enough for her to hear above her own gasps. From experience, Jim had learned his statement was one of her favorites. She rolled over and kissed him back, doing to him tricks she had learned worked as well. When he was sure the job was complete by both their standards, he kissed her on the forehead and rolled over.

Gwen fell asleep within minutes, but Jim tossed and turned. What he wanted to do was go back down to the garage to get clarification about Bethany's message to him, but somehow, he knew the attempt would be futile. Occasionally, Jim would awaken, so there was evidence that he too had drifted off, but more often, hoping to find answers to the nagging question, he studied the ceiling. There was more than one possible yet bizarre reason why a voice, pretending to be Bethany's, had spoken to him through his walkie-talkie, but one thing was for sure: the situation demanded investigation.

Gwen moaned in her sleep. Jim looked over at her, watching her intently. He expected a name to drift from her sleeping state into reality. Jim almost wished it to happen. At least then, he would know the enemy lurking between them. Through his years on the job, how many crimes had begun from problems in the home? A surprising number. Love twisted and transformed into an ugly creature too often. Is that what was happening? Was Gwen trying to make him go crazy?

Then there was Gabe. He had the other walkie-talkie. Gabe had a motive. He wanted to remain lead detective on the cases. If Jim got promoted when he finished his degree, that would change.

Investigators had searched the wooded area all day yet had not turned up anything. If the mysterious woman knew there was a body in the woods, had she helped put it there? Was Jim being set up somehow? The only fact Jim believed was that he couldn't trust anyone right now.

****

The following day, Jim plodded into the kitchen. His sleepless night had left him feeling lethargic. Gwen met him with a kiss on the cheek and handed him his cup of black coffee. Last night had done the trick. She was cured.

"Did I hear you tossing in your sleep?" Gwen asked while pouring egg whites into the pan on the stove.

"Yeah, lots on my mind."

"Want to share?" Her toast popped up. She placed it on the plate while continuing to scramble the egg. She then meticulously spread avocado across her toast, making sure she covered every crevice. Jim went to the pantry and grabbed the processed cereal he ate even though Gwen's breakfast looked appetizing. Gwen looked at the box and then at Jim. He tossed her a smile she managed to return.

Jim considered his thoughts from the night before. They seemed foolish in the light of day. "The missing college student. I just don't think it's going to end well," Jim said, cutting off any nutritional advice she was about to administer.

"It's such a shame. So young. Have the investigators searched the entire area already?"

Jim looked at his wife. Her back faced him as she dished up her meal. Had she said the word *entire* with emphasis? He shook off the paranoia. "The men searched all day yesterday."

"Were you out there?"

"No, we were interviewing the roommate." Jim took a large bite of cereal and spoke while chewing. "We've got some more people coming in today."

"You should go out there, too."

Jim privately grimaced. He hated when Gwen acted as if she understood anything about his work. Work was the one place where Gwen should have no say, but speaking these words would be a mistake. Instead, he clenched his spoon a bit tighter.

"If I'm assigned to interviewing people, then that's what I need to do."

"Well…"

After shoveling in a few last bites, Jim stood and dropped his bowl into the sink, knowing Gwen would sigh, think some derogatory thought, and then place it neatly in the dishwasher. "I need to get going. Maybe they'll get us out there later in the day." He gave her a routine kiss on her cheek and turned to leave.

Gwen grabbed his arm. "I'm sorry, Jim. I didn't mean to overstep my bounds." Her gaze was warm and kind. Jim couldn't look away. "I really don't want to fight," she added.

"You're not overstepping, Gwen." Jim forced a smile and gave another quick kiss on the cheek. "I'll see you at dinner. I'll fill you in then." Jim grabbed the keys off the key rack.

"I love you."

Jim responded by kissing her forehead. He thought of her soft eyes, staring into him, and for a moment, he longed to go back and look at them one more time. "I love you, too," he whispered as he backed down the driveway. But no one was there to hear his words.

Chapter 10

Present Day
Patient 541

The walls in my room are bare and white. My nightmares repeatedly play throughout the night as if my mind was a movie screen. Only tonight, with lingering thoughts of Dee—the Dee from before my fall—the memories tiptoe into my mind like a fawn might emerge from a forest, and I, for the first time in forever, allow myself to enjoy them.

After our night conversing under the stars, after I brushed my finger across her lips to remove the frosting, we crept closer to crossing the boundaries between Marine and reporter. The endless hours spent driving through the barren Iraqi land left us with voids of time to fill. We had our favorite go-to songs we belted out. Sometimes, the four of us Marines sang together, and other times only one man's voice could be heard, trying to be louder than the voice in his mind. But my favorite moments were when Dee sang along to the song, *I Like Big Butts*. Her smile and laughter filled me to combustible levels. From the front seat, Marshall and Toby could not see how our gazes locked on each other. They couldn't feel the energy between us rising to the surface and making me burn with a desire I had never experienced. The last words of the lyrics would linger in the air, drifting from the vehicle and take the mood of the moment with them, but Dee and I would still be staring at each other, transported to a place where explosions were not the background music to our story.

When we approached towns where sniper gunfire showered down on us from the crumbling buildings, I thought of Dee, positioned by the Humvee window, armed only with a pen and paper. My fighting had a purpose I had never expected to find amid the war. I had someone to protect, love, and envision a life with after all this hell was behind us. She made me believe I could be someone worth loving. When Shane shouted about hitting his targets as if he were playing a video game with computerized victims, Dee gently pressed her hand upon my thigh. I told myself her action was one of support as I pulled the trigger and took out my next target, yet something within me died with each victim. Her presence forced me to feel my actions. She kept one part of me in the world in which I sent bullets through the skulls of men I had never met. She made me feel the pain and guilt while keeping me grounded at the same time.

When the skies darkened, we stopped for the night. Minor gunfire sounded off in the distance as we pulled the camouflage netting over our vehicles. Only after securing the site did we tear into our bags of food. Dee was sitting alone. I considered sitting with her, but something told me that she needed space. When I looked away, I noticed Toby watching me. He was aware of the change that was happening. The quiet ones were always more aware of unspoken languages. Instead of blabbering on, they observed the nuances between people.

I wasn't surprised when Toby came over and sat

next to me, even though he had stopped doing such things long ago. He plopped down, and for a bit, he remained silent, as did I. Some of the guys grabbed a football and tossed it around in the moonlight. Part of me wanted to jump up and join them. As if I were a boy sitting outside the principal's office, Toby's proximity unsettled me. And in that same way, I knew I needed to stay put rather than try to escape the conversation that was sure to come.

I washed down a bit of food before it could stick in my dry throat. Without looking in my direction, Toby said, "You know your little thing with Dee is going to end badly, don't you?"

"There is no little thing with Dee."

"If you get caught, there's going to be consequences. No one was to cross a line with her. You know that."

"As I said, there is no little thing with Dee."

"For God's sake, it's so obvious." Gunfire breaks out somewhere in the far distance. Neither one of us flinches; the sound has become too common. "I can't say I mind it. At least I see a bit of the old you again. The one who had some soul."

As if on cue, the chaplain passed by, looking for the few men seeking his service. I dug into my bag, looking for food remnants, avoiding all eye contact.

"What the hell, Toby," I muttered. "We're in the middle of a war. We all left our souls at home, man. That's what you don't get. If you brought yours with you, then you had better prepare to lose it."

Toby stood. "And that, my friend, is why you and Dee don't stand a chance."

With our last drops of energy, we all dug our

foxholes before collapsing into the dirt shields. In a show of power, Dee generally dug her own. She would select a spot off to the edge of our makeshift camp but not too far. This night, I awoke to the sound of the earth crunching as her shovel punched into it. Forcing my eyes open, I saw Dee. Her silhouette in the moonlight hovered above me. I watched the strands of hair, which had freed themselves from her bun, as they swayed with her movements. My body ached, and my eyes struggled to stay open despite my surprise to find her beside me. I watched for a short time as if she were a dream, which seemed far more possible than the reality before me.

"Need some help?" My voice sounded gravelly.

"You sleep. I've got this," Dee answered. I sat up and began pushing into the dirt, hoping it would support my decision to stand. "I said I've got this. Go back to sleep."

"Now, what kind of Marine would I be if I let you dig your own hole?"

"A tired one." Her tone was determined. "Not to mention, I would prefer not to draw attention to my hole's location."

My tired mind struggled to find the correct response. Dee shoveled out three more large heaps of dirt. "Can I ask why you chose this spot?"

She tossed out another heap. "Does my closeness offend you?"

"Quite the contrary. It couldn't make me happier."

Dee flashed me a smile I could hardly capture in the dim light. She took out one final load and then rested her arm on the handle of the shovel. "I think that should do it." She walked away for a moment, presumably to return the shovel, and then eased herself into her hole. She was so close that I heard her breath, still a bit heavy from shoveling. For several minutes, I stared up at the starry sky, listening to the rhythmic sound of her breathing. Slowly, it softened, and I wondered if she had drifted off to sleep. Then her whispered voice broke the near silence. "Do you think I could hold your hand?" A tear formed in the corner of my eye, surprising me with its appearance.

"That would probably be okay." Our hands found each other. The softness of her skin was broken with fresh callouses. My fingers touched them as if they were wounds I could heal. What did Toby know? Nothing. How could he possibly understand my desperate need to hold her fragile hand in mine as I settled into a hole somewhere between life and death? I intertwined my fingers with hers. Only moments passed before sleep took me away from the heaven that had settled in a land where evil waited to destroy us.

****

2018
Jim

When Jim arrived at the office, Gabe was already busy at work. Over his computer, he gave Jim a quick glance. "Bethany's parents will be here within the hour. Her classmate, Brad Jennings, will be in shortly after that."

Jim cursed himself for having a second cup of coffee and giving Gabe a head start. "You could have shot me a heads-up on the walkie-talkie." As he said the words, Jim laughed light-heartedly, but he also watched for any reaction when mentioning his gift. Gabe raised an eyebrow at him, but otherwise, his response was unreadable. He continued to type. "What do you think of coming over later to work on the walkie-talkies?" Jim added. "Maybe we can get them working."

Gabe typed for a few more seconds before pushing back in his chair and looking directly at Jim. "You know, I think mine is working fine."

"You got it working?" Jim said with more interest than he'd intended.

"Yeah," Gabe answered dismissively, avoiding eye contact. His behavior seemed strange. Distant. "Bethany's parents will be here soon."

"You've made mention of that." Jim studied his partner. "What's up, Gabe?"

"What do you mean?"

"You seem off." Jim sat back in his chair, showing he was ready to listen.

"I'm just focused on our two interviews." Gabe looked directly at Jim. "As you should be."

"Doesn't Lieutenant Larsen want a briefing today?"

"I spoke with her this morning. She wants to meet with us again tomorrow. You might want to get in a bit earlier for that."

Jim eyed him suspiciously. "Your boxers too tight today?"

"Just need an extra cup of coffee." Gabe opened another file on his desk. "So, how's your class going?"

"Fine. A couple more to go, and I've got myself another useless piece of paper to hang on my wall."

"I'm not quite sure how useless it will be."

"Larsen say something? Is that what has your panties in a bunch?"

"We've got an interview to prepare for." Gabe headed for the coffee machine. "You need a cup?" he called.

"Sure," Jim said, although he wouldn't need coffee at all. His heart was already racing. Jim realized he had a chance at taking over as lead detective on future cases, but being a contender also made him a threat.

Gabe returned and handed Jim his cup. "Hey, Gabe, I hope this whole…"

"Jim, I'm not concerned. Let's focus on the interview."

"Don't you think we should check out the crime scene?"

"And where exactly is that?" Gabe studied Jim.

"If something happened to Bethany, there's a good chance it happened along her running route."

"Our guys have been searching the area for days. So, again, what crime scene are they overlooking?"

Jim hesitated. "I'm not sure, but if they haven't found her, and something happened to the girl, then they aren't searching in the right area. That's all I'm saying."

"There's still hope that she's okay. Don't you think? But yeah, when we wrap up these interviews, we're heading over to the campus."

Jim shook his head.

"Is everything alright, Jim?"

"Yeah, just something tells me we need to move quicker on this one."

Gabe leaned back in his chair again. "You're a real go-getter today." He sipped his coffee. "We'll get over there by noon, I'm sure."

"That'll have to be good enough."

Ginny Larsen rounded the corner. "The parents are in the interrogation room," she announced. Jim released a long breath and eased the tension the conversation was creating.

Gabe and Jim followed Larsen down the hallway.

Larsen was a twenty-year veteran of investigating. In fact, she could retire if she cared to, but because there was no obvious replacement for her and Larsen loved her job, she continued to show up every day.

Larsen had earned respect in the mid-2000s by solving a serial killer case that had haunted the area for years. She wasn't the type to sit on her laurels, though, and didn't respect others who were not as ferocious in their drive as she considered herself to be. If Jim continued to show up to work half an hour after Gabe, he would never be designated primary investigator on a case.

The three of them entered the interrogation room. Larsen introduced Gabe and Jim to the parents and expressed her sympathy for their situation.

Larsen's matronly appearance could put people at ease when she deemed it necessary. She was of average height, maybe five foot, three inches, with short, wheat-blonde hair, and had a plumpness to her that gave people comfort, as if she was about to sit you down at her kitchen table and offer you a fresh-out-of-the-oven cookie. When she turned her smile your way, the day felt warmer. But that same face could harbor a coldness that often made grown men shiver.

"I'm going to step outside of the room now and let Detective Hunter and Detective Castille take over. You're in good hands, Mr. and Mrs. Williams. We're doing everything we can."

Mrs. Williams was wringing a tissue. Occasionally, she would dab her nose after sniffling. She had yet to make eye contact. Mr. Williams sat with his legs slightly apart, his arms resting on his knees, almost in prayer. There was a distance between them that was undeniable. They suffered alone, without a gentle hand grazing the other's back or reaching to hold onto each other for support. Jim wondered if they had spent the ride over in silence, or instead, one or both had vocalized their judgment. He remembered the roommate describing the last conversation Bethany had with her father. Undoubtedly, the argument between father and daughter had come up in the past few days.

"Let me start by saying that we have people out there looking for Bethany as we speak, Mr. and Mrs. Williams," Gabe said.

Jim expected the typical "please call me" followed by their first names, but the invitation never came. Perhaps they were nervous, but Jim suspected it was something else altogether. He glanced down at the notepad in front of him and saw the names Austin and Paige Williams scribbled in his boss's handwriting.

"Up to this moment, we haven't found any piece of evidence to suspect foul play," Gabe continued.

"Except my daughter is missing," Mr. Williams said with evident frustration.

"Let's go back to the last conversation you had with Bethany."

"I called her. I'm not going to deny it. I was quite angry with her. She has such potential, and she's throwing it away by partying. Now, look what's happened."

Mrs. Williams began openly crying; her tissue was nearly shredded in her hands.

"We don't know yet what has happened." Gabe paused momentarily. "I'm assuming that Bethany was upset after your phone conversation?"

"Yes. The last she said was that she didn't care if I stopped paying her tuition. Then she hung up. She actually hung up on me." Jim could not help but wonder about Mr. Williams's wave of anger, still strong enough to overshadow what should be concern for his child.

"You were screaming at her," Mrs. Williams yelled. She was met by her husband's warning gaze, and she soon focused again on the tissue.

Jim leaned back against the wall, folded his arms in front of him, and studied Mr. Williams. He noted the control he maintained over his wife. She seemed almost afraid. Everything about her was perfectly in place, each strand of hair, and each stroke of mascara, if it was mascara and not those trendy fake lashes. The woman in front of him wore designer clothes, shoes, and jewelry, yet she still appeared nothing more than an ornate shell of a person. The question that screamed for an answer was whether it was solely due to her missing daughter or was there something more sinister going on in her relationship with her husband.

Gabe glanced over at Jim. He nodded ever so slightly, letting Gabe know he'd noticed the look. When pressed, Jim could play bad cop better than any of his colleagues.

"Did you attempt to reach Bethany after she hung up on you?" Gabe asked.

"What? Do you have children?" Mr. Williams raised his hand. "You don't need to answer that. It's obvious you don't. What parent would reach out to their child after they hung up on them? I waited for her to call with an apology. It didn't come that night as I suspected it would. And I will admit, I was a bit surprised it didn't come in the morning either."

"Did this raise a concern?" Gabe asked.

"To be honest, no. I was just frustrated. It was the first time Bethany had raised her voice at me in that manner. We were in unprecedented territory, so I suppose I didn't know what to expect."

"What did you do then?"

"Nothing. I just waited."

The door to the room swung open, and Lieutenant Larsen asked Gabe to step outside. Bethany's parents would be curious, as was Jim. Or perhaps Jim's frustration at the preferential treatment described his feelings better than curiosity.

"You got this for a minute?" Gabe asked him.

Jim nodded, but tension hardened his jawline. He scanned his notes and tried to find a detail that would give him the upper hand in the interview. There wasn't much.

"How well do you know Bethany's roommate?" Jim asked.

"Not well. We had only met her a few times," Mrs. Williams answered. "Bethany really seemed to like her though. I think she's a good influence."

"Except for the fact she left our daughter in a bar knowing she was intoxicated." Mr. Williams's face reddened as he spoke. His hands balled into fists.

When Gabe reentered, his expression was hardened. "Mr. Williams," Gabe said as he took the seat next to him, "I need you to explain one more thing to me."

"What's that?"

"Why did the campus security cameras record your car on campus right about the time your daughter went missing?"

****

Jim hadn't liked Mr. Williams from the get-go, but he genuinely hoped there was a good excuse for his car being on the campus. Fathers guilty of foul play of any kind involving their children sickened him. Every case he'd encountered of such made him question humanity.

Mr. Williams was silent for only a moment, and for the first time since the interview began, he appeared uncomfortable. "I just did what any parent would do when their child was about to wreck everything."

Chapter 11

Present Day
Patient 541

Journal Entry
Sometimes the desert was quiet. Oddly, the silence put me on edge more than the sound of explosions and bullets slicing through the air. The quiet tempted us to let our guard down and allow our minds to drift to pleasant places far away. I scanned the dunes, searching for movement. Nothing. Mile after mile. Shane was above me lazily singing "Coward of the County." *I was too tired to join in. Each time my head bobbed and sleep threatened to take over, an imaginary bullet whizzed by my head, jolting me awake.*

Eventually, sleep won the battle. One moment, the smells of the desert and the sound of the Humvee engine surrounded me and then I was back home in my mother's kitchen. My father sat at the table drinking coffee. He slouched over his cup and looked down at the table. He appeared vulnerable somehow, and an unexpected rush of emotion washed over me. "Dad," *my sleeping self said. He wouldn't look up.* "Dad, why are you here?" *Even my unconscious self knew that the question meant more than the face value of the words. I needed to understand why he was on my mind, why I hadn't left him to decay in the ground, forgotten. My gaze pleaded for him to answer. Finally, he looked up with tear-filled eyes. I dreaded the words that were sure to come from his mouth, yet I needed to hear them. Was he sorry for taking his life and leaving us alone, or was he fearful that I would rot in hell with him? Did he see me as a murderer or a hero? "Dad, please."*

"Movement half a klick." The voice on the radio yanked me from my dream. All the vehicles halted. I gripped my M16. Shane was no longer singing, and I pictured him above me, searching the dunes for movement, his turret ready to fire. Then I spotted them. "I got eyes on them."

"I've got them in my sights, too," Shane said from above.

"Are they armed?" Marshall asked.

"Affirmative," Shane answered.

Two men, their earth-colored thobes blowing in the breeze, ducked behind the dunes. From that distance, I could not decipher whether they held weapons or not, and I questioned Shane's ability to be any more assured than me.

"Am I clear?" Shane asked.

"Interrogative, are we clear to shoot?" Marshall asked into the radio.

"Roger. That's a go."

"Copy that."

Within seconds, the men became nothing more than flowing garments drifting downward into the sand where they would never stand again. Our vehicles moved on, leaving the corpses to decay in the desert heat.

I couldn't erase the images of them, imagining the flies buzzing and crawling over them, eggs being laid in their flesh. How many bodies had we seen already?

"Does anyone come to pick up the bodies?" To my surprise, I had spoken my question out loud.

"Probably not," Shane answered. "This desert is like a giant recycling center."

"What the hell are you talking about?" I heard the annoyance in Marshall's voice.

"These corpses, they get chewed up and spit out. They decay into the sand and become..."

"What? What do they become, Shane?" I asked.

"More damn Hajis, that's what they become. They just keep popping up out of nowhere. Been like that over here since the beginning of time."

I wanted to argue, but the evidence was hard to deny. One war just led to another. One act of hatred fueled another. When had it started, and what the hell were we doing to stop it?

Toby spoke, and maybe because hearing his voice had become such a rare occurrence, we all became quiet. " 'Returning hate for hate multiplies hate, adding deeper darkness to a night already devoid of stars. Darkness cannot drive out darkness; only light can do that. Hate cannot drive out hate; only love can do that.' " He paused, letting the words linger in the air. "Martin Luther King, Jr." Toby paused again. "He might have been on to something."

Toby's words stuck like glue to my curious mind. Maybe it was the way they poetically simplified how to win against evil. But how were we to end the hatred of insurgents with a pleasant smile and a message of hope? I pushed the wise words to the back of my mind, tucked them away for a situation that might benefit from the message.

"Where the hell did you get that shit, Toby? There

*ain't no place in this country for flowery phrases."
Shane ended the discussion, but even he was somber for
the next hour.*

*I welcomed the night. I even looked forward to
shoveling out the hole I would call my bed. When I had
my hole about half dug, I paused, taking in the solitude,
letting it wrap its arms around me like an old friend. The
evening sky was aglow with stars, and I closed my eyes
while I breathed in and wished myself elsewhere. As I
exhaled slowly, I sensed someone behind me.*

*"Do you mind having some company again
tonight?"*

*I could tell she was smiling before I even turned to
look at her.*

*"The ground's all yours." I motioned at the dirt next
to me. We both sat on the edge of my half-dug hole,
leaving the digging for later. Her arm rested against
mine, allowing her warmth to travel through me. I took
a swig from my canteen and then handed it to her. I
watched as her lips touched the container. After a long
sip, she gave it to me and leaned back on her arms. I
followed suit and gazed up at the stars staring back down
at us. The silence was comfortable but heavy with
thought.*

*"You were quiet today. Is something bothering
you?" Dee asked.*

*"No," I answered. "Nothing besides, you know, a
war and all."*

*Many moments passed in silence. "Forgive me for
asking this, but…" Dee took my hand in hers.*

*"But what?" I asked when she struggled for words.
I looked down at her thin fingers entwined with mine like
puzzle pieces.*

"Do you believe in what you are fighting for here?"

"What do you mean?"

"Well, you know, like what Toby said, about trying to chase out evil with violence, or do you think Shane is right? That the Iraqi people will never find peace?"

"I'm protecting my country. Of course, I believe in that." We were now staring into each other's eyes. Both, I'm sure, nervous that the following words would destroy a moment that had seemed magical seconds before.

"It's just... It's just that I worry." Dee looked back up to the sky.

"What exactly are you worried about? Because what we're worried about is making it home alive. That worry outweighs all other concerns, don't you think?"

"Yes, but it's the after that is worrying me. When you make it home, and the media discuss this war and whether we were right or wrong, all the killing and horror... Well, I'm just afraid that it will haunt you."

"Dee, are you forgetting what they did?"

"God no! It's the 'they' that bothers me. When I see the corpses on the side of the road, the children, the families...I wonder if innocent people are..." Dee stopped talking, leaving me to guess at the words left unsaid.

I took a large swig from my canteen and let the warm water slide down my throat as if it could rinse away the comments I feared would spill from my mouth, the words I wanted to scream not just at her but at every person judging our actions from the comfort of their homes. Did they forget that violence in a country clear across the ocean was one hijacked airplane away from knocking them to their knees?

I grasped her hand. "Dee, we live in an imperfect

world with imperfect solutions."

"Maybe, or maybe we're all just too lazy to try another way."

I released the grip I had on her hand and let her fingers slip away. "Why did you become a reporter? So, you could understand the war or criticize the people fighting in it? I assure you, you can't change a group of people intent on destruction."

"My father died in Grenada during Operation Urgent Fury. I guess I wanted to feel what he felt, to live it in a way, or at least the closest I could to it. I never had a desire to serve in the military, but journalism, that was my ticket into his world."

"So, I'll ask again. What's your purpose here?"

"I want a different world. I want the one from Toby's quote, but I know that I can't make a change without understanding as much as possible. I need to understand the Iraqi people. I need to know the Shanes of the world, the Tobys, the Marshalls, and especially the ones like you."

"What do you mean, the ones like me? Am I about to be insulted?"

"That depends."

"Depends on what?" Agitation was building, and I hoped—I needed—Dee to say something that didn't make me hate her.

"Are you okay with you?"

"Of course." Heat rose onto my neck and face. "I still don't know what you're getting at."

"You're lost. You say you're okay with who you are, but my guess is that you don't truly even know who that person is yourself. When you pull the trigger and watch a human body fall to the ground, what is that doing to

you? Shane is going to be okay. He'll leave this place, find a bar, and spend his years gloating about his kills. Marshall knows himself. He'll struggle, but his confidence in his mission and ethics are strong. Those characteristics will help him survive." She paused, and her voice filled with sadness. "Toby will struggle. I can see it now. But you, there is something in your eyes, something wild and terrified. I just can't tell what the byproduct of such unharnessed emotions is going to be."

An irritated laugh escaped me. "Why can't you just focus on the facts like a normal journalist, Dee? No one needs your amateur psychoanalysis shit here." My tone was harsher than I intended, but I didn't care.

"You don't understand what I'm saying."

"Please leave."

She stood, but before walking away, she turned back to me. "There's something broken inside of you. I recognize it because there is something broken inside of me, too. I came here to heal the pain inside of me, and I suspect you did, too." She paused and stared at me. "I'm afraid for you. I'm afraid the memories to come are going to haunt you, and broken people aren't equipped to win a war against ghosts."

As Dee walked away, I jabbed the shovel into the ground, scooping out mounds of sand, each movement harder and more agitated than the last. Our conversation that night would serve as a segue to her next article. She found a place to share her judgment, knowledge, and opinions where no one would interrupt her or disagree with her. Her voice would be heard above the explosions, sounds equally impossible to silence.

****

2018
Paige

As her husband, Austin, gruffly adjusted his tie, Paige had begged him not to go. "Austin, please, you're too angry right now. I'm sure the situation's not what you're thinking."

"The hell it's not. That professor has been stalking her since last year. It's about time we had a talk."

"Why do you think this has anything to do with him? Bethany didn't mention him in the conversation."

"She's never mentioned him. Nor would she. Bethany has been keeping secrets since she became a teenager. I warned her that while I pay the phone bill, I have the right to see and hear every conversation that takes place."

"She's in college. You don't have the right."

Austin turned abruptly toward Paige, making her skip a breath. He had never hit her, yet his tone slammed into her harder than a fist at times. While she was being more confrontational than was usually wise around him, someone had to stand up for their child.

"I have the right to know what's going on in my daughter's life," he said with a clenched jaw. "Why is a grown man texting her asking to meet for a drink? He's her professor, for God's sake. It's completely inappropriate."

"You said she told him no."

"Maybe she knows I'm watching her messages. All I know is she went out and came home past midnight, drunk. And guess whose class she has this morning. She probably figured she would have preferential treatment. And then she spoke back to me, ended the call, even."

Austin pulled his tie tight and made a final adjustment to his collar. "My daughter hung up on me. Someone is filling her head with crap, and I have a strong feeling it's him."

"What are you going to do? Go to his classroom? Start a brawl in front of his students?"

"No. I'm just going to wait outside the building and have a quick, pleasant conversation with the man. According to the text, she has been politely trying to get him to leave her alone. He's not hearing her, so I'm going to help her out a bit."

Austin grabbed his suit jacket off the bed and headed out of the room. Paige followed, not knowing what more she could say to stop her husband. When they got to the front door, she uttered, "Austin." She pleaded to be heard. He ignored her, continued down the walkway, and in a moment, sped down their neighborhood road.

****

As the detective began drilling her husband with more questions, Paige tensed. The memories of the event were still painfully fresh. She was glad Austin had warned her to let him do the talking. Somehow, she knew that her words would make her husband look guilty or at least make the detectives suspicious of him.

"Mr. Williams, you said you went to do what any parent would have done. And what might that have been?" Detective Hunter asked.

The other detective took a step forward as if readying himself, yet for what, she could not imagine.

"I went to talk to the man I felt was responsible for Bethany's behavior change," Austin answered.

"And who would that be?" Detective Hunter asked.

"Her professor. The man who keeps texting her,

asking her out."

"And what's his name?"

"He likes to be called Doc V or some stupid nickname. Bethany would just call him *V* on the texts, but his name is Vijay Patil. All I know is that he's way too interested in our daughter." This detail was about the only thing that Paige would agree with her husband about, and even though every part of the situation was unsettling, they were right to mention him to the investigators.

"Did you end up talking with him?" Detective Hunter asked.

"Briefly."

"And how did that conversation go?" the detective asked.

"I just introduced myself. Sometimes that's all that is necessary."

"You just walked up to her professor and introduced yourself? That's all?"

"Pretty much. I let the professor know I was visiting campus, and Bethany had mentioned his class."

"That's it?" Detective Hunter asked again.

"That's it."

Paige glanced over at her husband and looked for signs of deceit.

For the first time since the interview began, Detective Castille spoke up. "How'd you know what the professor looked like?"

"It's not very difficult to find his picture when you search his name."

Detective Castille paused for a moment. "We'll be speaking to the professor soon. Maybe he can fill us in on any details you might be forgetting."

Austin shrugged, but Paige didn't need investigators to tell her that her husband's interaction with the professor would not have been cordial.

Detective Castille stood, stripping away her husband's general air of authority. The energy in the room was changing, and a bead of sweat trickled down the back of Paige's neck. What was her husband capable of when pushed?

"Are we done here?" Mr. Williams said, never averting his gaze.

Detective Castille glanced over at his partner and exchanged a look of understanding. Detective Hunter stood and shook both of their hands. "Thank you for coming in, Mr. and Mrs. Williams. We'll be in touch."

Detective Castille nodded in an apparent attempt to be polite, then he spoke dismissively. "Mr. and Mrs. Williams, you're free to go." Paige felt their questioning gazes following them all the way home.

****

Lieutenant Larsen called them into the squad room. "What are your thoughts?"

"I think a few people need further investigation," Gabe replied.

On the whiteboard, they started what would be the beginning of a lengthy web connecting all people of interest to its center, Bethany. They added Mr. Williams, the professor, and the stranger from the bar. Then, they walked away, knowing the work had only just begun.

Chapter 12

2018
Patient 541

Journal Entry
*The next day, we spent endless hours watching the
desert sands pass by our window. Most of us allowed our
thoughts to drift into our minds until a new one, equally
unpleasant, filled the space. Dee, on the other hand,
captured her thoughts with her pen and sealed them like
prisoners onto the paper.*

*Marshall looked over and watched Dee scribbling
on her pad. "What you writin' about today, Dee?"*

*Dee glanced my way, hesitating before she
answered. I turned and looked out the window.*

*"I'm editing some work from yesterday." She riffled
through the pages of her pad. "I'm not sure if it's any
good yet."*

"Would you like some input?" Marshall asked.

"I wouldn't want to ask that of you."

*"My calendar is pretty clear for the next few hours.
Entertain me."*

*"Are you sure?" Something told me she was giving
me time to object, but I only would have been viewed as
rude by the others.*

"Go for it."

Dee cleared her throat and began slowly.

"As an embedded journalist, I set out on a mission to answer several questions that had burned inside me since my father died in Grenada. The little girl inside of me had never stopped asking, 'Why?' Why did he die, and why did people, strangers even, honor the man I knew only as my father, the one I ran to when he returned home, who tucked me in at night, who had pancakes waiting for me when I woke in the morning? That is until the day he no longer did.

"My column is written under the assumption that my readers also ponder the whys of war. I have been accused of being incapable of fully embracing the intricacies of war because I keep one foot firmly planted in a Utopian society that has never existed beyond our dreams. I argue that due to my idealistic views, my mind is forced to observe the harshness of war with fresh and honest eyes. As I recount my experiences overseas, I will be truthful and brutally honest. My hope is that when the next crisis arises, as we know it will, we might stop and think before we regurgitate an answer to the why question because nothing is as excusable or straightforward as we would like to believe."

"Put your seatbelts on, boys. It's about to get ugly." I spoke into the window, refusing to look her way.

"I can stop."

"Private, if you can't handle the words of a journalist, then Fallujah is going to be a living hell."

"I'm pretty sure Fallujah will be hell." I paused and waited. Dee didn't start reading again. *"Go ahead. Let us have it."*

"Are you sure? The next part gets more personal."

"Go ahead, Dee. We can handle it. Might be interesting to hear what you think of us after all this time

together." Marshall's voice was calm and inviting. Did he know what he was in for?

"Okay, then." Dee turned her attention back to her pad. "As the Humvee I travel in with four Marines, each different from one another in many ways, rumbles across the hot desert terrain, I listen. I listen to the conversations, the friendly and not so friendly banter, and try to decipher all that is not being spoken aloud."

"We should take that as a warning. She is always listening," I said.

"That's kind of her job. Let her continue." Toby was becoming impatient with my comments.

"Why are they fighting in this war?" Dee continued.

"Are you kidding me? Why are we fighting this war?" Shane's voice resonated irritation.

"Let her speak. Maybe we'll learn something," Marshall said.

"Humph." Shane and I echoed our responses.

"What brought them to a place where bombs light up the sky and friends transform from boys to men in conditions far from nurturing?"

Dee hesitated.

"Go on," Marshall insisted.

"The leader, the loner, the lost, and the bully are joined together by metal and circumstance."

"Oh, this is getting good. Can I be the bully?" Shane asked.

Marshall laughed. "She pegged you, didn't she?"

"Just go on." I didn't need all the titles analyzed down to where they realized she referred to me as lost.

"They came from homes far and wide across the United States, from families proud, terrified, and, for some, disappointed by their decision. At times, the

Humvee falls silent, and I see them asleep, their Kevlar vests holding in all the feelings I want to uncover. As I learn every day, it is a dangerous task because that Kevlar shield surrounding them is not just protecting them physically. The vest protects more than their bodies. They serve as security blankets, making them brave when everything around them tells them to fear. My questions, I hope, will never separate them from that security."

The Humvee was finally silent apart from Dee's voice.

"As I search the dunes for hidden secrets that I have come to realize even the young men willing to sacrifice their lives cannot fully know, I become overwhelmed with history. These dunes have seen so much fighting and death in the thousands of years preceding this one. There was a point, a beginning, and whether one believes in Biblical stories as actual history or not, there is proof that many people still do thousands of years after they were written. At least, there is proof that those stories are still at the center of the chaos in the Middle East."

Shane snored. Dee ignored him.

"The hatred that has branched out to encompass today's problems began with differing vantage points dating back to the Old Testament. Who owns what, and what is moral and worth fighting for? What are our obligations as a people? As I listen in on the conversations among the Marines who have allowed me into their world, one fact becomes apparent. They are not learned in the causes of the war they fight, but they stand by their trust in the government's agendas. When asked what they know of the Islamic religion, I receive answers ranging from honest ignorance to ignited

hatred. The intention of my column is that my readers will journey with me and become more knowledgeable and sympathetic to the many people caught in the middle—the Iraqi people and the men fighting for our freedom and security. If we want to find a solution, would it not be prudent to know the problem?"

"Shane, maybe you want to listen up. Good chance she's referring to you as the ignorant one." Marshall laughed, but we all knew Shane was the one taking the brunt of her statement.

"In the game of tennis, when the opponents do not agree with a score, they must go back to the last point where both teams agree. Nothing in history is that simple, but I will begin with an important moment of impasse and look at the colliding cultures from that point.

"To understand the Iraqi war, we must travel back before the division began—before Islam and Christianity existed. To do this, we slip back to Biblical times when God promises an elderly man named Abraham a son who would make him the father of many countries. Now a very old woman, Abraham's wife Sarah, lost faith in God's promise. This lack of belief led to Abraham having a child with his handmaid, Hagar. The child, Ishmael, was Abraham's firstborn, but Sarah regretted allowing her husband to father Hagar's child. She sent them off into the desert to remove them from her sight. They later traveled to Mecca, where Ishmael became the father of many descendants.

"In the meantime, Sarah became pregnant and gave birth to her son, Isaac. Isaac also fathered many children. Ishmael's descendants led to Muhammad, while Isaac's led to Jesus. Islam is the religion that

follows the teachings of Muhammad, while Christianity is the religion that follows Jesus. Muslims believe God spoke through the prophets—Adam, Abraham, Moses, and Jesus—but they think Muhammad was the last and most significant. Muslims also respect the Jewish and Christian religions for the most part because both are monotheistic and follow scripture.

"Muhammad was born to a merchant family. At the age of about five, he was orphaned. He became a caravan leader as a teenager and then a merchant himself. Muhammad, in the year A.D. 610, had a vision. In the dream, Allah told him to preach Islam and to destroy the statues of false idols.

"Muhammad was a skilled political and religious leader and used his power to spread the Caliphate vice Islamic State. The Caliphate vice Islamic State requires all Muslims to put the Islamic State above their tribes. He made Mecca a holy city of Islam, and by the time he died in A.D. 632, the entire Arabian Peninsula was part of his territory. The messages he believes he received from God over twenty years were written down after he died, and they formed the Quran or holy book of Islam. The Quran instructs Muslims to be honest, treat people fairly, respect parents, be kind to neighbors, not commit murder, not lie or steal, and obey Allah's will. They also abide by the shari'ah or code of law, which instructs them not to gamble, eat pork, or drink alcohol. Along with the shari'ah, Muslims have a set of customs based on Muhammad's words and deeds referred to as Sunna.

"Through the decades, many branches have grown from these two religions. To simplify a complex beginning, Christianity spawned the Roman Catholic Church and the Eastern Orthodox Church. Roman

Catholics accepted the Pope as their leader, while the Eastern Orthodox Church did not. Islam split into Sunni and Shi'a (Shi'ites). About eighty-five percent of Muslims (people who follow Islam) are Sunni, but Shi'a is the most popular branch of Islam in Iran and Iraq. Sunni believers felt elite members should choose Muhammad's successor.

"At the same time, Shi'a followers believe that Ali (Muhammad's son-in-law) is the rightful heir and that all future leaders should be one of his descendants. Both groups believe in one God, the teaching in the Quran, and the Five Pillars (belief, prayer, charity, fasting, and pilgrimage). From there, they differ on many issues. But just as Christianity continued to split into even more churches as different opinions formed and arguments arose, so did Islam. Some of the Islam branches are extreme groups who have twisted the teachings that began with love and devotion and ended with a focus on violence and control.

"If my explanation of the history of Islam sounded like a textbook, it was intended. Many people, I suspect, tuned out, feeling like a student bored by facts."

"Amen to that," Shane said.

Dee laughed softly. "You know I'm not coming at you, Shane."

"So, if I'm getting you right, the Sunnis want elites to elect their leader, but the Shi'as believe in descendants inheriting power. Sounds somewhat like a form of democracy and a form of royalty to me," Marshall added.

"Yes. I suppose you're right."

"Okay. Go on."

"I'm almost done." She flipped the page. "To a

young man full of energy and physical drive, classroom learning is tortuous, and reading history books is perceived as a punishment from authority figures. They will fight. They risk their lives. But do they know why?

"If there is one takeaway in watching how the thousands of years fertilized two seeds from one tree, I hope it is this. Branches grew. Some remain fruitful, and some remain crooked, but at the base of both trees remain similar foundations that some scholars believe are the answer to peace between our countries and our faiths. One principle—simple in words and challenging in reality—is to love, and yes, sometimes that principle is worth fighting a war over."

Dee paused.

"Is that it?" Marshall asked.

"Yes." I could see more words on the page. I reached over and attempted to take the pad from her. She looked at me and released her grip. Her gaze searched mine.

Marshall began clapping, and to my surprise, so did Shane.

"That was great, Dee." Toby kept his hands on the wheel. "I didn't know any of that history."

"Oh, so I'm not the only ignorant one?" Shane responded.

"I'd bet there's under a percent of us who could rattle all that off. Don't be too hard on yourself," Marshall added.

I remained silent as I scanned the paragraph Dee had chosen not to share.

"The men tossing in their sleep bring me back to the Humvee and the desert surrounding me. One of them jolts awake and scans the vehicle with fear in his eyes.

He is sitting beside me, yet he is so far away. I wonder if he fears that what he is fighting for might not be what he believes it to be. I fear that when he returns home, the images will remain with him for a lifetime. And when that day comes, when the memories haunt him in his sleep, I pray he will know his actions were necessary and honorable."

****

2018
Jim

Gabe and Jim went back to the interrogation room to wait for Brad Jennings to arrive.

"What are your thoughts?" Gabe asked as they both settled in the now empty seats.

"I think the world is full of sick people who lie to cover their asses," Jim replied.

"Can't deny that fact, but Bethany's dad, what's your take on him?"

"I think Austin's capable of many things that would make him a terrible husband and father, but I'm not sure murder is one of them. I'm interested to hear what actually happened when he visited the professor."

"You think Austin spoke to him?"

"I think he was too angry not to. He doesn't seem like a man to give up after driving out to the campus. My guess is that something took place, and Austin didn't feel like sharing."

The following interview would begin shortly, yet the minutes seemed to drag by. Jim needed to be out there looking for Bethany. He had to find out if the voice he had heard through the walkie-talkie was a lead or a cruel joke.

"Do I have enough time to look into something?" Jim asked.

Gabe looked up with a questioning gaze while taking the last bite of a protein bar and washing it down with a large swig of water. Gabe glanced at his watch. "Fifteen minutes, maybe."

Jim mentally kicked himself for not just saying he wanted to grab a snack, something that wouldn't raise questions. He hurried back to his desk, careful not to appear too anxious, and opened his computer. Within moments, Jim was studying an aerial view of the campus. Taking classes at night had made him familiar with much of the campus, but the areas students frequented were not the ones that interested him.

The dogs had searched around the woods near where Bethany was known to run. The location was expected, too obvious. Not to mention, if someone had killed Bethany and dumped her there, the investigators would have found her by now. The voice in the walkie-talkie had said near the fields. Jim scanned the screen for only a moment. The spot leaped out at him. The girl on the walkie-talkie must have been referring to the baseball field. There was a small road that didn't appear heavily trafficked. The woods were thick, and the field was far from the site. No one would find her for days, at least not without a bit of help. After a quick glance around, Jim dialed the phone.

****

Brad Jennings was escorted into the room by one of the officers. He wore a striped shirt and a backward UNF ball cap. Brad was obviously uncomfortable, but Jim sensed his innocence immediately. The young man looked around the room with fear in his eyes. Girls would consider him a cute guy more than a handsome one. Jim took him as the kind of kid who was every girl's friend versus their hook-up interest. If it weren't for the circumstances, Brad would probably have entered the police department and greeted them each with a jovial smile.

He'd probably never entirely understand why he was always in the friend zone. Jim wanted to pat him on the back and tell him, "You just can't be that nice, kid."

"Have a seat, Brad," Jim said, motioning to the chair across from him. Brad nervously followed orders. "We just want to ask you a few questions."

"Okay." Brad looked back and forth between the two men. "Have you found out anything yet? Bethany, she's great. I…it's just…I'm just really worried."

Years of investigating people had taught Jim how to read people. There was a stutter that stemmed from fear for themselves and one that was fueled by fear for the victim. Brad was afraid for Bethany; Jim would bet his career on it.

"Unfortunately, we don't have anything yet." Gabe folded his hands on the table. "Amber Cardin. You know her, correct?" Brad nodded. "She said you thought you saw Bethany in your Economics class Friday morning."

"I thought I did, but as time passes, I can't be sure. Sometimes, we would talk after class. Not always, but at least I would see Bethany walk out of the building. You know, my memories are blurry. When you try to recall things, no matter how hard you try—and I'm trying so hard—I feel like I'm confusing my memory at this point. I know we didn't talk after class on Friday."

"What makes you think you saw her?"

"Well, when we first got into the class, Doc V, that's

our professor, was acting all flustered, and I was sort of laughing to myself. I looked back to share a laugh with Bethany, and I thought it was her looking down at her notes, but really, I just saw long blonde hair hanging over a girl's face. Maybe it wasn't her. Then our professor, well, he seemed irritable, so I didn't dare keep looking back. The class was a bit high stress for some reason, and I was just happy to get out of there. I forgot to even look for her at the end of it."

Jim and Gabe exchanged looks before Gabe continued. "Was it strange for your professor to act rattled?"

"Yeah, it was. Generally, Doc V tries to act all cool, cracking jokes, trying to be one of us, I guess. He would even be seen in the bars sometimes."

"Did you see him out the night before Bethany went missing?" Gabe asked.

"No, but Bethany showed me some of his texts."

"What were the texts?" Gabe asked.

"Asking if she would be going out. Joking not to come to class hungover. Things like that."

"Did it sound like he was meeting her?"

"No, not to me."

"Do you know who she was dancing with at the bar?"

"Some townie. I'd see him out sometimes. I believe his name is Ben Adams."

"What do you mean by townie?" Jim asked.

"I mean, not a student anymore, but hangs out at the college-type bars. He's a bit older, maybe late twenties if I were to guess."

"Know anything else about him?"

"Not really. The guy's got short, dark hair and a

beard, but not a thick one. I think he's about six feet. Good enough looking, I guess."

"Did Bethany hang out with him often?" Jim asked.

"No." Brad paused. "I think she liked him from afar. A lot of the girls did."

"You sound like this bothers you," Gabe said.

"No. Not really. It's just maybe…well, maybe I just think the guy's too old to be hanging out in college bars." Something lit up in Brad's eyes. "That reminds me why she was hanging out with him that night. I guess some guy tried to buy Bethany a drink at the bar, and Bethany, well, she could have anyone, and when she wanted to get cold with a guy, it could be brutal."

"Did you see the guy?"

"No. But the guy did something or said something to creep her out, and the next thing I knew, she was clinging to the townie." Brad looked up at the detectives. "To be honest, I'd had a few too many. Things are a bit blurry." Brad buried his head in his hands. "God, I wish I could remember things better. I wish I could tell you something about the guy at the bar. I just thought it was girl drama, and she had someone to watch over her, so I just…I didn't think of it anymore after that."

Jim stopped taking notes and looked at Brad. "And what was your relationship with Bethany?"

"Friends. Just friends."

"Bethany's a beautiful girl. You never had any interest in her?" Gabe asked in a non-accusing way.

"I think everyone had a little interest in her, but no, not serious interest. I knew we were best as friends."

Gabe nodded, and Jim took it that his colleague believed Brad. Jim pulled out a card. "If you think of anything else, Brad, make sure you give us a call."

****

After the interrogation, Gabe and Jim went to the campus and tracked down Dr. Patil.

The professor, after eyeing the clock, had led them to his office and closed the door. When they brought up Bethany's name, the tension in the air increased as if they were watching an animal hear the latch being shut on its cage. Testosterone seemed to fill the room.

Fight or flight. Jim recognized the signs. Yet, he leaned toward the view that the professor had broken ethics codes more than committed murder. Jim kept his thoughts to himself, only hinting at his feelings with a shrug.

"I assume you know why we're here," Gabe began.

"I have a good idea, but let me assure you, I have no clue where Bethany is. The only reason I know anything is that Bethany's father came out of nowhere and accosted me as I tried to get to my class Friday morning. He shoved me against the brick wall and was breathing down my neck, accusing me of all sorts of inappropriate conduct. I'll tell you what I told him once he calmed down. I was home correcting papers, asleep by eleven."

Jim shook his head amazed at the human ability to lie to a detective. "Would you mind telling us specifically what Mr. Williams said to you that morning?"

Professor Patil sighed, preparing himself, Jim supposed. "I like to stay in contact with my students, be personable, so they know they can come to me for help. I don't like the line between professor and student. It's too stuffy for me, and I feel kids learn better when there is a respectful friendship involved."

"You didn't answer the question. What did Mr.

Williams say to you?"

"He was yelling accusations. Telling me I was stalking his daughter." Patil let out a deep breath. "I can't remember every word, but that's the gist of it."

"Are you sure?"

"That's it. I swear," Professor Patil said with emphasis. "I have never crossed the line. I have never done or said anything inappropriate."

"Then why did Mr. Williams feel the need to shove you against the bricks?" Jim questioned.

"Maybe in his time, professors were different, colder. He misread my friendliness, I suppose."

"Would you have a problem with us seeing the thread of texts?"

"No, I wouldn't." Patil reached into his briefcase and then suddenly stopped. "Actually, I deleted all my texts the other day. My phone was full."

"That's convenient," Jim said smugly.

"Seriously, it was full."

"No problem. I believe Mr. Williams has a record of all of the messages. I'm sure he would be happy to share them with us," Jim added.

Sweat beaded on Patil's forehead, and adrenaline surged through Jim. Moments like these—watching the fear of the guilty seep to the surface without invitation— had become addictive. Jim smiled. "One problem solved. Right?"

Patil tried to return the smile, but it appeared to be more of a grimace. The detectives let the awkward tension settle in the room before Gabe handed the professor a business card. "Call us if you think of anything that might be helpful."

"I will." Patil took the card and studied it until the detectives closed the door behind them. Jim got the sense that before the two of them got on the elevator, the card had been tossed in the garbage.

Chapter 13

2018
Patient 541

Journal Entry
That night, I slid into my hole and wrestled with sleep throughout the night. Sometimes I won, for an hour at a time, but more often, I found myself staring into the dark. Dee's words mingled in my mind. "There's something broken inside of you." Anger welled up inside of me like a protective coating keeping the parts of me that were tender from feeling the burn, yet the words kept coming. "I'm afraid for you. I'm afraid the memories to come are going to haunt you." Was she right? Was it true that broken people aren't equipped to win a war against ghosts? The truth was in every Vet hospital around the world. Evidence rose like a tidal wave threatening to drown me.

When I awoke in the morning, a sound rang out through our battalion like Christmas bells: The sound of children's laughter followed by the shushing sounds of adults. I climbed out of my hole and into the unfamiliar atmosphere. The morning air smelled less stifling than most days. Many Marines were already stuffing belongings into the Humvees and preparing to leave. Others scrambled out of their desert beds, looking around for the source of the young voices. That's when I saw a car broken down on the road a few dozen feet away. The man, who I assumed to be the father, looked under the hood as the mother attempted to keep two young boys from running too far from the vehicle.

Marshall headed over to them, and Dee followed. As Marshall approached, the boys froze in their steps and stared up at him. They studied him as if he were an alien creature. That's when I noticed he carried a football that he placed in the taller boy's hands. The boy hesitated, looked at his father, and after the father uttered some words in Arabic, the boy began tossing the toy to his brother. The laughter grew as they chased after the tumbling ball, which each of them proved incapable of catching.

Marshall looked under the car's hood. The father tried to explain the issue using hand gestures while Marshall tinkered with parts I could not see from my vantage point. Dee picked up the rolling ball. Her face lit up with joy as she tossed it to the younger of the two. The ball landed in his outstretched arms, and Dee clapped with delight. She threw it repeatedly, and the boys beamed with joy. Only when the engine rumbled back to life did I notice I had been frozen in place. After a brief exchange of gratitude, Marshall and Dee walked side by side back toward our convoy.

"You're lucky that son-of-a-bitch didn't blow both of you up," Shane said as they approached.

"I guess he could have," Marshall responded, "but something told me the man didn't intend to sacrifice his wife and kids to do so."

Shane spat on the ground in front of him. "I wouldn't put it past any of them,"

"Did you forget we're fighting for their freedom,

too?" Marshall said.

"Whatever." Shane turned to leave. "Let's get this convoy on the road."

Together, we removed the camo from the vehicle. All the while, Dee avoided me. Our gazes locked momentarily as we climbed inside, and we quickly looked away from each other. We all rode in near silence for several miles. Dee busied herself writing in her pad. The sound of her pencil and rustling paper filled the air.

"What the hell are you scribbling so much about?" Shane asked in the way only Shane could.

"Well, I was writing about those two boys and how happy they seemed despite all the craziness around them."

"They don't know any better. This shit show is all these kids have ever seen," Shane said.

"Don't you find that a bit sad?"

"Life is sad. Get used to it."

"Shane, were you kicked in the head as a kid?" Marshall asked.

"With all due respect, Corporal, screw you."

"I'll take that as a yes."

Toby chuckled. It was the first sound I'd heard from him all morning.

"You laughing, Private?"

"Never." Toby mocked Shane from the safety of his position.

"You best sleep with one eye open tonight."

"I always do."

The conversation felt more comical than intimidating, and in fact, I found it comforting to hear Toby join the banter for once, but then he fell silent again.

"We have a long journey. Do any of you care to give me something new to write about? I've just about run out of ideas."

I refused to speak. Instead, I waited and tried to predict who would take the bait. As expected, Shane spoke up. "What kind of crap you looking for?"

"I'd love to hear about what brought you here. Where were you on 9/11? That kind of thing."

"Me? I was sitting in my history class, trying to stay awake. The teacher, Mr. Bates, got a call, and then he turned on the television in our room. We watched the second plane go into the World Trade Center. The rest of the day was spent listening to the news, people guessing, rumors spreading. The typical after-disaster effect."

"Do you think you would have enlisted if it weren't for 9/11?"

"Probably. There's always some war waiting to be fought."

"Doesn't war frighten you?"

"I was born for this. Can't you tell?"

"Yes. I can."

"Thought so."

I shifted in my seat, trying to rid myself of the desire to reach out and touch her, hating myself for the thoughts that raced through my mind. Shane had no idea that Dee was insulting him, but I was becoming more aware all the time that she was insulting all of us. Even knowing this, my body betrayed me. I could feel her without touching her. Her energy reached out to me, called to me, and pushed me away all at once.

"Marshall? Want to share?" Dee asked.

"I always knew I'd enlist. I come from a long line of

military." Marshall tossed a handful of food in his mouth and swallowed it down with a swig of water. "According to my family, there isn't anything a man can do that's more admirable than serving his country."

Dee scribbled something. "Have you lost family members to wars?"

"Too many."

"Yet you still find it admirable."

"I wouldn't be here if I didn't." Marshall appeared to think a moment. "I guess in some ways, you have to respect a man when he's willing to die for what he believes in, even if his thinking is tainted."

"Are you saying you respect the insurgents then?" Dee asked. Everyone in the Humvee waited on his response.

"So many people die from far more selfish acts like drugs and drinking. Hell, people fall off cliffs they climbed for no other reason than to get a jolt of adrenaline. Nothing was won from reaching the top. The insurgents are misguided but loyal to their beliefs. I don't respect what they stand for, but I respect their dedication to their cause."

"Do you believe in what you're fighting for over here?" Dee asked.

"I believe our country is worth fighting for, most definitely. We'll never know everything that happens behind the scenes. Is our government ever wrong? Do we ever act out of selfishness? Most likely. But it's the big picture I look at. Our country is a damn good place, and if I end up dying to protect it, well then, it beats falling off a cliff I shouldn't have been climbing in the first place. Wouldn't you agree?"

Dee scribbled some more but didn't respond to

Marshall's question. I shifted in my seat, waiting to be called upon next. I need not have worried.

"Toby, where were you on 9/11?" Dee asked.

Toby cleared his throat before speaking. "I was home, sick with something. I can't recall that detail. I didn't even know anything had happened until my mom came home." Dee's hand moved over her paper. "I think that was the day my mom decided I would enlist after graduating."

"How about you?" Dee asked. "Did you know then that you'd join the military?"

"I was a sophomore in high school. I had no idea what I wanted." Toby's voice resonated with resentment.

"Did you want to enlist?"

"It was the best choice, I guess. Some of my cousins had already enlisted, and my mom thought it would be good for me. I think she worried about me not having a father figure and growing up with too much female influence."

"Well, it all makes sense now."

Marshall spun toward Shane. "Shut the hell up, Shane." I noticed the pulse in his neck.

"I'm just busting on him. You know that, don't you, Toby?"

"I wouldn't expect anything less."

"See? Toby enjoys my banter."

After a few moments, Dee's pencil quieted, and the Humvee fell silent. Dee was right about Toby. The war would forever alter his ability to survive in the world that awaited his return. How would his mother feel when her son came home a shell of his former self?

"You forgot someone," Toby said, maybe out of interest or perhaps to make sure the spotlight had moved

permanently from his past.

Dee didn't look toward me. "Did you want to tell why you enlisted?" She stared at her notepad—her pencil ready.

"When I hurt my knee, I lost my football scholarship. We didn't have money, so college wasn't going to work out for me." Dee wasn't writing, but something told me she was listening intently, trying to find where the new information fits into the image she had formed of me.

"Did any of your family members serve in the military?"

"No. But my family, well, they stopped being a part of my decisions long ago."

"Now look who's sounding like a hard ass," Shane shouted down from above.

"I never said I was a hard ass."

"Oh, but I think you did."

"Shane, sometimes you have the intellect of a twelve-year-old. Continue," Marshall said. "I'm curious."

"That's enough about me for the night." I could feel Dee's gaze on me as I stared into the darkness. "Are we pulling over anytime soon?"

"About thirty more klicks," Marshall answered.

Shane started singing "Coward of the County," *and this time we all joined in, happy to leave our old lives behind once again. The last hour passed uneventfully, or so it would appear to the other Marines in the shared Humvee. But in the back seat, a nonverbal exchange reignited my feelings. My stolen glances would catch Dee's. We awkwardly diverted our gazes at first, but then the mood softened, and we stopped avoiding each other.*

Her eyes searched mine, and for the first time, I wasn't afraid, and I let her snake her way into my heart. At that moment, nothing else mattered.

****

Once we had spread the camouflage netting over the Humvees, I saw the silhouette of Dee digging her hole. This time, I went to her. Without a word, I tore into the earth with my shovel. Once I had my hole dug, I helped her finish hers. We didn't speak while we worked, and we didn't talk when I lay down in mine. Had I purposely made mine just a bit wider and deeper than usual? I wasn't aware of doing so at the time, but I wasn't surprised when Dee slid in next to me. I turned on my side to face her. Our legs tangled just enough so that our bodies fit together perfectly.

The full moon's light shimmered off Dee. We were silent enough that I could hear my own heartbeat. We breathed in unison; her breath was warm on my face. I traced her cheek with my finger, still not sure where she wanted my action to lead. Dee squeezed the back of my shirt, forcing us to inch closer together. This is the memory I revisited the most. The second I knew what I had hoped for would happen, when our breaths would become one, and the warmth that was once hers would become mine. For years after, I craved that moment. Even in the dark, I could see her crystal blue eyes staring back at me. Surely, she had not crossed this line with Toby or Shane, or any of the other Marines. Men talked. She would lose all credibility if she were making her rounds. Dee claimed me the minute she crawled in beside me, and I willingly became subservient to her. She breathed my soul back into me, the soul I had left safe at home so that I could recover it when I returned.

We stayed in that position for what seemed like an eternity, maybe both of us knowing that once we jumped from there, we would be free falling. Neither of us would be able to control the outcome to follow. Dee rested her forehead on mine, edging us closer to the cliff. Our breaths had become one. Soft wafts of air circled our faces. For a moment, the closeness of our bodies was enough. How long had it been since someone's skin had touched mine in an affectionate manner? Too long.

Dee brought her lips to mine, ran her fingers through my hair, and pushed her body closer to mine, and I responded quickly, praying she would not change her mind and that no one would come upon us while we broke so many rules. Suddenly, we began clawing at each other like teenagers in the back seat of a car, forgetting that we were in the middle of a war, half-swallowed by the earth. My hands pried at clothing, which could not be shed entirely until we both found what we were seeking. In any other instance, the brevity would have been a disappointment, but we were on borrowed time. When the moment was over, she kissed my forehead and crawled back to her foxhole. Neither of us spoke a word, maybe because words tended to be too messy, and I needed to figure out what my heart was feeling.

****

2018
Jim

Finally, it was time to join the search team. Jim felt the same adrenaline a Blue Tick Hound feels when a rabbit crosses its path. This surge was common amongst investigators about to receive a break in a case. Only this time, Jim had given himself an advantage: He had contacts who weren't official members of the police force. Through the years, he had formed a shallow relationship with a tracker. Evans was his last name and the only name anyone used when referring to him. He did private investigative work on the side and trained dogs to track scents. Despite the confidence people had in his work, Evans's ego and his growing record of trespassing complaints had kept the force from bringing him on as an employee.

Everything Jim asked of his contact was legal, just highly frowned upon. Considering the bizarre circumstances of the case, working with a person without ties to the job or concerns about minor ethical discrepancies was precisely what Jim needed. Jim respected Evans for taking matters into his own hands and not waiting for a system to notice his talents. As one kindred, irritated spirit to another, Jim savored the moment he slipped Evans an envelope of cash and eagerly awaited what he uncovered. Evans and his dog Duke would soon be combing the parts of the woods that the department had yet to tape off from the public.

Walking out of the building, Jim was hit by a breeze. The air that encircled him had once spun around the woods and seen it all; it knew everything. Jim could feel it in his bones. Bethany was close, but the search team would take days to reach the vicinity where Jim suspected her body would be found. The windy weather made drones useless, and the K-9 unit would not pick up a scent if the perp had forced Bethany into a vehicle. If there was the slightest chance that the voice Jim heard on the walkie-talkie held some credence, then Evans was searching in the perfect spot. If Evans found nothing, Jim would not have lost face to a practical joker in the office. No one would ever know about the peculiar event that had cast suspicion on the woods by the fields. Jim would worry about the explanation if a body was discovered.

Not to mention, Jim had too many questions of his own. He needed some proof, even a glimmer, that what he had heard was real. And Jim had to figure out why someone would be feeding him information in such an unusual way. Yes, he told himself again, making a deal with Evans was the only way to proceed.

"You finally get to join the search team. Feeling better now?" Gabe asked.

Jim didn't appreciate his colleague's tone. "I'm not sure I would describe my feelings as better. I just think we need to get down there to get a better understanding of the case."

"Just busting on you. Don't get all defensive."

Jim shook his head and slid into the passenger seat, not in the mood for their typical banter.

Adrenaline rushed through his veins as he anticipated what was to come. His mind was already traipsing through the woods on the heels of a trained tracker. He noticed Gabe watching him out of the corner of his eye.

"What's got you all amped up? Your leg's twitching like you drank three espressos."

Jim looked down at the limb that betrayed him. He set his hand on his thigh to steady it.

"I guess I won't let you get my coffee for me next time."

"You're blaming me, then?" Gabe snickered. "Why the lack of trust, partner?"

Jim considered his answer. "Killing off your partner

before he gets a promotion isn't a novel idea. I'm sure someone somewhere has attempted it before."

Now Gabe openly laughed. "Oh, my friend, killing you off would be way too easy. If I thought you enough of a threat, I would be far more creative than that."

"Interesting. I'll keep that in mind."

"Remember that case when the guy buried his landscaper in the flower bed so he wouldn't have to pay his bill?" Gabe said.

"I remember." Jim chuckled. "He got caught when his dog dug him up and set the femur bone on the neighbor's front stoop."

"See, murder is too easy and ends badly." They both were silent for a moment. "In all seriousness, Jim, may the best man win."

"Agreed. It's not really up to us anyway."

They arrived at the campus police station and parked. As they began walking down the road to the path Bethany would have taken, Gabe spoke. "So, what's your take on Bethany's father?"

"Besides him being a prick?"

Gabe let out a small laugh. "Yeah, besides the prick thing."

"He's controlling. Too controlling. Bethany's father was hiding a temper. Possibly an abusive home, maybe not physically, but at least verbally intimidating."

"The question is: How bad is his temper?"

"I can't blame Bethany for wanting to escape to college. She probably had a miserable childhood with him constantly belittling her."

Jim let the conversation dwindle. His mind was intent on the detectives standing up ahead with the K-9s. The casualness of their stance suggested there wasn't any actual activity yet. But then, if Jim believed the voice that had spoken to him through the walkie-talkie, this would soon change. With each hour that passed, the voice he had heard faded in his mind, and the possibility that his imagination—or another person—had played tricks on him became more plausible.

Jim considered Gabe a friend, not just a colleague. Would Gabe really be so callous as to try and deceive him? Not to mention, a woman had spoken to him, not a man. He could be in on it with someone though.

Gabe was used to being primary detective. If Jim got promoted after finishing his degree, Gabe would be reporting to him. As much as Jim looked forward to the day, the transition would undoubtedly be awkward for Gabe.

Gabe and Jim were not the only ones who vied for the position. Anyone could be trying to derail him, and from Gabe's reaction after talking to Lieutenant Larsen, maybe others feared Jim's degree would give him an advantage.

As the two of them approached the group, Jim glanced around at each one of them. Detective Walburg, a young female detective, studied Jim. Walburg was known for her no-nonsense approach, but Jim would be lying to himself if he pretended not to notice her thick, brunette hair and long, dark eyelashes. At another time, the detective's attention might have interested Jim strictly as an ego boost, but today, he eyed her suspiciously.

"Morning," Jim said, not to be cordial but merely to hear her voice for comparison purposes.

She replied, "Morning," with a straight face. Her voice was similar, maybe, to the one he'd heard on the walkie-talkie. Jim would have to hear more.

"Found anything yet?" he asked.

"Only this." She held up a bag containing a small piece of cloth. "It was stuck to a fence on the side of the walking path."

"Can I see that?" Gabe asked.

She handed it over to him, and he turned it around while looking at the fabric. The material appeared to be nylon and was bright pink. "Nice work. We'll have her roommate look at it. See if it matches something of Bethany's."

"Where exactly did you find it?" Jim asked.

Detective Walburg pointed in the direction of the woods. "We have the spot marked off." Jim walked toward the area and stopped by the edge of the woods. Gabe didn't follow him. Instead, he stood next to Walburg. They were talking, but Jim couldn't hear their words from such a distance. He found it curious that his partner wasn't following him and chose to stay next to Walburg. *What were they talking about?* Jim had to listen to her voice again. He had to know if she could be involved.

When Jim approached them, they stopped talking and looked his way. "Did you find any useful prints around the area?" he asked.

"No. I'll walk down there with you."

Wasn't the voice similar? He still couldn't be sure.

Another detective, Williamson, joined the three of them. "What did you think of the marks around the fence?" he asked.

"We're heading down now to take a look," Gabe said.

"I'll show you the spot," Williamson offered.

The earlier breeze had calmed, giving way to another day of sickly-hot temperatures. Sweat dripped down the backs of Jim's legs. The path dipped a bit off to the side of the road and then headed into a slightly thicker wooded area and over a wooden walking path. About ten feet after that, the detectives guided them off the trail. Jim could see the fence.

"It was here." Williamson pointed to the area marked off with yellow tape. "We couldn't find any good footprints, just smudge marks. The ground was messed up around the area, but if there were footprints, someone was smart enough to rub them out."

"Did the dogs get a trail?" Jim asked.

"For a bit, but it ended at the road. If it was Bethany, she didn't complete her journey on foot. She got into a vehicle."

Jim thought of the voice speaking to him through the walkie-talkie and heard the haunting words again: "Because he killed me." She was here somewhere.

"Just because she got into a car doesn't mean she stayed in one. We need to keep searching all the woods around the campus," Jim said.

Something between excitement and fear formed a tidal wave inside of Jim. The voice couldn't be that of a dead girl. The idea was crazy. But what if whoever had spoken to him knew the truth regarding her whereabouts? A gust of wind picked up speed from somewhere and blew against Jim's back. A chill shot up his spine. He'd never believed in supernatural happenings. It wasn't so much that he didn't believe in spirits and the afterlife, but the mingling of this realm with the next was the stuff found in fiction, not in crime solving.

But what if he was wrong? What if Bethany had spoken to him using the walkie-talkie? The chill of the supernatural coursed through his veins. Had he really heard Bethany? He shook his head. This job was making him crazy. He needed to stick to the facts, the stuff he could touch and prove. The evidence thus far did support his assumptions. Bethany had been in these woods yet not disposed of in this spot. Where was Evans now? Just as Jim contemplated calling him, his phone buzzed in his pocket.

"Jim, you need to get over here," Evans said. His authoritative tone made Jim's neck hairs stand on end.

"What do you have?"

"My guess..." Evans paused. "My guess is that I found Bethany Williams."

"We'll be right there." Jim ended the call, looked at Gabe, and plowed through the part that was going to get tricky.

"Evans thinks he found her over by the baseball fields."

"Evans?" Gabe asked, suspicion in his voice. "Why would Evans be out here?"

"I had a hunch and went with it," Jim added while heading to the car. "You coming?"

There was silence, yet Jim was quite sure he heard something very distinguishable—the unmistakable sound of power shifting.

For a moment, Jim felt the power surge through him. He had been correct. Young Bethany had been tossed aside in the woods farther away. When the caravan emptied out at the crime scene, a solemnness hung in the air. Jim wanted to assume the mood was for the obvious reasons: A young woman's lifeless body lay only a short distance from them. But Gabe's tightened jaw said otherwise. Jim shrugged off Gabe's anger and followed Evans and the others into the woods. Solving the case was far more important than Gabe's mood.

In the sky above, Jim noticed two buzzards. More were sure to come. Another few hours, and the birds would have drawn the attention of everyone. A wave of satisfaction swept through him. He had acted just in time so that he would receive the credit. For a moment, he contemplated the fact that his emotions were not consistent with what humanity deemed appropriate, yet he chalked it up to the fact that years on the force had already hardened him.

Within moments, he was staring down at the female's body. He saw only that—a body with a patchwork of random bruises and scrapes consistent with someone who had been dragged through the woods against her will. This corpse was not a daughter, friend, or future never to exist. In this career, his coldness was necessary for survival. The other detectives must feel the same.

The crime scene investigators, dressed in protective gear to preserve the scene, circled the corpse and stated their observations as cold data—measurements, colors, and placement. There was a two-inch bruise on her thigh, a scrape along her hip, and bruising to the throat area consistent with bruises caused by hands. Bethany's pink shirt, no longer bright and cheerful, was covered with mud. The tear was visible. Another member of the CSI team snapped pictures as the details continued to be rattled off. And then the investigator stopped talking. For a moment, Jim didn't notice the pregnant pause. He was watching Gabe, who now refused to make eye contact.

"We have something."

Jim looked back at the corpse and the CSI team encircling her. One of them held something small in his hand. "It's a...I think it's a challenge coin."

"A challenge coin?" Gabe asked.

"The military hands them out to represent being a part of the group or honoring a heroic act, but you can buy knock-offs online." He looked closely at the coin. "It should say *PRESENTED BY THE COMMANDER* or *FOR EXCELLENCE* somewhere on it. This one does not."

The investigator stepped closer as the group circled around him. The coin was red, black, and gold. On the front was a design. The investigator flipped it over and let them know that the Marine Corps Creed was on the backside. "I found it tucked between her left cheek and her teeth. Either someone is trying to throw us off course, or they are giving us our first strong piece of evidence."

"If this guy is a former Marine, it seems pretty bold to leave a Marine challenge coin at the scene of the crime," Gabe said.

"The guy just murdered someone for no apparent reason. Bold is one of many words to describe the perp," Jim said.

"How did Evans know where to look?" Detective Williamson asked.

Silence filled the air as Gabe waited for Jim to respond. Thinking it best, he kept his words brief. "I had a hunch and called Evans in to help check out the surrounding areas."

Detective Williamson looked at Gabe, who responded with a shrug. Heat rose under Jim's collar, and his skin flushed with rage. *What did they know?*

153

On the way back to the car, Jim attempted to make conversation.

"Well, I guess we don't need to show the roommate the shirt sample." Gabe did not respond. When Jim looked at his partner, their gazes locked. Gabe's eyes were filled with something much darker than admiration or gratitude for a job well done. "I just followed a hunch. That's all." Gabe ended the conversation with a laugh and a shake of his head.

Despite Gabe's displeasure, Jim felt confident he would be a hero when they returned to the office.

"I guess it wasn't espresso that had you all worked up earlier."

"Gabe…"

"You know what? I'm glad we found her. Let's leave it at that."

Jim turned his attention to the world passing by outside his window. Random students and curious people strolled along the sidewalk not far from the site. Jim stared without seeing any of them in detail until he spotted one man. He wore camouflage pants and a black T-shirt. The man was unshaven and haggard despite appearing to be in his late thirties or early forties.

"Stop the car." Jim's voice held urgency.

"What?"

"Stop the damn car."

Gabe pulled over and Jim scanned the group. The man had disappeared in its depths. He pushed through the people.

"Jim, what are you doing?"

His heart was racing. He caught a glimpse of the back of the stranger slipping farther into the group. *What would he say when he caught up to him?* Nothing. He had nothing real to go on. Jim watched as he disappeared. In the last moment, the man glanced over his shoulder at Jim as if urging him to follow him.

"Jim, what the hell are you doing?" Gabe was breathless.

"Nothing. I thought I saw something."

"You okay, man?" Jim knew Gabe was studying him, but he refused to look in his direction.

"Let's get out of here."

He headed to the car. Gabe followed, shaking his head in confusion, but he didn't ask any further questions.

Jim had seen him before, in the crowd from the crime scene, and most likely, would see him again.

Chapter 14

Published in 2004
Article

Dee
Soon the battalion will enter Camp Fallujah. Once
there, the Marines will await their orders to invade a city
already destroyed in a battle that ended only a short time
ago. Camp Fallujah was created and used by the people
of the Majahadeen-e-Khalq, or MEK. These people
fought against Western countries being able to use Iraq
for their resources, but in 2003, the MEK had no choice
but to give up their residency and turn it over to military
troops. The military hunkered down in the modest
confines built amid the arid desert and awaited orders
throughout the Iraqi war.

After weeks of traveling through the desert and
sleeping in holes in the ground, the camp's history meant
little to me. Instead, the basic accommodations I envision
within its walls are an oasis, offering a new life with
amenities I will not take for granted.

Back home, United States citizens are preparing for
our presidential election. Here in Iraq, there is a sense
that much of our fate depends on the outcome. The men
are ready, as ready as they can be, to defend our country
from the populations that harbor hatred for any
American citizen. In the year following 9/11, 181,510

Americans enlisted in the military. This number doesn't take into account all the young men and women who would enlist due to that horrific day. Even more men and women, who were too young to enlist but were scarred from the attacks on our country, enlisted when they became eligible. The images of their homeland crumbling under terrorism carried them across the ocean. The moment the planes hit the towers, the development of our young men and women was altered due to the hatred of radical groups. These groups served as looming trees overshadowing the brightness of our world. They sowed seeds that would spawn revenge and plant hatred and fear in American hearts. As with all acts of greed, hatred, and revenge, the ripple effects have and will continue from one generation to the next.

Who can blame a person for being angry and wanting vengeance? The seeds of darkness, planted on that day, force us to fight hatred with hatred and seek blood for blood. Our country will forever need protection from countries seeking to destroy our democracy and take away the freedoms we are accustomed to, that would make our daily lives unrecognizable.

As we journeyed across the barren desert, the Marines shared their stories with me—one seeking revenge, one honor, one approval, and one direction. I am left wondering who will escape this desert with their coveted treasure. Who will leave this war at all? At times, the Marine seeking revenge speaks with such anger and hatred for all Iraqi people, unable to decipher one group of people from the next. He is young, and I suspect, not nearly as hardened as his words portray. His reactions come from a place of ignorance and from

157

a disinterest in understanding beyond what his job demands. Some would consider him the perfect soldier, ready to fight and defend without question.

We, as Americans, can point fingers at the tragedies of 9/11 for why we want revenge, but why do the Iraqis hate us? Is there any validity to their emotions towards us? How do we appear to the world on the other side of the ocean, and when did differing views grow to a death sentence for any group? These questions trouble many of us as images of the Twin Towers collapsing haunt the airways still. Are we hated because we have freedom, money, and privilege? Perhaps. Or is this a holy war? The hypocrisy of a belief based on love yet enforced with violence is nothing new to humankind if one reads the Bible. The Old Testament is full of brutal scenes that can trouble the most devoted followers. Not only is the past stricken with the sickness of sin, but the Bible also states repeatedly that we will continue to live in a fallen world until its final collapse, where all will be made new.

Troublesome words, yet these are the words we turn to for hope. Does this make sense? Images of the bloodshed and destruction constantly reverberate through my mind. I close my eyes and see the destruction and devastation of yesterday, and I open them and witness today's suffering. There is no escape. I wonder if the desert sand is perhaps the same sand that absorbed the bloodshed from the stories told so long ago. I hear callous words, spawned from hatred and ignorance, fly from the mouths of some of the men in the battalion, and there are days I need to fight with all that I am not to tumble down that same slippery slope of despair. How is it that we can find hope while living in hell?

But somehow, we do. It's in our nature to hope. The

Bible never sugar-coated reality. The stories that take us by surprise in a holy book are written for a reason. They prepare us and inspire us to keep on, fight for what is righteous, never fall, and believe that love will win in the end.

Is that message the same one with which Osama bin Laden fueled his followers? Yes. He and his followers are fighting a holy war between Islam and the Western World and what it stands for. And what does the Western World stand for? Who are we to an outsider? Why do they hate us?

In the 1950s, Gamal Abdel Nasser became known as "The Lion of Egypt." He stood for modernizing the Middle East. Much of the Middle East was on board with the change at one point. This enthusiasm waned with each failed attempt, and the hatred for Westernization grew.

The last hope of this modernization fizzled after Saddam Hussein invaded Kuwait. The idea of modernization was swiftly overtaken by the desire of those in power to invoke Islamic fundamentalism. The concept behind the movement is to return to the strict code of conduct set by Islamic law. Instead of seeing Westernization as a worthwhile goal, the United States became known as "Great Satan."

And so, Osama bin Laden and his followers prepare to die in what they consider to be a holy war where they are the light, and we are the darkness. They believe by fighting Westernization, they are fighting immorality, greediness, and selfishness. Back home, families share traditions, friends gather, and with the holidays approaching, people look to be kind. There is goodness in all of them. And there is darkness. I know that each *day these Marines risk their lives, they are fighting for the goodness that is strong in our country. But from the vantage point of the back seat of our Humvee, darkness hides in every corner, and the light seldom flickers. I remind myself, as I search for hope in this hell, that the Good Book saw this moment, knew this violence would come, prepared us with disturbing violence, and promised us that goodness will prevail. It's a promise I'm holding tightly to, despite all.*

****

2018
Jim

"Detective Castille, I need to speak to you."

Jim glanced the Lieutenant's way.

"Privately," Larsen said, quieting the excited conversation throughout the office.

Foolishly, Jim followed with a proud grin on his face. He entered behind her. Larsen had a seat at her desk as Jim shut the door. She placed her elbows on the desktop and made a steeple with her two index fingers, then pressed them against her lips. As Jim stared into the eyes of his boss, a smile tugged at his lips. Humble responses played through his mind in anticipation of the compliments soon to be bestowed upon him. He cleared his throat and straightened himself in his chair.

"Explain to me," she began, "why you felt you had the right to bring a non-officer into a search site without permission."

Jim's smile disappeared as he struggled to hide his surprise.

"Evans wasn't the only non-officer out there searching. Students have been searching in the areas that

160

were not restricted. I don't see why enlisting someone with experience would be a controversial choice. Our own office was recruiting people to help. That's all I did. And as much as Evans crosses the line sometimes, we all know he's good at what he does."

Larsen sat back in the chair. She placed her arms on the armrests and stared at Jim, her jaw clenched. His face burned with a rage that he hoped was not evident to his boss. If Gabe had been the one to enlist Evans, he would probably be receiving accolades.

"Evans tells us that you told him where to search. Can you explain this?"

"Check my search history on my computer. I scanned maps of the college. The area was remote yet had road access. It stood out to me, that's all. Experience, maybe. I knew the area where Bethany ran was being covered, so I chose an area that was not being searched by our guys, students, or family, and I sent Evans to start his search there. The spot made sense to me. I can't explain it any more than that." The silence was suffocating. "I'm a detective and a good one. I have been in the office interviewing while busting at the seams to do more. I found a way to be in both places. And it worked."

"This is a warning, Jim. If you try anything like this again, there will be a consequence. Run your ideas by Gabe, get an okay. Steps and protocols need to be followed, Jim, and you are not above them. Am I being understood?"

"One hundred percent," Jim said before turning for the door. His job would be in jeopardy if he uttered one more word of what was going through his mind.

Jim's hands clenched the steering wheel as he drove

home through rush-hour traffic. A song fit only for a club blasted his eardrums. He changed the station three times before hitting the off button with more force than necessary. His head throbbed as it often did when his stress reached the boiling point. *Deep breath. Hold it. Let it out. Repeat.* The pulsing sensation by his temples eased. *Refocus. Breathe again.* The tightness in his chest subsided.

The bottom line was Bethany didn't deserve to die, especially so young, and bending a few rules would not stop Jim from bringing her killer to justice.

****

When he entered the house, it was silent. Unless Jim had class, he often got home hours before Gwen. He generally appreciated the silence after the heaviness of his job, but today he watched the clock, waiting for her to pull into their driveway. Jim would tell her nonchalantly that his hunch had been correct. Of course, he would leave out Larsen's harsh reaction. Jim would wait for Gwen to compliment him while downplaying his accomplishment. As the minutes ticked by, he became more annoyed by his desire to please her. By the time she entered the house, the desire had all but fizzled into nothingness.

Gwen stood at the counter while pulling fresh produce out of her canvas grocery bag, which she neatly folded and placed in the pantry after emptying it. "How was work?"

"We found the missing college student. I had a suspicion, acted on it, and it worked out."

"Oh, really." It was what Gwen said when Jim suspected she wasn't listening at all, which wasn't lost on him, considering he had just been scolded for the same flaw. "I invited Paul and Trish over for dinner Friday."

Gwen didn't care about his success, but Jim refused to show his agitation. He had already promised himself to be nonchalant about it, yet a pulsing sensation began at his temple, and a headache loomed on the horizon. He grabbed a cup, filled it with water, and drank the entirety.

"Paul and Trish, again?"

"Is there a problem?"

He tossed the plastic cup into the sink. Again, Gwen didn't look his way, which was evidence she was aware of the problem.

Trish was quiet, *reserved* to word it nicely, *utterly dull* to be honest. Why did this matter? Because Gwen wasn't inviting Trish over. She was inviting Paul. He was a pilot at the airport where Gwen worked. The two had grown into what Gwen referred to as friends through the years. She had even once described him as her work husband, the statement followed by a slight chuckle. Jim would classify their relationship differently, guessing it to be less innocent than Gwen wanted to admit.

The night would involve uncomfortably listening to work stories, shared laughs, intricacies that only airport employees cared about or understood. As the wine flowed, it would become even more apparent that Trish and Jim were spectators to Paul and Gwen's evening. Jim and Trish would share an occasional sympathetic smile that would go unnoticed by their occupied spouses. The evening would end with Gwen, half in the bag, passionately taking charge in the bedroom, leaving Jim to wonder whom she envisioned when she closed her eyes.

"Did you think to run the dinner plan by me

beforehand?"

"You never seem to mind if I invite people over for dinner. Why would you this time?"

Jim had never addressed his suspicion that Gwen had feelings for Paul. Why would he bother? The imagined outcome of such a conversation never ended in any way besides Jim looking like a weak, unconfident spouse. He wouldn't give Gwen that much. But inside, a piece of him was boiling. "Whatever," he grumbled.

"So, how did you say your day was?"

"Not worth repeating." Jim went to the crockpot and threw a lump of chicken and vegetables into a bowl.

"Aren't we going to sit and eat together?"

"Grab your bowl. I'm right here."

Gwen grabbed her bowl from the cupboard. Her mind was obviously elsewhere. They ate in silence, rinsed their bowls, and put the dishes in the dishwasher. The sound of clanking dinnerware rang through the room.

"I'm going to grab a drink with Gabe tonight."

"Oh, great. I'm glad you two are doing something outside of work. Getting along with your co-workers helps, you know."

"Helps what?"

"Well, you know. It will help you get noticed."

He fought it. That boiling sensation inside of him. "I won't be late." Jim headed out the door, not knowing where to, just knowing he couldn't sit in the house while Gwen planned her dinner with Paul and pretended, only pretended, to notice Jim was anywhere nearby.

****

Jim wasn't exactly drunk when he pulled into the driveway hours later. Sure, he had had a few. A fog was lifting from his mind, a clearing. He would be able to hide any buzz he was feeling from Gwen, but to be sure, he decided to spend some time in the garage before heading to bed. She would be slightly irritated by a few too many on a weekday but pissed about the driving thing.

Jim ran his hand over the Jeep as if it were an old Lab waiting for his master to return. "Not today, my boy. Not today." Jim's gaze was already fixated on the walkie-talkie as if it was a new, overpowering love needing all his attention. He had the time. He could offer his new interest anything it needed. It took only moments of fidgeting before the static began to clear, and a voice sifted through the sands.

"It's not him." Jim recognized the same woman's voice. This time, Jim wasn't surprised or frightened by the words, but they were confusing. What was he missing? She must be talking about the father. Jim's mind scrambled over the conversation they had had with him and stumbled over the words that had jutted out like jagged rocks. "What do you mean? Are you saying it's not your father, or it's not the professor? Give me a little help here."

"You know who it was?" the voice whispered as if defeated and in its final moments.

Jim envisioned possible scenes between Bethany and her father. A young Bethany was probably repeatedly degraded, belittled by the power of an adult figure in her life, a person whose job was to protect her. Once used as weapons against his daughter, Austin's bitter words would become evidence they would use against him. Jim just had to dig a bit deeper. He set the walkie-talkie down gently. Who else could it have been?

Then Jim thought of the man walking away from the scene. He needed to find him.

"We'll get him, Bethany. I promise you. The truth is always revealed in each of us."

Chapter 15

Present Day
Patient 541

Journal Entry

The sun peeked above the horizon, alerting me to the new day. As I had drifted off to sleep, I hadn't thought about the other men stumbling across me and Dee curled up together. Fortunately, Dee had. Sometime in the night, she had crept out of our desert bed.

Fallujah was only a day's travel away, and despite the fact the battle had not officially begun, sounds of war rang through the air.

When I crawled out of my hole, I witnessed the other Marines rising from their makeshift beds as well. Dee had her back resting on the Humvee, eating what appeared to be a packaged cupcake. Her gaze met mine, and she nodded in such a way as to say, I see you, but it's best to keep your distance. *We had crossed a dangerous line, yet I wouldn't take back a moment of the encounter.*

Without warning, a shot pierced the air, forcing all of us to scramble for cover. Some Marine beyond my range of vision quieted the problem by firing off a few rounds. My heart raced within my chest as I scanned the area for Dee. I spotted her huddled with Toby behind the vehicle, and I ran their way.

"Are you okay?" I asked, my gaze never leaving Dee.

"We're both fine," Toby replied as he stood, shaking the earth off his pants. "That's one hell of an alarm clock."

"Sure is." Toby walked away, and I stood face to face with Dee. "I'll ask you again. Are you all right? With everything?"

"I'm good, but..." she paused.

"You don't have to say it, but can you promise me one thing?"

"Yes."

"When we get back in the States, can you give me one chance? You deserve more than a hole in the desert." I couldn't even be sure what I meant by one chance, but my life rested on the answer.

"Definitely." She smiled at me, and for a moment, only the two of us existed. That moment ended with the conversation lighting up the radio. With my focus on Dee, I only caught a few words, Fallujah being one. Then, the air shifted, and when I glanced toward the Master Sergeant, his face told everything. Something was building, but after weeks of traveling through the desert, fearing what was to come, a part of me craved it—whatever it was.

We loaded the Humvees with all the artillery and supplies. As adrenaline pumped through my body once again, I glanced around at the other Marines. Excitement darted through the air like static, but amid the buzzing energy, faces stood out. I looked away from the fearful gazes of the men staring into the hurricane of impending battle, so their weaknesses could not penetrate me.

"How about you? Are you okay?" Dee asked me.

"What do you mean by okay?"

"I guess I mean, are you ready for this?"

"I'm as ready as I'll ever be."

Dee walked away, grazing my hand with hers as she passed.

A rough hand slammed against my back and jolted me out of my stupor.

"You gonna sit around and stare at everyone, or are you gonna help pack this shit up?" Shane didn't wait for my answer. His broad shoulders split the crowd as he passed by.

"Let's move it," the corporal shouted.

The men worked in near silence, loading the Humvees. We traveled hours before stopping. A small town stood in front of us, its roads deserted. An eerie feeling slithered up my spine. Where was everyone?

"Interrogative, should we pass?" the first Vic leader asked over the radio.

"Affirmative. Cleared to go," the lieutenant answered. The sound of the Humvees moving forward made saliva stick in my throat. I coughed slightly. From the corner of my eye, I saw Dee watching me. Fear emanated from her, and I could do nothing to console her.

The caravan of Humvees passed down the quiet streets. We scanned the windows through the scopes of our guns. Sweat trickled down my neck, which was nothing new except for my awareness of feeling as if everything was happening in slow motion.

In one of the top windows, a figure moved. "I have movement," I called out.

"Most likely civilian," Marshall responded. "Which

building—?"

Like a fiery bomb, the Humvee in front of us flew into the air.

"Missile pointed straight at us," Shane yelled while letting off rounds of ammunition.

"Abort vehicle," Marshall shouted.

We scrambled out and crouched behind another Humvee. I inhaled deeply but the heavy air stuck in the back of my throat. The scorching heat encircled us as we waited for another sound. The missile whizzed by us and entered the building behind us, creating a cloud of stench from the debris and desert sand.

The bitter taste of fear filled the back of my throat. The attack gave away the sniper's location. Without thinking, I fired my M16, and the sniper disappeared. My shot had found its target. All went quiet.

While scanning the building, I stole a glance at Dee. Her face was ghostly white, and she was visibly shaking. All I wanted to do was protect her. That meant I needed to focus, be a Marine, and do the deeds that needed to be done. The door to the building creaked open, and a figure emerged. My eyes pulsed with adrenaline. The boy moved his hand. "He's armed," I shouted. All weapons were prepared to fire, but mine went off. My bullets shot through the air and took out a boy who was far too young to be a soldier of any sort.

Oh, my God, what did I do? *I didn't speak the words aloud, but my mind screamed them. I closed my eyes tightly to shut out the guilt and to reinvent the moment. When I envisioned the boy, without a doubt, he held a weapon, but I couldn't completely fool myself. This was war, damn it. My brain screamed the new mantra repeatedly, but when I glanced at Dee, something inside me broke. To her, I had become the enemy.*

"You killed him," Dee yelled. "You killed that little boy."

"He had a weapon, Dee. He could have shot you or any of us."

"I didn't see a weapon." Tears were streaming down her face. "He was a baby. You killed a baby."

"Shut the hell up," I screamed. "Just shut the hell up. You don't know anything about war. In war, a ten-year-old with a weapon is a soldier, not a baby."

Dee kept whimpering. Her whimper echoed through my mind long after she had quieted.

Medics, driving an M113, collected the burned bodies of our fallen Marines. No one touched the boy, not that day and maybe ever. Maybe if I had gone back and laid a gentle hand on his corpse or shut his eyes, so he looked as if he had only fallen asleep, the boy wouldn't have threatened to haunt me, but sympathy had no place in war. I glanced back at him one more time and then tried to forget him. Once the danger was over, we drove past the destroyed Humvee and continued our journey.

Hours passed, and Dee remained silent as our caravan of Marines, still awaiting official orders, made its way closer to Fallujah. The coldness burned deep. She had to understand. She had to forgive me. I reached for her hand, but she shifted away, resting her head on the window. For a woman who spent her life contemplating the evils of the world and how to conquer them, Dee had surprisingly passed over the only slice of heaven I'd experienced in Iraq. Our moment together was nothing more than debris in the road, debris not worth a second glance in the rearview mirror.

But it wasn't only Dee who was quiet. We all rode in silence, surrounded by the suffocating air. Just like before a storm, ominous and intriguing energy lingered between us. After some time, the rhythmic movement of the vehicle lulled Marshall and Dee to sleep. As much as I envied them, too many thoughts raced through my mind for me to drift off.

As Dee slept, I studied her, the contours of her lips that had sought mine out and then rejected me only hours later. She was a mystery to me in so many ways. Dee's head gently bumped against the window, yet she didn't stir. Her sleep was sound and deep. The pad in which she endlessly scribbled stuck out from her bag just enough for me to see a few words: Accident or not… *There was no doubt in my mind what she was referring to. A wave of nausea rushed through my body, increasing to the point that my saliva warmed in my mouth. A tingling sensation resonated through my lip, which commonly happened to me due to stress.*

Without care of her waking, I reached into her bag and pulled out the document. The article in progress covered many pages, and I frantically skimmed the paragraphs searching for the parts I dreaded would be there. Bomb…Explosion…remnants of the building flew through the air. The thud of concrete colliding with our vehicles…chaos…fear…We sought refuge behind the Humvee. The desert heat and unbridled fear caused sweat to trickle down the back of my neck.

My reading slowed as I reached the scene I feared would be replayed forever in her written word.

A young Iraqi boy emerged from the hollows of the crumbling building. Dark with sadness and despair, his eyes scanned the vehicles and debris. His youthfulness shone like a beacon of peace in the middle of a war zone. The young boy and I locked gazes, and I saw something besides sadness in his eyes. I searched them as a chef might sample a dish to determine an unknown spice. I was closing in on the emotion. The mystery behind his eyes was about to reveal itself from behind the cloud. We continued to stare, speaking a silent language. The boy then made a movement, slight as if he might wave. A shot rang out so close to my ear that I ducked, covering my ears that rang from the blast.

When I looked up, I witnessed the Marine, the lost and internally damaged soul I have studied for weeks, holding his weapon aimed directly at the doorframe. Slowly, I pulled myself back to a standing position, my gaze never leaving the Marine. His face was stone. When I could no longer ignore my need to look, I turned toward the building. The boy was a crumpled heap. Blood flowed from his small frame.

Tears stream from my eyes as I write these words, but the Marine stares out his window, his eyes as dry as the desert.

Another Marine says into the air as we drive away, "They are all enemies here."

I envision the child's limp body and wonder where we as a human race have gone so wrong because, as I stood amid hell on earth, there seemed to be only one truth that deserved our attention. Something…Everything has gone wrong when men, put in a position to shoot children for our country's freedom, are also men we call heroes.

****

The Lieutenant's voice came over the radio. "Last stop, 40 klicks ahead."

Dee stirred.

"Ten-four," Marshall responded. "It's about to get real, boys."

Dee rubbed her face as if trying to wake up. Her nails were broken and dirty. I didn't care that her notebook lay open in my hands. Her acknowledgment would save me from having to explain my anger. Dee's attention drifted my way, first to the notebook and then to my face. She didn't lose eye contact as she reached for the pad and guided it out of my hands. Not until she'd tucked it back into her bag did her stare break free.

She diverted her attention to the sand stretching out for miles on the other side of the glass. Could she feel the hatred burning inside of me? The darkness I had held at bay gained strength at that moment. Oh, Dee, *I wanted to ask her,* do you know the monster you have just released?

****

2018
Jim

Dreading the night to come, Jim entered the kitchen. Gwen bounced between the stove and the counter. She didn't notice him enter as she chopped and stirred to the beat of the music playing loudly in the background. Jim watched her for a minute, studied the glow of her smile, and knew who was responsible for the energy circulating the room. Of course, it wasn't him, her husband, the man who was never named primary investigator, the man whose salary paled in comparison. What if he had destroyed his chances of a promotion by bringing in Evans? Jim hated himself at that moment almost as much as he hated her.

Jim shut the door loudly so she would hear the thump over Alexa's music selection. Gwen looked up. The glow on her face didn't have the decency to fade. Wasn't there an ounce of guilt within her?

He placed his keys on the designated key hook. "Smells good."

"Thanks. It's just spaghetti and homemade meatballs, but it's a favorite," she replied.

"Whose favorite?"

Gwen looked up. "Everyone loves pasta. I have salad and French bread as well. You always seem to like pasta."

"Yeah, I do. It's just you usually think it's too full of carbs."

"It's too many carbs to eat all the time, but it's a Friday. Rules can be broken on Fridays."

"Good to know." Jim eased up behind his wife and kissed her on the neck. "Is that a new fragrance?" Playfully, he nuzzled into her skin, but she pulled away ever so slightly.

"Jim, I'm never going to have this ready and cleaned up before Paul and Trish get here. Could you set the table?"

A pounding began behind his eyes as it often did before a migraine. He grabbed a glass of water and then went for the pain medicine.

"Was that a yes?" Gwen asked.

"Yes, Gwen, I'll set the table."

They worked together with only occasional small talk. Jim set the table, prepared the garlic bread, and opened the wine. He poured himself a large glass so that Gwen might not notice how much he took down before she reached for her own. Just as Gwen placed the last pan

175

inside the cupboard and closed it, the doorbell rang.

****

Jim shook hands with Paul and Trish as they entered. He silently cursed Gwen for the hypocrisy her desires created. He hoped her infatuation was to be a foolish passing crush. If Jim made too much of it, the relationship would evolve into an actual affair. No, he had to play it cool, wait for the newness to wane like the sweltering sun that shone too fiercely on a summer day. Patience…and then all would return to normal.

The medicine hadn't calmed his debilitating headache. Gwen's voice pierced through his skull; her laughter vibrated within his brain. Paul's voice was a drum hammering a constant rhythm Jim could not tune out. The wine had not had enough time to have effect, but Jim could not deny the change in his wife's behavior. Gwen's drunkenness wasn't from the bottle. She was intoxicated from the adrenaline Paul's presence produced. Jim watched her, almost with pity but mainly with anger. The rage boiled like acid inside of him.

She was polite, as always, to Trish, who never stood up against the demoralizing conversation or called Gwen out on her pathetic attempts to get closer to her husband.

God, wasn't Jim being just as passive?

After about an hour of hellish chitchat, they went to the table. Jim and Gwen sat at the heads of the table, and Paul and Trish sat on either side. The glow of candlelight lit their ordinary dining room table and created a room that seemed foreign to Jim, even though he walked by it daily. When was the last time he and Gwen had used this room? Had his wife ever pulled out the candles for him? Jim couldn't recall.

With a controlled voice, Gwen turned her attention

toward Trish. "Trish, what did you say you do again?"

Gwen asked the question each time they were together. Then Gwen, the woman always in control of herself when Paul's presence wasn't creating some primal rush of adrenaline-enriched blood, would not be able to calm her mind enough to process Trish's answer yet again.

"I'm in real estate," Trish answered.

"Oh, yes. I think I remember you mentioning that."

"I believe I have," Trish added politely, yet Jim could see a tension in her posture.

"Jim, honey, would you mind opening the cabernet that's on the counter?" Gwen's gaze drifted to Paul as she spoke. "You must get bored with all her weeknight and weekend showings. I'm assuming that's when people have the time to look at properties?"

Jim stood and did as Gwen told him, listening as he walked away.

"I try to schedule my appointments when Paul is busy, but if he's not working, he enjoys a morning to sleep."

Jim returned and filled each glass. He went light on Gwen's pour, knowing his wife would lose control of politeness with one more drink, and Jim and Trish would blur into the backdrop. From the corner of his eye, he saw Trish check her watch. She knew, too.

"Would you like Trish and me to clean up so that you and Paul can catch up?" Jim asked facetiously, testing his wife. Trish's gaze bore into him with either curiosity or anger; he couldn't be sure.

"Seriously, that's so sweet, Jim."

Fail.

"No problem. Trish, I hope you don't mind that I

offered your services. Work talk bores the shit out of me."

"No, that's fine," she answered with tiredness in her voice, but she rose anyway and began clearing the table. When they entered the kitchen, their hands full of plates, Jim smiled and told her to have a seat.

"I wouldn't make you clean up this mess. I was just saving you from the conversation."

He reached for another unopened bottle of wine. With a lift of the bottle, he asked Trish if she wanted a refill. Her smile didn't cover the concern in her eyes, but she nodded and raised her glass.

"Thanks. It's good to know I'm not the only one who is a bit tired of it," Trish offered quietly.

"I'll make another sweep and grab the glasses."

After a short time, Jim had the dishes rinsed and in the dishwasher. He topped off his glass and had a seat next to her.

"So, real estate, huh?"

"I know, really exciting. I'm not landing 747s in lightning storms."

"Their stories are a bit more exciting to the two of them than they are to anyone else, especially by the third time they've told them." She glanced through the doorway into the dining room. "You should hear him go on about his years in the service."

"Paul's ex-military?"

"He flew in the Air Force."

"Interesting." Jim thought of the challenge coin. "I'm sure he shared those stories more than once."

Trish laughed softly and tucked a strand of hair behind her ear. Then a somberness settled over her face. When she spoke, she looked directly into Jim's eyes, insisting on his honesty. "Do you think we need to be worried about the two of them?"

Jim leaned back in his chair enough to glimpse Gwen and Paul, lost in conversation. Gwen's hands moved with every word; excitement gushed even from her fingertips. And then he did what his training had taught him to do to calm the victim: He lied.

"Nah. They're just a couple of co-workers happy to be outside the confinements of their job."

He swallowed a swig of wine and smiled at the poor soul before him. "Nothing to worry about at all."

By the time Jim closed the door behind Paul and Trish, he was exhausted: exhausted by listening, exhausted by trying not to, and exhausted by containing all the emotions that had threatened to spew forth at any moment. Gwen was obviously beyond tipsy. Jim walked behind her as she stumbled to the bedroom while declaring that the night had been a success. She then repeated her statement in question form as if making her husband agree with her would wash away any hidden guilt.

"Jim, don't you think it was a good evening?" Gwen slurred. She reached down to pull off her high heel while simultaneously balancing herself on the wall.

"It was great, Gwen." Jim forced the words through his clenched jaw.

"Really?" Her dress hit the floor. "Do you honestly think so?"

"I already answered you."

Not bothering to complete the rituals of brushing her teeth or washing her face, Gwen crawled between the sheets.

He remained standing in the doorway.

"Aren't you coming to bed?" she asked.

"I think I'll leave you to your dreams tonight," Jim said, but she was already asleep. He had no intention of being used as a prop anyway.

His brutal headache was only getting worse, and even though he recognized that he was also heavily buzzed, it didn't explain his mental fog over parts of the night. Perhaps he'd just mentally willed himself away from Paul and Gwen's after-dinner conversation. He recalled tidbits, enough to annoy him, but their words were a blurred memory for the most part. On the other hand, the image of Gwen laughing at Paul's every word like a giddy teenager was crystal clear.

Jim walked back through the dark kitchen and fumbled for the garage light. He needed the secret world the walkie-talkie linked him with, maybe now more than ever. Nothing in his life seemed to be making sense otherwise.

"Jim, where are you?" Gwen was in the kitchen, calling to him. The walkie-talkie was cold in his hand, silent as a stone.

"Damn her," he said to the air. "I'm in the—"

The garage door opened. "What are you doing? Why aren't you in bed?" Gwen looked pale and disheveled.

"I couldn't sleep. Why are you up?"

"I got sick. I guess I drank too much. I hope I didn't act like an idiot."

Jim looked at the walkie-talkie one last time before setting it down. "I'll get you some water and something for your headache. Try to fall back to sleep. It will make the misery pass quicker." He brushed past her into the kitchen and opened the cabinet door.

"I'm sorry, Jim."

"For what?"

"If I acted poorly."

"I didn't think you were acting at all. That's the problem."

"What's that supposed to mean?" Gwen asked, but without any fight in her voice.

"It means you have some things to figure out, Gwen. Now let's go to bed."

They walked silently to the bedroom—Jim's thoughts still with the walkie-talkie. Gwen's mind, Jim was sure, was scrambling to decode the messages hidden within her conversation with Paul.

Gwen stood in Jim's way of discovery, just as he stood in hers.

Chapter 16

Present Day
Patient 541

Journal Entry
When I next walk into the chaplain's office, I'm not the man he met with before. I'm a blend of the man looking for answers and the man who has them. The answers aren't clear yet, but the terror is building within me as my journal writing loosens my memories.

I sit in the chair, and the chaplain greets me with his smile, but his expression changes quickly.

"What's happened?" he asks.

"The journal."

"What do you mean, the journal?"

"I'm remembering." My hands are shaking. "My dreams are starting to reveal things. I see the war. I see the dead Iraqis, but the faces…"

I wring my hands and stand up. The chaplain straightens in his chair.

"The faces aren't the Iraqis' any longer. I see the women." My voice rises. "I'm seeing the women."

Suddenly I'm shouting words I can't even remember. The next moment, I'm being escorted back to my room. It's days before I dare to write again.

****

The stars above us had begun to peek at us as the

world wobbled between day and night. Together, we set up our makeshift camp, concealing as much of ourselves as possible. We were so close to Fallujah that we could see the city in the distance, yet it was far enough away that one might think it tranquil. I envisioned the dreaded images of the days to come—bloodshed, loss, and destruction.

My sanity teetered on a tightrope that shook beneath my feet. The energy I needed to remain balanced made my head throb and my vision blur. Dee was unpacking some supplies and still refusing to glance my way. I needed her to grab hold of me, to apologize, to tell me she had overreacted. I needed her to tell me I wasn't a killer. Maybe if she did, the ugliness growing inside me would lessen from a full boil to a slow simmer. I could handle a slow simmer. I could recover if she just looked my way and smiled.

"Dee," I said into the darkness. She continued to walk away, not witnessing me punch the seat and curse into the air. I breathed slowly, trying to calm myself. "Dee," I called, but she was gone.

Any day now, I would be fighting for my survival, yet I couldn't stop my hands from shaking. How could I hit my target if I couldn't control my nerves? My only chance of survival was falling from reality and becoming something this world could no longer hurt. Insignificant details like Dee's words on a page could not be allowed to burn into me. My eyes closed, and I watched myself falling away from the desert into a dark abyss. Farther and farther, I drifted into the darkness. I was almost gone when Toby nudged me.

"We've got to set up camp." Toby's voice was gentle. "She's not going to understand. Hell, would you

if you hadn't trained for this? Give her time." Toby had read my thoughts and rescued me from them.

Hours passed as we ate, dug our foxholes, and covered our vehicles, forming a makeshift home. Exhaustion, like I had never experienced, came over me. My mouth craved more water than I could offer it, and my legs wobbled like gelatin under my weight.

"Look up," Toby said.

I looked up to see the sun setting behind Fallujah. The buildings were ablaze with color, and for a moment, it was beautiful. Several Marines rested their arms on the handles of the shovels and marveled at the image of the city. For the moment, the picture before us was not that of a war scene. Fallujah imitated a place altogether different, something peaceful and beautiful. As the sun set behind the rubble, we heard the sergeant calling us.

"Get some sleep, men. You don't have many peaceful nights left," he said.

I curled into my foxhole still wet with sweat and coated with desert sand. I stared up into the night sky and tried to force my fears from my mind. My thoughts drifted to Dee, sleeping somewhere nearby. I closed my eyes and pictured the contours of her face, her bright blue eyes, her smile...My thoughts of her lulled me to sleep.

****

All we had accomplished the night before was taken apart in the morning. The time was fast approaching when we would be tested beyond what most of us had ever experienced in the past. The training, waiting, and preparing mimicked a balloon pumped with air to the point of popping. One way or the other, the tension had to be released.

Before noon, we pulled into Camp Fallujah, and in the strangest of ways, arriving there was the closest I had felt to home in weeks. We unpacked in the tents, where we each selected a cot to call our own. We ate at a table and used a latrine instead of a hole in the sand. Many of the Marines unwound by throwing around a football. So much of me wanted to join in and act as if all my wiring had not melted inside my mind, but I couldn't bust through the damaged shell. Shane yelled out to me, "Private, get your ass in the game." I waved him off. At first, he stared at me as if he would give one of his snide remarks and then his shoulders slumped. He shook his head and mumbled under his breath. Could he see the crazy behind my eyes even then?

Three days later, the US reelected President Bush, and all hell broke loose. We received our orders to penetrate the city, sparking the Second Battle of Fallujah, otherwise known as Operation Phantom Fury. The day was November 7, 2004. I can't recall many conversations in the three days spent at Camp Fallujah. I only know that neither Dee nor I spoke to each other.

Once the orders were handed down, Camp Fallujah resembled a kicked anthill where we all scrambled to prepare for war. Weapons and ammunition filled the vehicles, along with water and food. I stood outside the Humvee, stuffing supplies into a duffel bag. Toby opened the driver's seat door, paused, and looked me up and down. His expression held concern, not judgment, which unnerved me.

"You ready for this?"

"Bring it." My words were harsh and short. When I met his glance, Toby nodded. His fear showed clearly in his eyes. "You?" I asked.

"I don't think we can ever really be ready for this, but it's going to happen anyway, I suppose."

"I suppose it is."

The backseat door opened on the other side of the vehicle. Toby and I both looked in shock as Dee crawled into the Humvee.

"Dee?" Toby asked.

"That's me."

"You can stay at the camp, you know."

"I know my options."

Toby glanced back at me with a look of concern. I only shrugged.

"I think you're making a mistake, Dee," Toby said.

"It's my decision."

Toby shook his head and crawled into his seat. Marshall slid into the passenger seat. "We're about to pull out, men. Get settled in."

Shane grabbed Dee's door before she could close it. His frame blocked the sun.

"Seriously," Shane commented.

"It's her choice," Marshall said. "Jump in, Shane."

"Do you know the shit you're about to see?" Shane hovered at her door as she stubbornly adjusted her seatbelt.

"I've seen plenty, and I'm still here, aren't I?"

Shane stared at her in awkward silence for a long moment. "And how did that go over?"

"I reacted. Yes. I'm human."

"Shane, it's been discussed. Leave it." Marshall's voice was stern.

"Well, I hope she knows she could lose her life with the rest of us." Shane climbed up to the turret. "Not one of us is promised a return flight from this adventure, my

dear."

"I'm well aware of the dangers."

I remained quiet as we moved forward toward our fate. We weren't alone. The Iraqi and British military had joined us to rid Fallujah of the trained fighters and Islamic insurgents hiding within the city, yet inside of me was complete aloneness and emptiness. I was nothing short of a hollow shell full of white noise.

The vehicles left the camp, kicking up dirt along the way. Everywhere I looked, the world was the same brown and gray; the land, the buildings, and the sky blended into one. We drove with a seriousness that before now had come in spurts. This conviction would not leave us until someone was declared a winner, and for the first time, I doubted that the winner would be us. No military forces had entered the city in the months after the first battle. The US troops had attempted to control the comings and goings of Fallujah, but we weren't fools either. We knew that the enemy supplies would be plentiful. Only after the battle was complete did the officials truly see how abundant their collection had become: PMKs, RPGs, SA-7s, SA-14s, older Communist Bloc or ComBloc weaponry, and anti-aircraft missiles would later be found in the debris once called a city.

But on that day, as we focused on our mission, we knew nothing of those supplies. We expected the insurgents had spent the quiet months drawing battle plans and filling caches with weapons of some sort. We anticipated that improvised explosive devices, or IEDs, would be buried throughout the city. We had been warned that the enemy, hunkered down in spider holes, awaited our arrival, and snipers, watching in eager anticipation, stood guard in buildings.

My back remained to Dee as I scanned the area. With all my energy, I forced the knowledge of her existence from my mind. And I succeeded, for a bit. I existed in a bubble where the world hummed around me. The quiet only lasted moments, it seemed, and then the world crashed down on me. The first loss is the hardest. The first ding on a Mercedes, the first touchdown from the opposing team, the first scar on a youthful body—each one rips away the dream of being invincible and knocks us down to reality. We are not untouchable. We will feel pain. We will not walk out completely victorious because there will be loss. But in war, the losses are enormous, and the scars never heal.

****

2018
Jim

Gwen suggested a weekend away in Helen, Georgia. She insisted the mountain air would breathe new life into their relationship. A part of Jim wanted to say no, but ending a marriage wasn't something to be taken lightly. Jim hoped that Gwen's invitation meant she hadn't already given into her temptations with Paul. He couldn't forgive that. If Gwen wanted to put in some effort, he would meet her in the middle.

They drove the many hours north and pulled into the driveway of their rented house. Mountains served as the backdrop, but the town encircled them. Gwen looked apprehensive one moment and excited the next. Jim even thought she had a glow about her despite Paul being nowhere around.

After settling into their weekend home, they decided to walk through the town, stopping at the local shops and grabbing drinks and appetizers as they went. The experience transported Jim to a time when their relationship excited them both. In the beginning, the conversations began slowly due to nervousness and not knowing each other. Now, the quietness sprung from knowing each other too well and becoming strangers all over again. He hoped that as the beers kept coming, the words would flow easily, just as they once had. Jim reached for Gwen's hand, and they walked hand in hand, laughing over silly memories and making new ones as they went. For the first time in too long, Jim remembered how much he loved his wife.

They ended their day by stopping at a nearby pub for dinner. They sat at a picnic table overlooking a small brook. The water flowed over a rocky bed, and children hopped from rock to rock as their parents watched from the patio area.

"It's been a great day, hasn't it?" Gwen said.

"It's been good."

Gwen quieted and looked out over the water. When she turned back, Jim saw tears in her eyes. "You know I love you, don't you?" she asked.

"I know you try to."

She nodded but didn't add anything to his comment.

"I love you too, Gwen, and I know I'm not easy. I'm not much of a romantic."

"You don't need to be." She wiped the tears away. "Or at least, you shouldn't need to be."

"I'll try to do better. I know you're missing something. We're missing something."

Gwen began to openly cry. She grabbed her napkin and tried to hide her tears from onlooking customers.

"It's both our faults. Or maybe it's neither of our

faults. Life just has its way of carrying a person in the current. It's impossible to stay in one place, and almost as hard to make this journey at the same pace and path as the next person."

"Jim, what are you saying? Do you think it's not even worth trying?"

"I think we've drifted a long way from each other. Together, we have to decide if it's worth all the effort to make our paths connect again."

"Isn't that why we took this trip? Because we decided our marriage is worth it?"

"This trip was to help us decide if what's left is salvageable." Jim chugged half of his beer and then set it down. "I'm not ready to give up, but I'm not going to be made a fool of either."

"What's that supposed to mean?"

"You know what it means, Gwen. If your heart already belongs to someone else, let me help you with the decision. I don't want us anymore."

Gwen grabbed his hand. "Jim, my heart doesn't belong to anyone else. We just need more of this. More you-and-me time to remember why we got married in the first place."

"I'm willing to do that. We'll do more dates. How's that for a start?"

"Sounds great."

Jim glanced at his watch. "It's almost ten o'clock."

"Time has flown by today, hasn't it?"

Jim smiled at his wife. "It's been a good day."

Their gazes locked, and Jim was overwhelmed with longing.

"Let's get back to the house before we're both too tired to enjoy the time alone."

Jim waved down the waitress, and when he placed his hand back on the table, Gwen placed hers on top of his. She rubbed his hand with her fingers. "I love you, Jim. You do know that don't you?" Gwen repeated what she had said minutes before, but this time Jim heard a goodbye hidden in her tone.

"I love you too, Gwen."

****

The walk back to the house was quiet. A pain in Jim's heart stung yet simultaneously felt good. For months, he had felt nothing for his wife but a growing animosity. This weekend, he remembered the woman he had fallen in love with, which made the fact that he might lose her hurt even more. Jim savored the pain as if its presence was proof of life left in their marriage.

They walked into the house, and Gwen turned to him. She caressed his face, looked at him like she was seeing him for the first time. Jim wrapped his arms around her lower back and pulled her closer to him. Their lips met in the middle, both seeking the other. Jim picked her up and carried her to the bedroom. One moment, the kissing and tearing at each other's clothes was fierce and demanding, and the next, he or she would slow it down by tracing an arm, abdomen, or face with gentle fingers, slowly and softly as if uncovering a treasure that could disappear at any moment.

They fell asleep in each other's arms. Neither woke throughout the night. When the sun broke through the blinds, Jim opened his eyes. Gwen, still sleeping peacefully, lay naked next to him.

Gwen's phone buzzed on the nightstand. Jim didn't want to look. He told himself not to the whole time his hand reached for the phone. When he flipped it over, he saw a picture of Paul and Gwen in their work uniforms. Paul would have selected the image on his end, but why was Gwen in it? Why not Trish? Maybe he had a work phone and a personal phone. The message was cut off, and Jim couldn't recall Gwen's passcode. What he did see was, —*Don't enjoy your weekend too much.*—

The message could have been platonic. Hell, Jim could ask to see it when Gwen woke up. But he wouldn't. He had to trust her if there was any hope of saving their marriage. His headache started to rear its ugly head. He went to the bathroom to search for his medicine and realized he had forgotten to bring it. There was only one other solution: He needed to run. Without a sound, he put on his running clothes and slipped out the door.

Chapter 17

Present Day
Patient 541

Journal Entry
The launched mortar hit the Humvee beside us, blowing it apart. Our Humvee blew over from the blast. We scrambled out of the wreckage, each of us scanning ourselves and each other for injuries. By some miracle, no one showed any critical damage. Marshall waved for us to follow him. He may have spoken as well, but my ears were ringing, and my mind swam with confusion. We grabbed a few essentials and ran for cover behind another vehicle.

Rounds of bullets whizzed by our heads and hit unintentional targets behind us. Clouds of dust and debris enshrouded us. All we could do was fire back. There wasn't time for strategizing, only reacting. Even thoughts of Dee and her safety were squeezed from my mind. I was vaguely aware of her hunkered down near Shane and hugging her knees. She shouldn't be here. We all knew it, and I suspected she knew it as well.

"We need to get in a building," Marshall shouted over the din. A few seconds later, he yelled for us to follow his lead. "Dee, stay close."

Still firing our guns, we ran to another vehicle, crouched down, and fired off several more rounds before running again. Marshall kicked in a door of one of the intact buildings. We filed in, checking each corner for insurgents. We went our separate ways yet stayed relatively close to each other. I heard gunfire come from Shane's direction, and then he yelled, "Clear."

Dee stayed between Shane and Marshall, and we crept up the stairs, weapons in the ready position. On the second floor, we found an empty room with a window overlooking the city. "In here," Marshall told us. "Push the dresser against the door. It won't keep them out, but at least we'll know they're coming."

Toby and I followed orders. When I turned around, Marshall was squatted down in front of Dee. "Take a deep breath." Dee listened. Her skin was ashen, and she looked close to passing out. "In and out. That's it. You got this."

"I shouldn't have come."

"Damn straight," Shane mumbled.

"But you did, and now you need to breathe." Marshall reached behind him and pulled out a Beretta M9. He placed the black handgun in her hand. "It's not much of a weapon, but I want you to keep this on you. Understand?" Dee nodded. "Only use it if it's life or death. You are not here to fight this war. You hear me?" Dee nodded again. "Do you know how to fire a gun?"

"No." Her voice was shaky.

"Toby, give her a quick lesson while I assess our situation." Toby settled in next to Dee, their backs against the wall. They spoke softly, so quietly that I could still hear my beating heart above the sound of their voices. I moved toward the window and slid down the wall where I would await orders. The fact that bullets were not busting through our window was evidence the

enemy did not know of our location. But there was still plenty of fighting going on in the streets. Each explosion, each pull of the trigger on the other side of the window could be ending a life of a man I'd spoken with only hours before.

The radio was quiet. Whose voice had been quieted forever, and who was too busy surviving to speak? Shane reloaded his M16 while Marshall attempted to survey the area without being seen.

"I only see the two vehicles destroyed. Some have been deserted, though." Marshall turned from the window, his M16 raised and ready. He stared into the room before him, and his Adam's apple moved as he swallowed hard.

I didn't want to ask my question, but I did anyway. "What's the casualty count?"

Marshall focused on me. Before he spoke, I knew the answer.

"Too many to count without getting my head shot off."

I nodded, and for the first time, my gaze met Dee's. If she was searching for comfort, she wouldn't find any.

"What's the plan?" Toby asked.

"For now, we fight from here. We have a good view of the street, and the insurgents don't know we're here yet. No reason to move out."

That room became our home for several days. We had minimal food, a bathroom across the hall, and a hard floor for a bed. At night, we took turns keeping watch and listening for noises in the house. Hardly a moment passed without the sounds of gunfire in the distance. When it was light, Dee scribbled into her pad, and when it was dark, she tossed and turned, trying to find sleep. When it was my turn to stand watch by the window, I stole glances at her and the pad in which she wrote her judgments. I wanted to burn every word she had ever written. I needed to make her thoughts disappear before they could poison people's opinions. And still, even more, I wanted her to change the configuration of her letters into words that made me forgive myself. I needed her words to be a salve on the burning thoughts in my mind.

When I woke the next day, Toby sat next to Dee, reading from her journal. His face was somber, and she watched him with what appeared to be anticipation. My stomach clenched with anger. I should be the one curled up next to her, but my bitterness toward her made that reality impossible.

"You're pretty educated in politics and history," Toby said as he closed the journal.

"After my father died, my mom closely followed politics. Maybe that was her way of finding answers, but you know how that goes. Sometimes, politics can seem more like opinion and bullshit than answers."

"You got that right," Shane interjected.

"You don't agree with this war?" Toby asked Dee.

My spine stiffened at the question. I wanted to shut Dee up before she could even open her mouth.

"I agree with protecting our country. I agree that the attacks on our country were wrong, but there are many reasons why being here, fighting this war, are wrong as well."

"Oh, shit, here we go." I envied Shane and his ability to say whatever was on his mind. I, instead, listened with gritted teeth. Perhaps what was on my mind was safer staying contained.

"We don't have permission to be in this war," Dee said. *"There are steps to follow, and we didn't follow them."*

"Go on," Toby encouraged.

"Anyone have a damn drink?" Shane asked.

"I'll take one, too." Dee shot me a look, which I ignored, as I tore into my breakfast bag.

"The UN Security Council needs to determine if force is necessary. It's in Articles 41 and 42 of the UN Charter, and we ignored those rules developed to keep the peace."

Dee looked around at her audience. Shane and I were purposely ignoring her. Toby appeared intent to take in her every word, and Marshall stayed quiet. Being the one in charge, Marshall should have told her to shut her mouth since we could very well be dead in the next few hours. I didn't need to hear that the reason for my death was bogus political crap.

"This war isn't even supported by the Arab world. In fact, Iraq and Kuwait just signed a promising pact. And as for weapons of mass destruction, no one found any."

"You know what I think? I think you are a traitor who should live in Iraq for a year and see how well you like it then." Shane shoved a piece of muffin in his mouth and swallowed it down with a swig of water. *"How many towers are you ready to see blown to pieces before you think we have a right to defend our country? Or do your loved ones need to be in the next tower for that to sink home?"*

Dee was quiet for a moment, but I knew she was only contemplating what words were safe. "Do you know that none of the hijackers were Iraqi? In fact, none of the big-

time leaders of Al Qaeda can be traced to Iraq, and no one can trace funds coming from Iraq to Al Qaeda."

"Dee, know your audience." Marshall stood and began scanning the streets.

"Sorry, I—"

"Let's just leave it right there. These men have a long day ahead of them and filling their minds with political shit is going to get them killed." He glared at her. "Do you hear me?"

"Yes." Dee was silenced, and to my knowledge, she never spoke her accusatory thoughts aloud again.

Marshall whipped away from the window. "We've got three insurgents heading toward the building."

We all scrambled into position. "Have they entered yet?" Shane asked.

"They're crossing the street. Be ready." Marshall aimed and fired. As soon as he did, the quiet building lit up with activity. Shots rang out; all seemed to be aimed directly at us. Dee's words were behind every pull of the trigger. Righteous Dee hovered safely to the side while we risked our lives to save hers and the lives of countless people across the globe. All the while, she judged us, always judged.

At some point, the battle quieted, and we rested our backs against the walls.

"Everyone okay?" Marshall asked.

"Perfect." Shane sounded exhausted. "How about you, Dee? You feelin' good over there?"

Dee looked at Shane. At first, I didn't think she would respond at all. "I'm sorry."

Shane just nodded. Maybe he forgave her. Perhaps they all did. But of the many feelings that flooded me when I looked at Dee, forgiveness was not one of them.

****

2018
Jim

Monday morning began with a briefing. Lieutenant Larsen had every detective in the squad room. The whiteboard served as the puzzle board they all stared at, hoping to make sense of its contents. In the middle was Bethany's name. Around the center, connected with strings, were the names Austin Williams, Vijay Patil, the man at the bar, and Ben Adams, the townie who had walked Bethany home.

"Men, it's been over a week, and we've made no progress. Gabe, what did you find on the father?"

"He's got a temper, but his alibi checks out. He'd been at the campus harassing the professor."

"Are we sure? If Bethany went for her run around six that morning, the father could have still gone to see the professor." Larsen looked around the room and her gaze settled on a new guy, Gibbs. "Gibbs, start checking more of the video footage. I want to know every time his car shows up."

"On it," Gibbs answered dutifully.

"What about the professor?"

"He doesn't have an alibi for the time." Jim cleared his throat and continued. "The students said he was visibly shaken in class, but that could be because of the confrontation with Mr. Williams."

"We need more. Start pressing." Larsen turned and stared at the board. "Hunter and Castille, find out who that guy at the bar was and locate the townie. Today."

"Will do," Gabe answered.

"And men, when you find something like a

challenge coin stuffed inside the victim's mouth, I'll guarantee you one thing." Jim knew what she was going to say before the words left her mouth. "This will not be the perp's last kill."

The men filed out of the room. Gabe caught up to Jim. "Let's head over to the bar where the mystery man tried to buy Bethany a beer."

"Now?"

"No better time than the present." Gabe clapped Jim on the back. "You can fill me in on your romantic getaway on the way over."

"Good thing we don't have far to travel."

Gabe snickered and grabbed his jacket from the back of his chair. "Why am I not surprised?"

Once in the car, Jim dreaded the conversation. He wasn't ready to admit to his so-called friend that his marriage was in trouble.

"So, let me hear the gory details."

"Sorry, no gore. We drank, ate, and had sex. Which part do you want to hear more about?"

"I'll pass." Gabe set the address into his GPS. "Seriously, man, if you ever want to talk, I'm here."

"Are you?"

"Of course. Let's not let this work thing get in the way of a good friendship."

Jim gave Gabe a sideways glance. "Why don't we do dinner tonight? Bring Susan. I'll even treat."

"Why do you want to do that?"

"Because the tension between you two is driving me crazy. You just need to get to know each other a little. You don't have to be best friends but learning to be civil would be nice."

"Who am I to turn down a free meal? I'll get the first

round of beers. We're going to need one after today."

"Perfect. I'll text Gwen." Jim waited for the response but was quite certain she would agree. She was still coming off the weekend where she'd decided she liked him and probably wondered if he had read the text from Paul. Only a few minutes passed before she texted that dinner would be fine.

Jim and Gabe parked on the side of the street and headed down toward the bar. The sounds of the ocean mingled with the sounds of traffic. Beachgoers carrying chairs strolled past businessmen and women grabbing an early lunch. Jim and Gabe walked up to the bar. A miniature surfboard stood beside the door, covered by a tiki hut-style roof. The sign on the outside stated they weren't open for several more hours. Through the dirty glass, they spotted the bartender inside stocking the liquor shelves. Gabe knocked, startling the man holding a vodka bottle.

Before ambling toward the door, he looked over his shoulder toward a back room. Most likely, he considered alerting someone to our presence. After unlocking the door, he opened it just enough to look us up and down. When Gabe showed his badge, the bartender allowed us to enter.

Jim's eyes adjusted to the lighting, which was much dimmer than the outside. The dancefloor where Bethany once danced was behind the bar.

"Do you have a minute? We have a few questions about the Bethany Williams case."

"Sure." The man motioned to a booth. "Would you like to have a seat?"

"Great," Gabe responded.

Once settled, Jim pulled out a notepad, and Gabe

began asking questions. "Did you know Bethany Williams?"

Jim pulled out a picture and slid it across the table.

"I knew of her but didn't know her."

"What do you mean you knew of her?" Gabe asked.

"She was a bit of a regular in here. Good looking. Got lots of attention. You know the type."

"Yes. We all know the type. How about Ben Adams, the man she left with? Did you know him?"

"Oh, yeah. Ben and I go way back. Good guy. He just needs to grow up a bit."

"So, you know him well?"

"I'll say. He's my roommate. That's partly why he comes in so much. He figures I'll throw him a free drink here and there, which I do."

"Your housemate." Gabe glanced at Jim with the *well this is working out better than expected* look. "Did you see him leave with Bethany?"

"Yeah, I did. I was a bit surprised, but whatever. I wasn't surprised nothing came of it, though."

"How do you know nothing came of it that night?"

"He was back at the bar within the hour. Gave me a thumbs down and asked for a beer."

"How long did he stay after that?"

"Until we closed. I generally have to give him a ride home after a night out."

"So, he stayed at his house all night?"

"Definitely."

"Was he there in the morning?"

"Definitely."

"How can you be sure?"

"Because we fell asleep watching television. I woke up around eight, and he was still passed out on the other couch."

"What do you know about the guy who Bethany was scared of at the bar?"

"Yeah, Ben said something about him. I didn't notice anyone. Whoever the guy was, he wasn't here long because no one else saw him either, or at least they didn't have any memory of seeing him." The bartender shook his head. "It's a damn shame about Bethany. We've all been wracking our brains trying to remember details about that night that would help, but it's chaos behind the bar sometimes. Unless you walk up naked, you're most likely just another face in the crowd. Everyone just blurs together."

"I can only imagine." Jim glanced at his notes. "What did you say your name was?"

"I don't think I did, but it's Tyler McCabe."

"Are there any cameras around the bar?" Jim asked.

"Only outside, in the back. We've had some issues with fights back there. Might be time to get some cameras inside as well."

"Never a bad idea." Gabe handed him a card. "Tyler, if you think of anything, even if it seems insignificant, give us a call."

"For sure. I don't think anyone feels settled right now, knowing there's a murderer lurking around."

Jim studied Tyler's posture, relaxed and confident. He noted that Tyler's eye contact didn't waiver unnaturally.

"It's disturbing for sure." Jim shook Tyler's hand, confident that he was not a suspect or knowingly covering for someone. "Thanks for your time."

****

Gwen and Susan met Jim and Gabe at City Ale

House. Gabe and Jim had already finished a tall draft and had ordered another. The two women were acquaintances at best, and Jim knew that if he and Gwen were not on such good terms, Gwen would have scoffed at the idea of going to an ale house on a Monday with people she cared little about.

"Gwen was just telling me about your weekend away to the Georgia mountains. It sounds amazing," Susan said as she slid into the booth next to Gabe.

"It was pretty special." Jim squeezed Gwen's thigh under the table, and she returned his act of affection with a smile.

The waitress came to the table. She was laughing at something that had happened on the way to their booth. The laugh in and of itself was innocent enough, but her other mannerisms irked Jim from the start—the toss of her hair, the sideways glances at another waitress as if they shared a private joke. Gwen's leg tensed beneath his fingers. The condescending air of the waitress was a characteristic that could trigger Gwen. Jim found this irony, which overshadowed his own annoyance, amusing. Waiting to be entertained, he watched the interaction.

"Would you mind telling me the specials?" Gwen asked. Only Jim recognized the question as a test. This was not a high-end restaurant where the wait staff rattled off the menu down to the smallest ingredient—all of it sounding French to Jim. This was a step above a pub, and if you didn't bother reading the sign on the way in, you missed your chance.

The waitress looked toward the door and turned back to Gwen with a glance that said, *Seriously, lady.* "We have chili and cornbread."

"How's the cornbread?"

"I don't eat carbs, but if you like bread, then you would like it."

"Well, wouldn't you do well in sales."

"Excuse me?"

"I'll take the Greek salad. You didn't make the chili sound that appetizing."

Unbothered, the waitress glanced at Jim. "You?"

"I'll take the chili." Jim handed her the menu. "And give me extra cornbread."

Jim could have sworn he saw her eyes roll. Gabe chuckled and asked for the same as Jim.

"I'll have the cheeseburger and fries, please." Susan's words were polite, but as soon as the waitress and her blonde ponytail disappeared around the corner, Susan let her real feelings be known.

"What a piece of work that one is."

"I want to speak to the manager." Gwen leaned in across the table and spoke softly. "Seriously, he should know that his employee is chasing off the customers."

"Chasing off the customers?" Gabe laughed. "You really wouldn't come back here because of a little attitude? I would think you of all people wouldn't flinch from someone like her."

"Excuse me?"

"Oh, here we go," Jim said, sitting back and removing his hand from Gwen's leg.

"What's that supposed to mean?" Gwen's glare was fierce.

"Not talking about you, my dear." Jim glanced at Gabe. "I think maybe we're just getting off on the wrong foot here. Let's start over." Jim smiled at Gwen. "How was your day?"

"Fine," Gwen answered, but she was clearly not amused. The waitress returned with their drinks. "I'm sorry. I didn't catch your name." Jim knew exactly his wife's motivation for asking. Gwen wanted to let the waitress know that she was considering talking to her boss.

"My apologies. My name's Tori." She finished setting each glass in its spot. "Is there anything else you need?" The waitress's tone shifted enough to appease Gwen for the moment.

"No thanks. We're all set," Jim said, hoping all the sparks at the table had cooled.

"You're sure you don't need another beer?" Tori said. "I think you might have a hole in your glass."

Gwen smirked at Jim as if to say, *See, bud, you're not safe from her attitude either.*

"I'll let you know if I need another." All eyes were on Jim as Tori walked away. "What? I never said I disagreed with you. The girl has issues."

Once everyone was allowed some time for their alcohol to ease the tension, dinner passed uneventfully. Gwen appeared to be relaxing, and Jim even looked forward to getting home and having some time together before bed. He slid into the passenger seat of Gwen's car since, to save time, he had ridden with Gabe to the restaurant. Gabe assured him he would rather do it that way and pick him up in the morning than drive all the way back to the office for Jim's car.

"Well, that wasn't so bad, was it?" he said once they were settled.

"Are you kidding me?" Gwen's voice was just shy of a yell. "That was hell. Between Gabe and that waitress, you're lucky I didn't lose my mind and strangle one of them."

"Gwen, you're overreacting."

"Don't," she said while pointing a finger, "ever tell me I'm overreacting. And how embarrassing. That little snob had to point out to you that you were drinking too much."

"I had three beers. Don't come at me for three beers."

"I'm not even going to discuss it with you. I'm over the whole thing." Gwen flipped on the radio, and just like that, any remnant of connection dissipated into the air.

Chapter 18

Present Day
Patient 541

Journal Entry
We needed to move. If we stayed hidden behind these walls any longer, bombs would blow what had been our shelter, along with the people in it, apart.

"Where next, Corporal Marshall?" Toby asked.

"Sergeant Major is three klicks down the street. We need to get to him." Marshall looked around the room. "Gather the stuff up. We leave as soon as the sun sets."

I wanted—no, needed—to see other people, other scenery than the walls we had holed up behind, but three klicks were a long way to travel on foot. We had to expect that the enemy had night vision equipment, which meant traveling at night was almost as risky, but staying in this building meant death.

When darkness fell, we crept out onto the street. Always, lone gunfire could be heard in intervals. For now, the sounds remained somewhat distant. The hours passed slowly. Adrenaline flooded my body so often that my heart received no downtime. We sought cover often, and on occasion, the snipers' shots seemed directed at us, but if that were the case, their bullets would have eventually found us. We pressed on for about two klicks until we were spotted. How the shots missed us was nothing short of miraculous, even though I did not believe in miracles. We ducked inside a building and sought cover. The bullets pummeled the door. Once again, we scanned the premises, this time finding no one. We burst into an upstairs bedroom and made our way to the window.

For a moment, all was silent. Through the night vision glasses, I scanned the buildings across the street. When I set my gaze on the sniper, he had his weapon aimed directly at me. We fired simultaneously. His bullet ricocheted off the window frame. The debris from the building floated to the ground, and all went silent. For a moment, we all sat with our backs against the wall, waiting for a sound, for something, anything. When I dared to peek through the window again, the sniper was no longer visible. Since the enemy would not quietly lay down his weapon, the only possibility was that his lifeless body lay beneath the windowsill, out of sight.

"I think it's best if we camp out here tonight. We'll go the rest of the way tomorrow."

No one argued with Marshall. Instead, we curled up in our corners, shoved our packs under our heads, and sought a sleep that would not come easily.

Hours later, Marshall woke me for my shift. The time passed without event, and at times, my head bobbed, threatening sleep. I pinched my fingers, inspected my weapon, ate dehydrated food from silver bags, and studied my companions as they slept. The moon's light illuminated Dee's face and created a halo. Perfect Dee. In my mind, I cursed her and the universe that appeared to be taking her side.

The clock struck 4:00, and I shook Toby awake. "Your turn."

He rubbed his eyes and stumbled to the window.

"Stay awake," I said.

"Got it."

I turned toward the wall and woke to a voice on the radio.

"Vic Two. Time is limited. How far out are you?"

Marshall jumped up and grabbed his radio. "One klick out. Is there time?"

"Affirmative. But hurry."

"Affirmative."

We all scrambled for our belongings.

"But it's still..." Dee let her half sentence linger in the air. No one looked her way or responded. Out of the corner of my eye, I saw her throw the last of her things into her bag.

The streets were quiet. We crept out the door, and seeking cover, made our way to a flipped-over vehicle. Still nothing. We scanned the windows and saw no movement. As the distance passed, we became bolder, walking down the street, spread slightly apart. Dee stayed in the middle, protected as best we could.

Enemy bodies lay about the streets. Medics, what the Marines referred to as corpsmen, had at some point gathered our fallen and wounded, making it appear to have been a one-sided battle. We all knew better.

Our journey took two hours, and as with almost all endeavors, this one was not without incident. We would walk for ten minutes in silence before being engaged in combat. Then we would continue for another ten or so minutes without bloodshed. We found Sergeant Major Samuels on the third floor of a now abandoned building. A hand waved us up, and we clambered in, our heavy boots pounding up the stairs. One Marine lay wounded, a gunshot wound in his thigh.

"Have you seen the corpsmen out there?" The young Marine winced as he spoke.

"No. We haven't seen any for miles, but they've cleared out the streets." Marshall bent down next to the Marine and examined the wound. "Don't you worry. They'll be back around soon."

"We're running out of time," Sergeant Major Samuels said. "They'd better be quick." As if on call, the sound of a vehicle drew our attention to the window. "Let's get him downstairs."

Marshall lifted one side of the young Marine and Samuels the other. I trailed behind them and Dee behind me. Outside the door, an olive-green tracked vehicle screeched to a halt, and two corpsmen ran to the Marine's aid.

"See you back home, Private. I'll buy you a beer." Private Allen patted his apparent friend on the shoulder.

"And it won't be that watered-down shit you drink."

"Wouldn't think of it."

About as quickly as the vehicle pulled up, it disappeared down the street. For the first time, I envied the wounded. They were on their way home, and for a moment, as I watched the dust from the tires settle, I traveled with the men escaping the hellhole of Iraq.

"We need to move." Sergeant Major Samuels spoke with authority. "The worst is yet to come, and if we want to live to witness it, we'd better find the rest of our battalion real fast."

His words broke my trance and brought me back to the men surrounding me. Moving forward was the only option, so I forced my legs to move, to take me farther into the unknown where for some of us, certain death awaited.

****

2018
Jim

When Jim woke up, his head throbbed. Sure, the beer didn't help, but the lack of sleep was what curled like a fist around his brain, clenching it with each step he took. Gwen hadn't said a word to him after the yelling incident in the car. She'd gone straight to the room, and Jim had headed for the garage. For some time, he'd pleaded with the walkie-talkie to speak again. The device had remained silent.

Each time this happened, he questioned whether he had ever heard anything at all, but he knew he had. But had the walkie-talkie spoken to him, or was he hearing voices, for God's sake? The voices of dead people? What a gift a voice from beyond would be if it were possible. But Jim didn't believe that to be the case. His feet were planted in a reality where voices from the grave did not belong.

Jim went to the fridge and grabbed another beer, which led to another. Gwen would not be seeking his company tonight; therefore, his consumption of alcohol was his own business. Truth be known, he lost count of the number.

When Gwen awoke, she was still grumpy but not as adamant about being that way. She offered Jim scrambled eggs, and he accepted them. They were being cordial, which was better than the alternative. When she went to leave, she even kissed him on the cheek and said goodbye. Once the door closed behind her, Jim breathed a sigh of relief. He was placing his coffee cup in the

212

dishwasher when the front door opened. He looked up, expecting to see Gabe.

"Did you drive my car last night?"

Jim's eyes narrowed. "No. Why would I have driven your car?"

"I don't know, but the seat is moved back."

"Well, I can't explain why your seat is moved."

Gwen thought for a moment. "You know, I might have moved it. My lipstick fell out of my purse, and I was trying to find it."

"Well, there you have it. No need to accuse your husband."

"Sorry. I guess I'm just stressed. I'll see you at dinner."

"I'll be late. I have class tonight."

"I'll wait," she offered. "Oh, and Gabe just pulled in."

Jim followed her out of the house and this time, met her for a kiss. When he climbed into Gabe's car, Gabe had a smirk pasted on his face.

"So, all is well in the Castille home. I wasn't quite sure if Gwen was still worked up about the waitress and just faking her good mood."

"She seems good enough to me, but who knows?" Jim didn't feel the need to share the actual events of his night.

As soon as they entered the headquarters, Lieutenant Larsen opened her office door and demanded they all meet in the squad room. The men cast questioning looks around the room, and then one by one, they followed their leader down the hallway. Larsen's expression was somber, which was never a good thing.

"There's another Signal 8, relatively the same age,

blonde. Other than that, no connection." Larsen hit a few buttons on her computer and up flashed a picture. "She never made it home from work last night. A coworker found her phone in a bush near the restaurant when he went to open for the day."

"Holy shit." Everyone turned to look at Gabe. "That's our waitress from last night."

Jim looked back at the picture. "Holy shit," he said, mimicking his partner's surprise. "That is her."

The picture of the beautiful young woman showed on the screen. One couldn't see the attitude in the posed photograph, but Jim knew it was there. Why could he already picture Tori's corpse? His mind must be combining the memory of Bethany with the image of the waitress. A part of him prayed it wasn't a premonition, yet another part... How could he verbalize it even to himself? A part of him just viewed the victims as pictures, lifeless, meaningless images that paid his bills and offered opportunities for advancement.

While going through training, several men hadn't been able to tolerate the smells, the visuals. Jim had watched their faces and secretly made predictions of who would disappear before graduating. Every time, Jim was correct. The men would find their way in life, Jim was sure of it, behind a desk, serving the world in some other way. Coldness was necessary for survival in Jim's line of work, not just normal human behavior but necessary human behavior.

"The victim was last seen leaving her waitressing job on Atlantic Boulevard." Larsen hit another button, and a video showed a young woman getting into a blue Camry. She appeared to drive away uneventfully. "After that, she disappears from the camera. The troubling part is that her car was found in that parking lot in the morning. Whoever parked it knew exactly where the cameras were located and where the blind spots were."

"A co-worker?" Gabe asked.

"It's where we'll begin our search. You and Jim head out there this morning and start asking questions."

Gabe drove them, as usual. The restaurant was snuggled between small businesses in a plaza one could easily pass by.

"Our waitress. Can you believe it?" Gabe shook his head. "Really, what are the chances?"

"It is a bizarre coincidence."

Gabe shook his head again. "You think Gwen did it?"

Jim chuckled despite himself. "Not many things surprise me, but that would."

"We probably should call Evans. You've got his number on speed dial, don't you?"

"Are we still going there?"

"Hell, yeah. I haven't bled that one dry yet."

"Sorry if it wasn't cool with you to contact him. In hindsight, I guess I should have brought you in on the plan, but then again, if Evans didn't find anything, well, you know," Jim rambled, hoping to be interrupted.

Gabe took a few turns and merged into traffic on I-95. He drove in silence for a moment. "Well, it did pay off."

"I'm not sure it helped me earn any respect."

"Hell, I don't know why I should be upset about it then. You keep pissing off Larsen, and I'll keep being named lead detective on the cases." Gabe pulled into the parking lot and parked in front of the building. "But I get it. Next time let's follow protocol. Makes things easier in the long run."

Jim swallowed a lump of pride caught in his throat. He had to let the matter go. Reaching for the door handle, he managed to mumble, "Agreed."

****

When they entered the dark restaurant, which smelled of yesterday's beer spills, an eerie silence fell over them as if the funeral was already taking place in the co-workers' minds and speaking loudly would be disrespectful.

"How many?" the young, dark-haired lady asked.

"We won't be eating," Gabe answered, showing his badge to save conversation.

"We're here to help find Tori, your co-worker," Gabe said in a comforting tone Jim seldom heard.

"I'll get my manager." The young girl turned, eager to get away.

"Hang on. We'd like to hear from you as well."

"I'm pretty new. I only met Tori a few times. We weren't really friends," the girl said while adjusting her glasses on the bridge of her nose.

"You weren't friends, or you weren't friendly together?"

"I don't know what you mean," the girl answered with a blank stare.

"Did you not like each other?" Gabe asked.

The girl paused. "I didn't know her." She was silent again, and Jim pitied her a bit. "Would you like me to get my manager?"

"That would be great," Gabe replied.

She disappeared down a hallway and reappeared followed by a large man, in his mid-forties, Jim would guess, fit with a layer of Friday night appetizers and cold beer covering his would-be sleek physique.

His gaze somber, the man stretched his hand out to Gabe and then Jim. "I'm glad to see you here, detectives. I'm Robert Burger." At another time, Jim might have been amused by the last name of the restaurant manager. Instead, he was too busy sizing up each twitch of his eye, deciding if he was a good actor or sincere.

"I'm Detective Hunter, and this is my partner, Detective Castille. Do you have a place we can talk?"

With the wave of his hand, Robert indicated a back table. "We'll have privacy there at this time of day."

They followed Robert through the dimly lit restaurant, their feet sticking to the floor despite the *Caution, floor is wet* sign off to the side. Whoever had mopped clearly took zero pride in his or her work. Jim shuffled in along the bench, letting Gabe slide in next to him. Robert took the bench across from them.

Robert nervously clenched his hands as they rested on the table in front of him. "Any luck tracking Tori down?"

"Not yet," Gabe responded. "We were hoping you could help fill in some of the gaps." Jim pulled out his pad to jot notes on and could not help but notice how Robert tensed. Seeing the pad had that effect on people as if everything had suddenly become real and definite, each word etched in the history of the crime. The pressure could bring out the smallest crack in a criminal's persona, hardly noticeable unless one was trained to detect the nuance.

"Tori was a sweet girl, hard worker. I'll help in any way I can."

"Is," Jim said.

"Excuse me?" Robert responded.

"Tori is a sweet girl. You spoke of her in the past tense."

Robert's eyebrows lifted. His mouth fell agape momentarily as he tried to claw himself out of the hole he'd just dug.

"Of course. I didn't mean to insinuate otherwise."

Gabe and Jim let silence settle, allowing the awkwardness to jostle any details wavering on being divulged. Robert instead regained his footing.

"There's been too much talk today among the employees. I've tried to hush it the best I could, but the fact is, people talk. The restaurant employs many young teenagers who seek the drama. Happy endings can't satiate that desire. I've overheard too much, I guess."

"Who's been doing all the talking?" Gabe asked.

Jim scribbled some meaningless gibberish onto his pad as he eyed Robert. The act did not go unnoticed.

Robert began to stutter when he spoke. "There was a dishwasher who worked here. He and Tori butted heads a bit. The other night, she complained after some woman's beer mug had leftover lipstick on it, and the couple was rude to her. When I discussed Tori's complaints with Bill—Bill Decker's the dishwasher's name—he threw a dish and walked out, giving her the evil eye all the way. As he left, Tori just smirked at him. She had a strong side."

"Has," Jim reminded him.

"Yes, yes, my apologies." Robert looked down at his hands, and when he spoke, there was a solemnness in his voice that hadn't been there before. "I feel responsible. The people working here become like family to me, and sometimes family just doesn't get along no matter how hard I try." Robert rubbed his forehead, and they gave him a moment to regain his composure.

"Beside Bill, did Tori have other enemies?"

"Not enemies, but, well, Tori had her share of both people who didn't care much for her, as well as people who admired her, that's for sure."

"Continue," Jim urged.

"Where to start? She could be moody. People didn't always know what to expect from her. Sometimes Tori can be flirty and friendly. She knows how to use her looks to increase her tips. She will feign interest in the guys at the single tables and give sleepy bedroom eyes to men while their wives scan the menu. She does what suits Tori at the time. Other times, she can be abrasive, if I'm to be honest."

Jim jotted notes, and Robert squirmed in his seat.

"Listen, it's uncomfortable saying negative things about someone who might be in trouble. It's just…well, Tori has offended many people in the short time she's worked here, and I think that it's best I give an honest account of who she is. Maybe it will help you figure out where she is and why she isn't contacting anyone."

Tori was exactly the kind of woman Jim couldn't stand. He knew her games, and the idea she toyed with her customers infuriated him to his core.

"What are your feelings for Tori?" Jim asked.

"What exactly do you mean by that?" Burger's agitation shown through his tone.

"Exactly what I said: your feelings. Did you like her? Dislike her? Did she make sleepy bedroom eyes at you?"

Burger glared at Jim. "As I said, my staff is like family. Sons and daughters. Tori was the daughter who had some maturing to do. I thought she would turn out okay, but she needed to have life knock her down a bit for that to happen." Burger paused, and Jim thought he was pondering how his words would be perceived. "I liked her the way a frustrated parent likes his teenage child despite the fact she is not always likeable."

Jim nodded, scribbled something. "Yeah, I get it. So where can we find this dishwasher?"

Chapter 19

Present Day
Patient 541

Journal Entry
About a week into the fighting, I had already witnessed more horrific sights than I had imagined possible. Our numbers grew as our battalion joined together and then shrank as we watched our friends fall. Before entering Fallujah, I had envisioned the battle. I pictured myself aiming my M16 and shooting running targets in the back or shooting snipers in windows at a distance that made them appear shadows of humans. I had not imagined the look in a man's eyes as his soul departed from his body, a body I had, with the pull of a trigger, made incapable of supporting life.

My first kills did not happen in the city. In fact, before our battalion had entered Fallujah, I had killed a dozen or more men from a distance. One kill weighed on me heavily, though—the boy. When my mind drifted back to the moment, he always held a weapon. I can picture the moment clear as day. The boy held a Glock. He started to raise the gun toward my head, a smirk on his face. Part of my mind knew this memory to be false, but without the small adaptations, the memory would be my death. Not due to the next insurgent aiming a weapon at me, but that memory.

*Every time I took aim and the insurgent's features
tried to morph into the boy's, I envisioned that smirk and
the weapon he'd planned on killing me with, and I pulled
the trigger. My body, with my created memories, kept
moving forward, searching for the next victim, while my
mind pulled a curtain between the two realities. I moved
like a robot, well-trained in carrying out my mission, but
when my eyelids became too heavy to hold open and
dreams took over my mind, the images haunted me,
waking me at all hours of the night. I squeezed my eyes
shut, trying to escape, but the boy's face appeared, a
young, innocent face with eyes full of fear. Dee's words
echoed through my mind and made my temples pulse and
my head pound. My heart thumped violently within my
chest. I could hear the gushing, rhythmic sound of the
beating in my ears. I took a deep breath and held it for
the count of four before releasing the air slowly out of
my mouth.*

*I drifted back to sleep only to jolt awake as a dream
bullet hit me in the back. Somewhere in the darkness of
the room, one of the Marines must have woken to similar
nightmarish images. His muffled cry lingered in the air
despite an obvious attempt to keep his emotions
contained within his pack being used as a pillow. I
wondered if it was Toby, but I didn't care to know for
sure. The moment was too personal. How many of the
Marines surrounding me pretended to sleep, trying not
to let their tears fall. Eventually, slumber rescued me and
held me without interruption until morning.*

*The next day, we headed back outside. In a sick way,
the streets were akin to a frat house after a party. We
walked along them as if in a hungover state, but instead
of empty beer bottles and pizza boxes littering the way,*

we stepped over bodies. There were so many of them. Why had I not expected to see them still lying where they had fallen? Most civilians had left the city, so there was no one to remove them or respectfully bury them.

Flies danced around the corpses. The sound of buzzing grew to such a degree that I'm confident the volume manifested from a place within my mind. I tried not to look at the faces of the dead—cold, bloodied, with dark eyes staring back at me. I stepped over the lifeless hands, somehow threatening to grab me and pull me down with them, stretched out on the gravel. I stumbled over a sandal. An eerie sensation crept over me as I stared down at the lone shoe, and I wondered if there could ever be a story with a happy ending that involved a lone shoe, for at that moment, it seemed impossible.

Suddenly, unbearable loneliness overtook me, and I drifted to another realm. A voice behind me brought me back.

"Damn, I can't take this smell."

I glanced back and saw a Marine I didn't know burying his nose into the sleeve of his camo. At that moment, the putrid odor hit me as well. The death in the air had begun to circulate, and I wondered, as I breathed in the air, what caused an object to have an odor, what was the actual substance entering the lining of my nose, and at what point in my life would I ever be able to stop smelling death. A fly danced upon the fingertips of the corpse. Is this what we become—a bacteria-filled carcass left to rot in the sun? Is this what I would become?

We walked in silence most of the time, partly for safety and partly because we had no words other than a few that seemed appropriate. At first, I, being lost in my *thoughts, didn't notice the silence. Then the quiet became strange and ominous. A few yards in front of us, something metallic reflected the sunlight. I could not be sure if the object was a coin or a lost piece of jewelry. In a daze, I studied it with absent-minded curiosity. Shane was a few steps ahead of me. He'd noticed the bright, metallic object as well. The juxtaposition of its brilliance against the dusty background was impossible to ignore.*

When Shane reached the spot, he bent down to pick up the item. I took a step closer to him and the mysterious object. As I did, Shane faced us, holding the piece of metal out to Dee.

She looked at Shane quizzically. "It's a challenge coin." She studied it in his palm. "You earn them for being loyal to a group."

His hand started to fold around it before she could take it. "Do you think you've earned this?" he asked.

"I'm here, aren't I?"

Shane's fist opened, revealing the coin again. I could see that it was a Marine challenge coin. "Doesn't mean you've earned it yet, but it's yours anyway."

Dee lifted it from his hand and smiled. "Thank you."

Shane nodded.

My gaze drifted from Dee's face to Shane's. At that moment, he resembled someone younger and more innocent. I saw a different Shane, and that made me wonder if I could be friends with him after this bloody war. In that instant, one shot rang out, and the world went into slow motion. I watched Shane's expression, soft and likable, as a bullet formed a hole in the middle of his forehead. Blood splattered my face and clothes, yet I stood watching Shane's body drop. His hands fell, palms upright, and joined the other hands clawing at us from another world.

What seemed like minutes were only seconds. Toby jumped on me, bringing me to the ground, where we scrambled for cover. Along with the other Marines, we found an overturned car and hid behind it. Bullets pelted against the metal for several minutes, and then all went silent.

The silence, interspersed with more bloodshed, would come and go throughout the day. After Shane's death, the killing did not bother me, and for the first time, I might have even considered it enjoyable.

When the sun threatened to leave us in the dark, corpsmen loaded Shane's body, along with some others, into the tracked vehicle. Our fallen comrades left the city forever, while the living, exhausted and beaten in every way a man could be, sought cover.

When I lay in my corner that night, I envisioned Shane, the day I had met him in the chow hall, cocky and full of life. I remembered the sensation of his hand slapping me obnoxiously on the back and saw that same hand as it dropped into the dry dirt. Death for Shane had been incredibly instantaneous. Alive one moment, and without warning, dead the next. My tomorrow could bring the same ending for me. A shiver ran up my spine as I pictured my corpse deserted in the streets. Fellow Marines would stare out their windows at my remains. Would their shock stem from my loss or merely from their fear of death?

****

2018
Jim

Bill Decker opened the door wearing only his jeans,

which settled low on his hips, unbuckled and half zipped. The smell of pot rolled out of his apartment like a billowing cloud, and he eyed the detectives with unamused boredom.

"Yeah," he said, daring them to give him shit.

Jim felt himself salivating at the opportunity, but he refrained. "We need to have a little chat with you, Bill."

"What about?" Bill said, again unamused. Jim and Gabe simultaneously showed their badges, and Bill's shoulders stood a bit more erect as he apparently contemplated his next move. "Let me grab my shirt."

The door closed between them, and Jim heard Bill shuffling around the apartment. No doubt, he was trying to hide his bag of weed as if the fact that he was stoned wasn't evident enough. A few minutes later, the door reopened. Jim was hit with the smell of toothpaste and cheap cologne. Bill now wore an old, gray T-shirt with a stain on the front. Jim suspected the stain was sauce, most likely from the last late-night pizza binge.

"How can I help you?" Bill said, his demeanor suddenly polite.

Gabe pulled out a picture of Tori. "We're looking for this young woman. Have you seen her?"

"Tori? She's missing?" He let out a small laugh that fell short of amused.

"Something funny?" Jim asked. His reaction proved his dislike, but Jim didn't sense guilt.

"No. Not at all."

"You didn't know?" Gabe asked.

"No. I quit working at the restaurant almost a week ago. I haven't seen any of those people since." Bill slid his hands into his pockets. Jim took this as a sign of nervousness.

"Want to explain why you quit?" Jim asked.

"Too many attitudes. I'd just had enough."

"Who had the attitudes?" Jim asked, studying every facial twitch.

"To be honest, Tori. Listen, I have no clue where she is, but to tell you the truth, she was a bitch. She irritated people just for her own amusement. She was always coming into the kitchen, laughing about this person's outfit, weight, or behavior. And it wasn't a fun laugh. She was vicious. I don't think anyone actually liked her. They were just too scared to stand up to her. I quit because I couldn't take her attitude anymore. I didn't just hate her comments to me, but I hated the way she poisoned the air around her. I couldn't stand her, but I wouldn't do anything to her. I just needed to get the hell away from her. I'm sure you've both met your share of Toris."

Jim shook his head as he jotted down a quick note. Yes, he had met his share of Toris. Hell, he'd married a Tori.

"We appreciate your honesty, Bill, but we would like you to stay local in case we have more questions. And by the way," Gabe added, "that cologne isn't hiding anything."

Bill stayed silent, a smart choice, as Jim and Gabe turned and headed down the steps leading to the parking lot.

When they were out of earshot, Gabe asked, "What's your take?"

"Just a guy sick of women's bullshit." Jim could feel Gabe's eyes on him, and he tried to soften the tension in his jaw.

"Rough day with the missus?" Gabe asked.

As Jim opened the car door, he met his partner's gaze over the roof of the vehicle. "Wasn't speaking for myself."

Tori and Bethany had similarities, but until Jim and Gabe knew more, they couldn't link the young women's cases. They had to find Tori, but something dark had settled over the office. Something told all of them that Tori would not be found alive.

When Jim finally walked into the kitchen, Gwen had a tofu stir fry waiting for him and a bottle of wine ready to be poured. His hangover had healed, so he accepted the invitation.

"You know that waitress from last night?"

"Oh, don't bring her up again. Please."

"She's missing."

"What? You can't be serious."

"I'm very serious, and I know this won't surprise you, but she wasn't well liked."

"Do you think someone killed her?"

"I don't like the fact that she meets the description of Bethany Williams. Serial killers have types."

"Oh, my God. Now I feel terrible."

"Unless you killed her, you don't have anything to feel terrible about. Not everyone is a nice person. Tori was who she was, and that's on her."

"I know, but still." Gwen took a drink. "I forgot to tell you. The neighbors were talking outside. They saw this homeless man lurking around the neighborhood last night. He was wearing camo pants."

Jim set down his fork. His appetite disappeared as the lump in his chest grew. "Where did they see him?"

"Just walking up and down our street. Barb told her husband, and when he went out looking for him, he was gone. I bet that's who was in my car." Gwen ran to the key hooks. "You know what? My extra set of keys was in the car last night. I'm lucky he didn't steal it."

"Yeah, you are. How many times have I told you to lock your doors? Cars get broken into in all sorts of neighborhoods." Jim's voice sounded gravelly as he held back his frustration.

"I know. I know. I will from now on." Gwen studied Jim's face. "I'm sorry. My car is still here, so please don't be so angry."

Adrenaline pumped through Jim's veins. He took a deep breath to rid himself of some of the tension. "You got lucky this time."

"I'll keep it locked, but can you do something about that guy?"

"I'll get someone to send a patrol car around tonight, to keep an eye out for him."

"This whole thing has me on edge. Would you mind if I take my glass of wine up to the bath?"

"Sure. Go ahead. I'll clean up."

Without another word, Gwen disappeared up the stairs while Jim downed his glass of wine and poured another. If the homeless man was the same guy Jim had seen earlier, this was evidence that he was following Jim. He picked up his phone to call for a patrol car and then put it back down. Something told him he needed to take care of the problem on his own.

After her bath, Gwen watched television in bed. She didn't argue with Jim when he told her he was going to stay up and keep an eye on the goings-on outside. In fact, she thanked him and gave him a lengthy hug.

For hours, Jim alternated between the front windows and the garage. The world outside remained silent. He went into the garage and picked up the walkie-talkie. It too was silent. He set it down, sat back in his chair, and took another swig of wine. How many glasses had he had? He'd lost count after he opened the second bottle.

Frustrated, he grabbed the device off the table and yelled into it. "Talk to me, damn it!" Jim swore the object warmed in his hands. "Are you there?"

Silence.

"Bethany, are you there?"

The red wine had sucked all hydration from his brain, and tomorrow's hangover was already pecking at his eyeballs. Jim massaged his temple with one hand while the other gripped the device.

"Bethany?" He was about to give up when the static became louder and then dimmed to a nearly inaudible level.

"She's not here."

Jim's eyes flew open. "What the hell," he said to the air. And then into the walkie-talkie: "What do you mean? Who's this?"

There was a silence and then a voice unlike Bethany's. This one was angry. "You know who I am."

"Where's Bethany?"

"She left."

"Who is this?"

"I'm right there," the voice challenged through the haze.

"I'm not following you," Jim said, almost begging for clarity.

"In the water, behind the…"

The voice cut off, but Jim knew exactly where investigators would be searching the next day.

Chapter 20

Present Day
Patient 541

Journal Entry
I could write a million words about the days and weeks that followed, but I will never be able to explain to anyone what I experienced. The tolerable moments were the ones when I floated above myself, not even experiencing it all for myself. Below me was a man who shared my appearance, my name, and my past. He walked through the rubble, breathing in the dusty, arid air. He held his gun, ready to shoot his target. He kicked in doors and searched buildings for men hiding within the walls of the destroyed city. He was a stranger to me, and for me to survive, he would remain someone separate from the man who hibernated inside of me.

Since the incident with the boy, Dee and I had only coexisted. I watched her from a distance, trying to see the woman I was sure I once loved, but there was something cold about both of us now. One night, we sat with our backs against the walls of the dusty room we sheltered in, eating from our bags of food. Her hair drifted down, covering one side of her face, and on that evening, I was too tired to hate her. I scooted over to her spot. For some time, she said nothing to me. The silence was comfortable, though.

Dee took a swallow from her canteen. "I want you to know I need to publish the truth. I won't use names, but people will know what happened here. They'll know about the boy."

The challenge coin sat on the floor in front of her. "Shane should have never given you that. You know nothing about loyalty."

I stood and walked away.

At night, before falling asleep, Dee would spin the challenge coin around in her fingers. Tears would stream down her cheeks, yet she never wiped them away. I wondered if she was contemplating my words, if she might possibly change her mind, but I doubted it.

Once, Toby sat beside her, and she cried on his shoulder. How she was alive, and Shane was somewhere decomposing was a question my mind struggled with each time I looked at her, each time I heard her scribbling in her pad. My mind succumbed to sleep while hearing the scratching of her pen and the rustling of her papers. The sounds followed my subconsciousness into my dreams, but the dreams slithered from my mind, unwilling to reveal themselves to me in my awoken state.

Dee slept soundly still when I opened my eyes. Toby was at the window, his hands sliding back and forth over his M16. He looked somber, lost in thoughts I dared not imagine. I had my own to weigh me down.

"Any activity?" I asked.

He took a knee and peeked out the window. "Holy shit." Everyone jumped up from where they sat. "They're entering the building."

"What the hell, Toby," Marshall yelled. "Why weren't you watching?"

"I just looked away."

The room was in chaos. Everyone scrambled to get a weapon in hand as heavy footsteps sounded on the stairs.

"Guard the door." Just as Marshall shouted the words, the door flew open. Close-range fire surrounded us. Blood spurted from the wounds of the men around me as those of us standing continued to fight. There were about seven of them and ten of us. The exchange lasted minutes and claimed the life of each insurgent and half of our men. Marshall, Toby, and I were unharmed and rushed to the aid of the men around us.

To this day, I can't explain why Dee went unnoticed. Perhaps we overlooked her because she had partly hidden behind the door when the enemy burst into the room. There were so many injuries: headshots we tried to avoid looking at; chest wounds we applied pressure to without much hope of success; and leg wounds we tried to treat with tourniquets.

How much time had passed before we heard her whimper? I ran to her first, pressing a dirty jacket a Marine had shed in the night against her wound. Her shirt was darkening with blood.

"Help me," Dee begged.

"I'm trying."

"I'm scared."

I pressed harder. "I know." I heard a vehicle stop outside of the building. Marshall had communicated with the corpsmen, and I prayed they were coming to rescue the wounded. Boots pounded up the stairs, and our men rushed into the room. They must have been close by.

I looked around the room at all the men struggling to survive, men who had given all they had for our country. Toby and Marshall were carrying out a Marine with a bullet wound to his leg. As they passed us, they noticed me leaning in front of Dee.

"Private, what's her condition?" Marshall asked, his breathing heavy with the weight of the wounded Marine.

"I have it covered. She'll be all right."

"Dee, we're coming right back. Hang in there," Toby said as he headed through the door. Dee mumbled an "okay" that I'm sure Toby couldn't hear.

On the other side of the door, the other Marine moaned. I needed to help him.

Blood was gushing from Dee's abdomen. The Marine let out a cry. I needed to get to him. I watched as my hand covered her mouth. A tear trickled down her cheek, and the crystal blue eyes stared up at me petrified. I stared back until she went still as if she had fallen asleep, and then I tucked the coin into her mouth. Even now, I cannot explain why besides the fact that I wanted her to choke on the very thing she mocked with her writing. She didn't have loyalty. She had no clue what it was like to be a Marine.

I ran over to the one remaining person and helped him down the flights of stairs. The stairs seemed many and the task tedious. As I reached the bottom, shots rang out once again. Someone yelled, "Grenade." We all ducked for cover as our gazes followed the second rocket-propelled grenade's path into the upstairs window. Within seconds, the room disappeared.

Toby screamed Dee's name, and then he turned to me. "Did you get her out?"

I stared blankly at him.

"Did you get Dee out?"

I shook my head.

"Why the hell didn't you help her out? You were right there next to her." Toby was screaming.

"She was already gone, Toby."

His expression fell as if he just now grasped that she was gone either way.

"I saved the living." The lie seeped from my lips as if spoken by someone else. "She was already dead."

"You said you had it," he screamed.

"I only said that because she was scared."

We were huddled behind a vehicle, firing our weapons at unknown targets between words.

"We need to be sure. We can't just leave her."

"She's gone, Toby."

In time, the dust settled over the exchange. Behind us, the building still stood, despite the damage.

"I can't leave until I'm sure," Toby insisted.

"Be quick," Marshall responded.

Toby looked at me.

"I know the truth," I said. "I don't need to see it."

Toby stood and headed to the door. He glanced back at me once before entering. His gaze accused me of betrayals he had no right to assume, but then Toby always seemed to know more than he should. What would he see when he found her? Would he find the coin in her mouth and demand an explanation?

We waited for an immeasurable amount of time. Toby finally appeared in the doorframe, his face downcast. He walked over to his weapon and picked it up. "We can go."

One of the corpsmen laid his hand on Toby's shoulder. "We'll make sure she gets home."

Toby, for the first time, led the group as we walked

down the road. Everyone was somber. The air was dark with sadness and hopelessness. I should have shared the feeling, but I didn't.

I felt nothing.

****

2018
Jim

In the morning, Jim slipped into the garage for one final attempt to reach the mysterious woman. After several tries, he went into the kitchen and poured his bowl of cereal. He didn't want Gwen to know he was back in the garage. She might find it odd that he needed to tinker before work. Avoiding her questions was best.

After Gwen left, Jim slipped back out to his man cave and pulled out a whiteboard he sometimes used at home when a case was troubling him in the off hours. But the case that troubled him now was not so much about the victims. Rather, it was about who would be speaking to him through the walkie-talkie. First, why would they? There were only two logical reasons that Jim could think of: one, they were messing with him to be funny, or two, they were trying to wreck his chances at earning a promotion. If it were the latter, who could it be? Was it Gabe or Detective Walburg? Maybe they were working together.

He added their names, but the action did not trigger any understanding. It was difficult to believe they would be manipulative in that manner, but still possible. But to believe them to be murderers was impossible and so unlikely that Jim could, with almost one hundred percent assurance, take the idea off the table. If they weren't murderers, then they must only be assuming the missing women would be found dead. Then again, the voices had not given any information that was definite. Jim had used his detective skills to find Bethany, and he would for Tori.

Who else would have it in for Jim? Paul? What was really going on with Paul? How many times had a murder investigation ended with a spouse in jail? He wrote Paul's name and circled it in red.

Jim placed the dry-erase marker on the tray and was about to head out. He hesitated and then picked the marker back up and wrote "the drifter." He studied the board for a moment and slid it behind a cabinet. The only other possibility was that someone wanted him to earn a promotion and was trying to give him a heads-up on solving the cases. But who? Jim could think of no one who would be rooting for him in that way besides Gwen, but how? How would she pull off the voice? The voices never gave away too much information. Gwen was never with him when he heard the girls, and she would have the best chance of knowing when Jim was in the garage. Whoever the owner of the mysterious voice was, he or she was either out to help him or destroy him, and he needed to know which one it was.

When he walked back into the kitchen, Gwen was standing there.

"Why are you back?" Jim tried not to look startled, but she was eyeballing him with suspicion.

"I forgot my lunch. Why haven't you left yet?"

"I'm leaving now."

"What are you doing in the garage this early in the morning?"

"Just messing with the Jeep. I was going to order a paint color and was trying to decide which one."

"Want some help?"

"No. I think we're both going to be late."

Gwen hesitated. "Is everything okay?"

"Of course. What could be wrong?"

Jim and Gwen walked to their separate cars, the questions and secrecy forming a wall between them. As Jim drove to work, the air of the morning began shifting his mood. By the time he reached the office, the thoughts had formed a foulness he couldn't shake. All aspects of Jim's life balanced on threads: his marriage, his promotion, his friendships. Threads of trust had been stretched to the breaking point, and Jim existed in a realm where he floated alone, not able to find a safe place to land.

Gabe greeted Jim with a "You're late," as he entered the office.

"Traffic was shit." He wasn't going to tell his partner that he'd been trying to communicate with missing people through a walkie-talkie.

"Well, you're unusually chipper," Gabe said sarcastically.

"I'm glad you noticed. Now take note of it and let me do my damn paperwork."

Jim could sense Gabe staring at him.

"No word on the missing girl yet, in case you were wondering."

"I figured I would have heard if there was a development in the case. No news is good news. Isn't that what they always say?"

Jim's head was pounding; the migraines were worsening.

"You okay, Jim?"

Jim took a deep breath. "Sorry, migraine's acting up

again. Didn't mean to take it out on you."

"You need to see someone about those things."

"Nothing helps." Jim attempted to rub his migraine away by massaging his temple.

"Think you'll make it?"

"Yeah." Jim sat up in his chair. "What's on the agenda?"

"We have people watching Bill Decker's apartment. Does that interest you?"

"Lieutenant Larsen thinks he's a credible lead, then." Not looking up as he spoke, Jim searched water sites near the restaurant.

"Credible enough to have men watching his house." Gabe shuffled some papers on his desk. "We found out his girlfriend, Quyen Nguyen, plays soccer with Tori. She wasn't a big fan of Tori either. Apparently, there were several tiffs on and off the field."

"Are we going to talk to her?"

"She suddenly took a trip to Richmond, Virginia. Her car is parked at Bill Decker's apartment. He drove her to the airport."

"That it?"

The job-related conversation cooled Jim's temper like a cloud covering the sweltering sun. Jim managed another deep breath and blew out the last of the morning's irritation. "Can we speak to Quyen's family?"

"We can, and we will." Gabe glanced at his watch. "In fact, they're expecting us at ten. Meeting with them in their home might give us more insight into this girl."

By the time Gabe and Jim climbed into the police vehicle, they were back to their typical candor. Jim, wanting to make the tracker jabs less painful, thought it might help to make light of the topic.

"Ya know, if using my tracker friend doesn't work for Larsen, maybe she would agree to bringing in Diligent Dave from Major Crimes. What's his name, Dave Spiller? He was always good at digging through the garbage leads and throwing us the worthwhile suspects. Come to think of it, I haven't seen him in the office for a while. He leave?"

"Oh, you haven't heard? He was granted a transfer," Gabe said with a smirk.

"Granted? What's the scoop on that?" Jim buckled his seatbelt, happy for the distraction the story would bring.

"Wait'll you hear this." Gabe chuckled. "Dave's squad had been after him to go to happy hours with them, but he always begged off, saying that he had reports to finish. He doesn't put in for OT. He just likes to make sure he's gotten his work done."

"Brown noser."

"Exactly." Gabe paused as he maneuvered through the traffic. "But a couple of weeks ago, his wife took the kids to visit her sister out of state, and it dawned on him that he had a weekend to himself. So, when the squad invited him to happy hour, to their surprise, he tagged along."

"Okay. So, is this where Mr. By the Book goes astray?"

"It's always the quiet ones. Isn't that what they say?" Gabe laughed again and slipped in between two cars that parted ways to give him room. "They were joined by a couple of female officers from a squad from across the hall."

"I like where this is going."

"Yeah, you will. One drink led to another, and one

of the female officers was in no position to drive home. Ever the nice guy, he offered to drive both women home, particularly as it was on his way.

"So, they pile into his car, and he drives up to the house of the first officer. She staggers out and immediately trips on the sidewalk or something. The other officer gets out, says that she'll help her friend into the house and to bed. He says sure and waits in the car. Time passes. More time passes. He's wondering how long it's going to be, and if anything's wrong. He shuts off the engine, gets out of the car."

"You're really milking this story, Gabe."

"Oh, it's worth it. Stay with me. Dave opens the front door, walks in and goes up the stairs to see if everything's okay. He opens the bedroom door, and things are okay. Really okay if you know what I mean, and I think you do. So, Dave's just standing there, admiring the festivities, and thinks, 'We're all adults. I have a free weekend. My wife will never know,' and proceeds to join them. For. The. Entire. Weekend!"

Jim laughed. "Sounds like a brilliant idea. Nothing could go wrong there."

"Well, come that Monday morning, Dave wanders into Human Resources, and asks for a transfer to another division."

"And they just gave it to him? No questions asked?"

"They didn't have too many questions since rumors were flying around the office. Some of the other officers saw his car at her house that night and kept checking back. The two women officers were known for being a bit free-spirited, put it that way. Dave confided in one person who confided in one person. You know how that goes."

"Well, I haven't done anything that juicy to confide to anyone."

"Can't say that I have either. Dave told HR he couldn't stand the guilt of seeing either of those women in the halls. They didn't put up a fight. They just transferred him out. He's probably lucky he didn't suffer other consequences."

"No joke. Must have been a busy week in HR. They just needed to shove that problem under the rug, or in this case, to another office."

Gabe slowed down and pulled into the driveway. "We're here. Glad I could entertain you for the trip."

Jim laughed. "As always."

****

Quyen's home was middle-class Jacksonville, Florida—stucco, lanai, pool surrounded by much of the same. Gabe rang the doorbell, which set off a dog's frantic barking.

"Hush, Pepper," a female voice uttered on the other side of the door. "Sit."

Once the barking quieted, the door opened, revealing a slender Vietnamese woman in her late forties to early fifties. A small Bichon-Yorkie sat faithfully at her feet. Behind her, a fit man wearing a suit stepped into view. He approached Jim and Gabe in a businesslike fashion, introduced himself as John Nguyen, and after placing a hand on his wife's back, introduced her as Cam.

"Please come in and have a seat." John led them to the kitchen. With a hand gesture, he invited the detectives to have a seat at the table.

"Can I get you some coffee? It's freshly brewed."

"No, thank you," Gabe responded.

Jim let the response speak for both. She nodded and then gracefully slid into one of the seats beside her husband. Without having a purpose, Cam's hands fidgeted until her husband gently placed his hands on top of hers. Jim did not take her nervousness to mean guilt or his calmness to mean innocence. Mr. Nguyen was too practiced of a businessman to be read that easily.

"We're here to ask some questions about your daughter, Quyen," Gabe began.

Jim pulled out his pad and pen and noticed Cam watching him closely.

"Yes. That's what you mentioned on the phone."

Jim flipped the notebook open to a clean sheet. Only then did John glance his way in the slightest recognition that his words were being recorded. "Unfortunately, Quyen is visiting friends out of state. Now that she is in college, I'm afraid I don't know as much about her life as I would like to. I'll try my best to be of help, though." Cam's fingers tangled together, and John gave them a squeeze.

"Has Quyen ever mentioned a girl named Tori?" Gabe asked. "I believe they play soccer together."

John snuck a glance at his wife, who returned his look with a hint of panic. "We know of Tori." Gabe gave him a moment to continue, but he did not.

"Do I sense they were not exactly friends?"

"To be honest, no. They weren't very friendly." John took a deep breath and let it out slowly, and a hint of Listerine and expensive cologne wafted across the table. "Quyen is different than Tori. The two young women are both competitive. The difference is Quyen is competitive with herself, always fighting to be better than she was the year before. She can be a bit single-minded in this endeavor. Tori, on the other hand, is competitive with everyone around her. She has to be the best, and when she is not, well, let's just say, she can make people regret their successes."

"How do you mean?" Jim asked after scribbling a few more words into his pad.

"Sports teams can be much like a sorority. The members of the team become a family. Tori, though, she has a strong personality. People fear her rejection, and when she decides she doesn't care for someone, other members follow suit. And to be frank, Tori does not care for our Quyen."

"And what about Quyen's boyfriend, Bill Decker?"

John just shook his head. "We've never cared for him. Maybe that's why Quyen has only let us meet him a couple of times. He has a temper."

"Have you seen this temper?" Jim asked.

"Not personally, but I've heard how he threw a plate and got fired," John responded. "But it's not just that. He just seems shady. He won't shake my hand and look me in the eye. I don't trust him."

"If it weren't for that Tori girl, Quyen would never have dated him. They connected over their dislike of her," Cam said. "Tori made her feel ostracized by her soccer family. Bill was the only one she felt understood her feelings."

"How did Quyen and Bill meet?" Gabe asked.

John's face showed disappointment as he spoke. "They met at the restaurant. Quyen didn't say she was in there drinking, but we assume so. Bill stood up for her when Tori was being rude and ended up giving her a ride home. The rest is history."

"Why did Quyen leave town right now?" Gabe

asked.

"She's visiting friends from her Richmond high school team." Cam smiled warmly at the memory. "She loved that team. Bill actually encouraged her to go."

"Whose idea was it for her to leave?" Gabe asked.

"Ours. We bought her the tickets months ago. We can show you that." John moved his hand, maybe sensing that his wife's nervousness was subsiding while she spoke. "She's coming home in a couple of days. I'm sure she would be happy to speak to you if you would like."

Gabe took out his business card. "We would like that. Have her contact us at her earliest convenience."

Chapter 21

Present Day
Patient 541

Journal Entry
That evening I dreamed of Dee. We were in the chow hall where we had first met. Shane was there, too. My subconscious fought becoming as callous as the outer version of myself, for in my dreams, I still searched for what other humans craved: connection and love. In my dream, my gaze met Dee's. Her blank eyes searched mine for a person she believed, at one time, was in there somewhere.

Dee stood to leave, gesturing for me to follow her. I floated ghost-like behind her as she left the chow hall and walked into the dark, open air. She walked at a pace that kept her distance. Every now and then, she would turn and beckon to me once more. Before she could disappear into a tent, I called out to her.

"Dee."

She turned toward me, her gaze soft and inviting. Then, on tiptoed feet, she kissed me gently on my cheek. My heart twitched, trying to come back to life.

"You're here," she said.

"What do you mean?" And then the past caught up to me even in my sleep. She would not find what she was looking for in the depths of my gaze. I was as gone as she

246

was—transformed into another being, another species, capable of unthinkable things. She must have sensed the transition. Her expression hardened, and her eyes shone with hatred.

"Why did you do it?" she asked.

"You were dying. I couldn't save you."

"You know the truth."

"I couldn't save you both."

Dee began fading, and the sounds of whimpering woke me again. The dream ran through my mind as I drifted between a state of sleep and wakefulness. For moments I couldn't move, and without permission, all the anger raging inside of me shifted into precisely what she wanted me to feel: guilt for surviving, guilt for fighting to survive, guilt for not choosing to pull her out before the Marine. I had no way of winning the battle in my mind. The fact that I saved a Marine before the grenade went off meant that I didn't save Dee.

The next day, our battalion fought again. The battle got bloodier each day, far bloodier than the First Battle of Fallujah, yet despite our efforts, it was not clear whether we were winning or losing. The troops were growing weary, and all the deaths, especially Shane's and Dee's, had taken a toll on us. In the middle of the bloodshed, we had no way of knowing that by the end of the battle, one hundred and seven Marines would have died, and six hundred and thirteen would have been wounded. Why would the death of Shane, a man who'd irked me more than most, bother me more than all the others? Was it because I saw his death happen with too much clarity? Perhaps. But it was more than that. Shane made people believe he was invincible. While his ego had made him a few enemies, his courage had made people *feel protected.*

With just one bullet, the insurgents had taken him out. They'd made all of us feel more vulnerable and aware of our mortality. We needed hope. For me, that hope came in a dangerous form.

****

2018
Jim

Gabe and Jim returned to the office, and Jim immediately went back to searching the aerial views of the area. Trees behind the restaurant blocked the view of a retention pond. He printed off the map and headed to Larsen's office. On the way, he stopped. He couldn't add any more fuel to the fire between him and Gabe.

"Hey, I found this site on the maps. Just a heads-up, I'm suggesting to Larsen that we search the area."

"Thanks for the heads-up, partner. Let me know what she says." Gabe's tone held more humor than admiration.

Jim knocked on Larsen's door, and she waved him in. "Do you have something?"

"Just a hunch." He slid the picture in front of her. "Thought I'd run it by you this time."

Larsen looked at him over her readers and then picked up the paper. "Want to explain?"

"It's a retention pond behind the restaurant. There are just enough woods that it might have been overlooked. Thought we might want to take a closer look at it."

Larsen sat back in her chair. Again, she eyed Jim over her glasses. "You know I'm rooting for you, Jim. I see potential." She tapped the picture with her finger.

"It's things like this that give you an edge."

Jim imagined his whiteboard at home and all the names of people who would be trying to destroy him. Lieutenant Larsen was the only person he could think of who might be trying to help. She would at least have the knowledge to make him look like a good detective. After all, he reminded himself again. The voice never said anything a good detective couldn't guess at.

"I'll get a search team over there right away. Good work, detective."

Jim turned to leave. With his hand on the door handle, he turned back to Larsen. "Do you happen to have a walkie-talkie?"

"Excuse me?"

"Do you own a walkie-talkie?"

"That's a strange question."

"Yeah, I guess it is. Pretend I didn't ask."

"You okay, detective?"

"Just working out some hunches."

"I guess you'll tell me what you find when the timing is right."

"For sure. Thanks for following up on the retention pond idea."

Jim left Larsen's office before he could say anything else to make him look foolish in front of his boss.

Within an hour, Jim and Gabe stepped out of their car and headed through the woods to the pond. Before they could reach the bank, a dank, moldy smell greeted them.

"It smells like death here." Jim swatted away the flies that buzzed around his head.

"Perfect place to hide a body."

A team of divers stood by the edge of the murky

water. As Jim stepped closer, his foot sunk into the muddy bank, creating a squishy sound. An old beer bottle stuck halfway out of the mud, probably left behind by teenagers. Yellow tape marked an area next to the water's edge.

"What do you have?" Jim asked as they approached.

"It looks like footprints, but I don't think they will be usable. We'll cast them in case, but it's just too muddy. The shape will be too distorted, is my guess."

"How deep do they go?" Gabe asked.

"Six inches. Maybe eight."

Gabe went over to an untouched, yet similar, area. He stepped onto the muddy bank and then stepped back. "Whoever left that print weighed a good deal more than me."

Jim studied the marks. "Or they were carrying someone."

"That's what we're afraid of."

Two men in wetsuits walked up to the water's edge. "Let's hope all of our suspicions are wrong," the taller one said as he stepped into the water.

The two divers waded in up to the waist and then stopped and looked at each other. The taller one called over his shoulder, "We've got a body."

She had been tossed in with a rope and brick tied around her waist. With no current in the pond, her body sank to the bottom where it was thrown. They carefully brought the corpse to the shore and placed the remains of Victoria Jensen on the bank. The detectives stood back, letting the CSI unit begin their work. Within minutes, the team had located the challenge coin tucked inside her cheek. And after that, no one on the force could deny they were dealing with a serial killer.

The air thickened around Jim, and for several heartbeats, he couldn't breathe. Tori's death, her body lifeless in front of him, bothered him more than other deaths he had investigated, perhaps because he had met her. Images of the young woman flashed before him; the way she'd strutted around the restaurant, cocky and confident. The memories collided with the bloated remains before him. Instead of the beautiful, physical creature that she'd been days before, she was now repulsive to gaze upon.

Jim stood to the side, watching as the experts went over every inch of her body. They took pictures of the bruises around her neck and on her cheek. The perpetrator had punched her several times before finishing the job. Once again, there wasn't a murder weapon; the perpetrator had only used his hands.

Whoever had done this to Tori had not liked her. They wanted to feel the life leave her body. They wanted to know they were responsible for her death.

Oh, Tori, Jim thought, *why did you have to make so many people hate you?*

****

Jim and Gabe spent the afternoon going over college schedules, trying to find a class or friend connection between Bethany and Tori. Both young women were working on a criminal justice major, which led to them being in several of the same courses. Dr. Vijay Patil's wasn't one of them, but the fact they were both taking some of the same classes was something to work with, at least. So far, it was all Jim and Gabe had that linked the women. That is, besides the fact that they were both about the same age, had the same hair color, and were about the same size. After an exhausting day of interviews with college professors and classmates, Jim and Gabe did not have any leads.

Back at the office, they studied the whiteboard. The pictures of the two women were the centerpiece of the puzzle. Lines shot out from the photos and led to pictures of Austin Williams, Dr. Patil, Ben Adams, Quyen Nguyen, and Bill Decker. There wasn't one strong lead. Whoever had committed the crimes knew what investigators looked for and had managed not to leave so much as a hair.

Jim returned home exhausted. As he called out Gwen's name, he heard the upstairs shower running and Gwen singing. The table was set, and the kitchen smelled of onions and garlic. The timer on the stove ticked down the last twenty minutes. His stomach rumbled as he riffled through the mail, separating the recycling from the papers of interest. Almost everything went straight into the recycling. One piece of mail stood out since it was addressed to him yet had no return address. As he went to open it, a phone began vibrating. Gwen had, in a rare moment, left her phone on the counter instead of carrying it with her wherever she went.

"Yeah," Jim said curtly, assuming the caller would be a telemarketer since the number was unknown.

"I'm sorry. I was trying to reach Gwen Castille. Do I have the wrong number?"

"No. That's my wife. Can I help you with something?" Jim remained short with the caller.

"I was calling to let her know that she forgot a sweatshirt in the room. We will hold it for her at the front desk."

"I'm sure she will be grateful. I can swing by and get it for her." Jim grabbed a piece of paper and a pen.

Even before the caller told him the address, he sensed his world was about to change. "The Days Inn on Baymeadows. The address is—"

"That's okay. I know where you're located." Jim crumpled the paper and tossed it into the recycling. "I'm on my way."

The entire ride, Jim searched his mind for reasons why his wife had left her sweatshirt in a hotel room. Her colleague is having an affair, and Gwen let her use her credit card so she wouldn't get caught by an abusive husband who had it coming. There was a conference in the hotel that Gwen had forgotten to mention, and when the person on the phone said room, he was referring to a conference room.

As he walked inside, Jim almost had himself convinced that there was a good explanation. He still believed in the possibility when he introduced himself as Gwen's husband, and the hotel attendant paused. But when the young man handed Jim the blue sweatshirt with the airport logo on it, the truth slammed into Jim with a force that knocked him to his knees.

Chapter 22

Present Day
Patient 541

Journal Entry

We began using white phosphorus to help us see at night. White phosphorus, or WP as we called it, was the equivalent of napalm, and using it against insurgents was illegal and considered inhumane. The possible effects of WP were unsettling to say the least. Anything that could melt a person's skin demanded respect. We used WP to create smoke screens so that we could move without being seen. At night, it aided the use of night gear by increasing clarity.

Shake 'n Bakes were different. Shake 'n Bakes involved combining WP with mortar, and their goal was not to illuminate the night sky. The battles were intense, the death toll on both sides was rising, and spirits were down. Shake 'n Bakes offered a power boost, so to speak. They gave us leverage when the scale seemed to favor the wrong side.

After a devastating day, Sergeant Major Samuels gave us the orders. WP had a new duty, and that duty involved ending this war sooner than later. Death surrounded me, and at the time, what caused it meant little to me. Samuels briefed Toby and me on our mission. A couple klicks down the road, our sources had pinpointed a headquarters of sorts. Our job was simple. We would "illuminate" the building so our night vision could get a better look at the enemy. And I was more than fine with the job. In the hallway of our latest hideout, Toby pulled me to the side.

"It's not right. We know they're in there. We can't use WP on them."

"But we can shoot them in their backs, and that's okay."

Toby looked at the ground while taking an audible breath. "There's rules in war, too, and this is breaking a serious one."

I put my hand on Toby's shoulder and smiled. "Shake 'n Bake, my man. Shake 'n Bake." I turned from him.

"Are you going to feel the same way when you're back home? What will you tell your future children? Will you mention the fact that you melted innocent women and children to defend our country?"

"Anyone left in this city would shove that WP up your ass if they had the chance. Don't you doubt it for a second." I took a couple of steps toward the room. "And Toby, if we don't make it out of here soon, you won't have any children to tell your war stories to anyway."

Occasionally guilt attempted to worm itself inside my mind, but I knew what I told Toby wasn't just coming from a warped mind. We needed to get the hell out of this city, and WP gave us an advantage.

"Gear up, men. We're heading out." Marshall would lead the mission, which included only the three of us. We grabbed our supplies and stepped out into the bright sunshine. Toby stood next to me. His presence stung like alcohol on infected flesh. I wanted him to go

away, but my annoyance faded as bullets buzzed our heads. We sought cover. One klick, one small kilometer, could seem impossible when faced with what we were facing.

Everywhere I looked, a building was turning into another pile of rubble. The bodies in the street were putrid and bloated. I was in hell, and in hell, ugly things happened. In my bag, I hid the hope we needed. The image of Dee's face haunted me, fueling my hatred and anger. Wouldn't she find it ironic that her judgmental attitude helped me complete my task? Still, I pushed her from my mind and worked on autopilot.

As we approached our target building, we saw rifles sticking out of the windows. Behind the walls were insurgents along with, we believed, a healthy number of weapons. Getting close enough to use the WP would not be easy. Improvised explosive devices hid under the streets, waiting for some poor soul to step on the pressure plate created to trigger the explosion. Some Marines had the job of Explosive Ordnance Disposal, which involved going ahead of a battalion and finding the IEDs. Often the missions were successful in the way success is easily measured. Other times, the Marines discovered mines by inadvertently stepping on them. We never knew what fresh young face would give us a final nod before being blown up in front of us. Today, we traveled alone, and alone, we would learn if bombs had been buried under our feet.

Eventually, we saw a clear path. We crept out from behind a vehicle, running from cover to cover as we approached the target. The insurgents knew we were coming. The gunshots followed us, but we managed to avoid getting hit. By the time we reached the building, everything was oddly quiet. The insurgents were planning something; of that, I was sure.

Marshall signaled for Toby and me to stand back. We slid against either side of the door with our weapons in ready position. Marshall then kicked in the door, setting off a firestorm of gunfire. Bullets pinged off the walls and whizzed through the air. Marshall fell to the ground, screaming. Blood gushed from a hole in his thigh. Toby grabbed him and pulled him to safety. That's when I ran in and threw the WP into a room full of insurgents. As the grenade flew, I caught a glimpse of the people in the room before I darted out of the building.

We ran to the next cover, dragging Marshall as best we could. Breathless and exhausted, we paused behind a truck. We heard people screaming and running from the building. Toby peeked around the vehicle and then ducked down quickly. He stared straight ahead. He wouldn't look at me, and his voice came from far away.

"They're women and children."

"They're insurgents, Toby. The kids had guns."

"You saw them holding guns?"

"You know that they train the children to kill. You know that we're to assume twelve-year-olds are insurgents if they stayed in the city."

"You saw them with guns?" he asked again.

"Yes," I said defiantly, but in truth, once again, I couldn't be sure. We could hear the screaming. I still hear the screaming.

Toby's skin was ashen and sweaty. "We need to get to the building," he insisted.

"Not yet. Wait for the firing to stop."

Toby tried to stand once, but his legs caved underneath him.

"Wait, Toby." I knew then that he was not trying to escape the gunfire but rather the sound of the screaming.

"We need to go now." Just as Toby stood, he fell again. Only this time, the cause was a bullet in his abdomen.

"Holy shit. Toby, I told you to wait."

Three of us were behind the truck seeking cover, and now two were wounded. I pushed down on Toby's wound to stop the bleeding. The insurgents continued to fire at us, and there was so much blood.

"Toby, you need to keep the pressure on your wound. Do you hear me?"

Toby nodded.

Marshall was tying a tourniquet around his leg. When he saw me looking at his wound, he said, "You've got other things to worry about," and nodded toward the building the insurgents were firing at us from.

I pulled my attention away from the injured Marines and took aim at every moving target I could find. Bullets ricocheted off the side of the vehicle. I took turns between shooting and ducking until there was a break in the battle.

"I need to get you to the building."

"Take Toby first. I'll hold them off the best I can."

I handed Marshall his weapon, hoisted Toby up the best I could, and as soon as Marshall gave me the signal, I took off in a run. The sounds of gunfire followed us with each step, but we made it to the building. As soon as I had Toby propped up against the wall, I ran back to the door. Several insurgents were approaching the vehicle, and Marshall was struggling to reload his weapon. Adrenaline pumped through my veins, and I acted without thought. I burst through the door, firing and taking fire at the same time. Each bullet found its mark, and one by one, the insurgents fell.

I raced to Marshall, grabbed him up, and together we hobbled backward toward the building. Both of us fired our weapons at the insurgents who kept emerging from their lair.

Marshall and I each took a window and continued to battle. The rounds of ammunition were dwindling quickly, yet the insurgents kept coming. Out of the corner of my eye, I saw Toby's pack. I reached for it with my boot and dragged it over to me. With one hand, I searched the contents until I found what I had only hoped was inside: a grenade. But there was something else inside the bag, which in the present situation I had no time to worry about: A pad. Dee's pad. It had to be. No one else kept a pad with them in the middle of the war. I grabbed the grenade and waited until the moment the potential was at its max, and then I threw it in the middle of the incoming enemies. Within seconds, limbs lay along the street, and men ran for cover.

Silence rang in my ears louder than the sound of the grenade exploding. Then, I became aware of another sound. A Humvee was heading toward us. The vehicle screeched to a halt in front of the building, and Marines filled the room. They pulled Toby and Marshall into the vehicle. Once they were loaded, I squeezed on top of other Marines as we rode until we found help.

After Toby was whisked off by the corpsmen, I never saw or spoke to him again. Neither Marshall's nor Toby's wounds ended up being fatal. Instead, the injuries served as their tickets home. There were times, through the years, I considered reaching out to Toby, but in truth, a rawness to our relationship always existed. Being in his presence exposed truths about me that I didn't want to face. Once we transferred our wounded men into the tracked vehicle, and I watched them speed down the road away from us, my experiences with Toby ended.

Marshall, on the other hand, would enter my life on occasion with a Christmas card or a phone call. These attempts at connection faded with time but never disappeared completely. Marshall, opposite of Toby, made me look at myself as a hero. My mind battled his perception just as much as Toby's perception of me riddled my consciousness. Toby's perception proved far more accurate, but false perceptions, like Marshall's, soothed the soul better than the truth.

That night—because it always seemed to be the nights that allowed my old self to creep in—an emptiness lingered in the room and made me feel hollow inside. Toby had reminded me of home, of another lifetime, another me that didn't belong in that arid desert. Toby deserved far better in life than having a mind destroyed by war. Getting shot was the best thing that had ever happened to him because maybe he'd gotten out in time before an irreversible transformation occurred within him. As I closed my eyes and begged my mind for sleep, I also said a small prayer, the first in a very long time, that once he returned to the other side of the world, Toby's mind, body, and soul would begin to heal.

****

2018
Jim

When Jim returned home, he did the only thing he could think of doing. He ate dinner, washed his plate, and retired to his man cave. When Gwen asked if he wanted to watch a show with her, he told her that he was too stressed with work and needed some time to himself. Once Gwen went to bed, he retrieved the sweatshirt and hid it in a corner of the garage where the whiteboard also remained out of sight.

Jim's mind swirled with hatred for his wife and for Paul. As he envisioned them together, curled up in a hotel bed, laughing together, enjoying the feeling that only secrets can create, he wanted them both dead. The memory of past victims was vivid in Jim's mind. Couldn't Paul be walking in a park when a punk kid jumped him for his wallet? Could Gwen be home alone when a drifter in need of cash entered their home and killed her in a robbery attempt? Jim envisioned Gwen smiling at Paul the night of the dinner. Jim hated her for what she was doing, but was his hatred enough to slip a homeless man money to get rid of her? He knew the answer.

In the end, all Jim could do was savor the taste of such crimes as if they were morsels of imagined sugar. He knew what the treat would taste like as it melted on his tongue. He could close his eyes and feel the sugar slide across his tongue as it turned to liquid. If he tried hard enough, could he satisfy his hunger with his imagined sensations? One way or the other, Jim needed to act, and his line of business had taught him that if he chose to kill them, there would be a strong possibility of ending up in prison. History proved that law enforcement did not fare well when confined with other criminals.

Jim swallowed his last swig of beer just as the garage door squeaked open.

"It's almost midnight. Why are you still up?" Gwen's voice was raspy, showing Jim that she had woken from her sleep.

"I can't get the shitty things people do out of my mind." Jim tossed his bottle in the recycling bin. "Are you thinking about the shitty things people do, too? Is that what woke you up? Thinking about shitty things?"

"Are you drunk, Jim? You have work tomorrow."

"I'm aware of my schedule, Gwen."

Jim slid past his wife while she stood in the doorway. His shoulder bumped her with a hint of weight behind it.

"You can't even walk straight." Gwen sounded disgusted.

"I'm going to bed. Why don't you do the same?"

"Going to work hungover is a great way to get a promotion. I can't believe—"

Jim snapped around, startling Gwen. With his finger pointed in her face, he spat out his words. "Don't you ever talk to me about my work again. Do you hear me? I can handle my own damn job, and I don't need you telling me how to solve cases."

Gwen's petrified expression empowered Jim. He turned away from her and ambled up the stairs. Long after Jim had drifted off to sleep, he was awakened when Gwen climbed into the bed next to him. When he woke, the house was empty, but a note on the kitchen table announced they needed to talk.

****

When Jim entered the office, there was a hum of conversation. Something had happened. Gabe was holding a cup of coffee and talking to a man Jim didn't recognize. The man stood a few inches taller than Gabe and had a thick head of dark brown hair. When Gabe noticed Jim, he tilted his head toward him saying, *Come*

262

here.

"This is Special Agent Brent Foster."

"Special agent? You're with the FBI?"

"That I am." Brent offered Jim his hand.

"Detective Jim Castille. So, to what do we owe the pleasure?"

"It appears there's a serial killer lurking around the area."

"We have two victims with similar appearances. Both found with Marine challenge coins in their mouths."

"Correction. You have three victims."

"Three?" Jim asked.

"A woman in Georgia. Same description. Same Marine challenge coin."

"Georgia. The perp crossed state lines. Well, that explains why the FBI is involved now."

Lieutenant Larsen stepped out of her office. "I'd like all detectives and investigators on the case to meet me in the briefing room."

The conversation quieted to whispers as the crowd flowed from one room into the next. Jim took a seat, and Special Agent Foster sat next to him.

"Any good leads?" Foster asked.

"Nothing to speak of. We've exhausted the few leads we've had, but I can't say I felt that strongly about any of them."

Lieutenant Larsen stood to the side of the whiteboard. "It's been weeks since the first murder, and this is all we have. You are probably all aware, but we will now be working with the FBI since the murders were committed in multiple states." She placed a third picture in the center of the board. "Her name was Carrie Mullen.

Blonde, twenty, blue eyes. The detail that connected Carrie's murder to the others is that investigators found a Marine challenge coin in her mouth."

Lieutenant Larsen studied the board. "I'm going to let Special Agent Foster take it from here."

Brent scanned the whiteboard and cleared his throat before addressing the room. "Carrie Mullen had no ties to UNF. From what we learned from the family, she has no ties to anyone in the Jacksonville area." He looked over the whiteboard again. "We have used Analysis of Competing Hypothesis software to categorize the evidence, and we don't believe our killer is one of these people. The ACH matrix shows that when looking at time, dates, sources—none of these people fit all the criteria. We're overlooking the perp's connection to the victims.

"Carrie left Roanoke, Virginia, to get away from a bad breakup. According to her parents, the ex-boyfriend was not a threat. He ended the relationship. Carrie was the one who couldn't get over him. She moved to Helen, Georgia, to start over. She had just started a job working as a waitress. When she didn't show up for her third shift, her boss assumed she'd quit without telling him. No one else knew her well enough to be concerned.

"Her body would have gone undiscovered if it weren't for a dog that ran off the trail. He returned to his owner holding a hand. Wild animals had destroyed much of her body, making time of death very difficult to pinpoint. Fortunately, investigators were able to recover the challenge coin. After searching the database, the Helen investigators discovered the two similar cases here in Jacksonville."

"I guess we don't have to waste our time questioning

Quyen," Jim whispered the words to Gabe, but his partner didn't respond. In fact, he wouldn't even look in Jim's direction.

"There are no witnesses. No suspects in the area, but according to our profilers in Quantico's Behavioral Analysis Unit, we are looking for a white, middle-aged male. He most likely fits into society, holds a job, maybe even has a family. So far, we cannot find any past crimes matching the same criteria as these murders. We believe we have someone new to killing. Something has triggered our perp, and he is looking for a place to unleash his fury."

After the special agent wrapped up his summary of the facts, people filed out of the briefing room. Jim stood waiting for his partner to follow suit, but Gabe remained sitting.

"You coming?"

"Nah. I'll catch up with you."

"You just going to hang out in the briefing room?"

"I want to speak with Foster."

"Now who's being secretive?"

Chapter 23

Present Day
Patient 541

Journal Entry
*After the WP event, my memories began to blur.
Reality was a concept I could not grasp no matter how
hard I tried. I floated through the streets where bodies
lay bloated, threatening to burst open, like balloons at a
hellish fair. Marines vomited on the roads due to the
putrid smells. Master Sergeant Brady gave another
order: Burn the bodies. If we did not, disease threatened
to take even more lives.*

*We dragged corpses into piles. Even as I retell the
story in my mind, I feel my sanity, the little thread of it
left in my mind, slipping away. I envied Toby and
Marshall, and every military man sent home with an
injury. I even envied the ones who had died. My heart
was empty of gratefulness to be alive. Images of
watching Shane die in front of me filled me with longing.
What realm did Shane inhabit as my every sense—sound,
sight, smell, touch, and even taste—experienced death
all around me? Could hell be worse than what we were
living through? No. No, hell could not compare.*

*We poured gasoline onto the heap. One of the
Marines searched his pocket for a lighter, and that's
when I saw movement in the heap. "Wait," I yelled.*

"Someone's alive in there."

"There is no damn way someone is alive in that heap. We just dragged each body, and I can tell you, not one of them had a heartbeat."

"I swear. I saw something move."

The group of us stared intently.

"I don't see…" another Marine said. "Holy shit, there is something."

The world went silent as we stared so hard the image in front of us began to blur. Then, out of the rubble, a squirrel scurried to the surface and scrambled down the side. We watched it disappear behind a building.

"Light the damn thing." The words came out of my mouth as I watched the flame touch the fuel. The flames didn't catch immediately, but soon the human bonfire lit up the city. I watched long enough that the faces of the corpses blurred into the faces of Shane, Dee, and my father, and then I turned away and tried to outrun the sounds of flesh burning. To this day, I have never run far enough.

Beyond that, I will not put into words the horrors of that day. It's a day I have refused to relive until now, and as my mind is flooded with visions, I am reminded why.

After the mission was complete, several Marines, including myself, hunkered down inside a building. My body and mind ached with exhaustion. I sipped from my canteen, which held only a dwindling amount of lukewarm water. Swallowing was difficult despite my desperate need for hydration. I rested my head on the wall and concentrated on my breathing, if for no reason but to stop my mind from thinking.

Back home, Christmas trees stood decorated,

cookies warmed in ovens, gifts teased young, excited children. As families curled up by their warm fireplaces and watched It's a Wonderful Life *for the fiftieth time, did they think about us overseas battling for our lives and what we believed to be theirs as well, at least for their way of life? Did they know we were scared at times? Did they know we wanted to come home, but we also feared the ringing in our ears would be with us for so long that every Christmas season would be scarred by memories of bloodshed? Did they care?*

Something thumped against the wall outside, and we all grabbed our rifles. We waited in silence for another sound. A blast sent my body flying until I slammed into a wall. My ears rang, and my head throbbed. I saw the bodies of the other Marines. And then I faded into darkness.

When I woke, I was receiving care in Camp Fallujah. A bandage covered half of my head, and my muscles ached from being tossed into the building. The muscles would heal quickly, but the concussion would take some time.

I remained there as battles continued to be fought. About a week later, on December 23, 2004, the powers that be declared the city safe for civilians to return to. When I heard the news, I laughed, a sad, defeated laugh not only for myself, but for the Iraqi people who would soon be returning to a place no one should need to call home. The road to what even Iraqis considered normal would be long and painful. For me, my journey would be just as difficult in different ways. Many months ago, I had left home lost and desperate for direction and purpose. Now, I would be returning in a condition far worse than that.

****

2018
Jim

The tension between him and Gabe was palpable. *What the hell was Gabe thinking?*

Jim searched the aerial views of Helen, Georgia. Pictures of the creek, which babbled by the restaurant where he and Gwen had eaten, popped up on the screen.

What the hell, Gwen? Why did you have to go and wreck everything?

Jim rested his head in his hands. He dreaded going home. Somehow Gwen would make him the bad guy. It would be his fault that she'd crawled into bed with her pilot friend. It would be his fault that he'd yelled at her last night. It would be his fault that catching his wife in her lies had made him drink too much.

"Tough day?"

Jim's head snapped up. Brent Foster stood next to his desk.

"Want to talk about it?"

"I wouldn't put you through that on your first day in our office." Jim chuckled, but Brent didn't. Instead, he pulled up a chair and had a seat next to Jim. The special agent had a calming presence, making Jim almost want to trust him.

"What's your take on these murders?"

"No one stands out as the one."

"I know what you're saying. I looked at that board, and it seems like we're missing something, an important clue that might be right under our noses." Brent looked Jim in the eyes. "You know those cases when the solution is so close that everyone is looking right over it."

"I'm in the boat not seeing it. Even before the Georgia case, we only had the one connection: UNF. This last case destroyed that lead."

"I heard you recently traveled to Helen. Beautiful area, isn't it?"

"Yeah. My wife and I had a great weekend."

"And…?"

"What do you mean, and? That's all there was to it."

"You didn't look very happy for a guy who was describing an enjoyable getaway. Is there more to that story?"

Jim began to squirm under the special agent's scrutiny. As a detective, he'd been trained to read squirming as an admission of guilt. Jim decided sharing a bit might make the guy understand that his mood came from something else altogether.

"To be honest, we went away to work on our marriage. Things aren't all they should be between us."

"Sorry to hear that. Did the weekend help?"

Jim looked around. No one was in earshot. "I try to keep my personal life personal, but no. Things are far from all right. The weekend went well, but nothing changed when we got home."

"That's unfortunate."

"Yeah. It's unfortunate all right."

"So, when you were in Helen, were you together the whole time?"

"Yeah." Jim remembered his run, but Gwen had been asleep when he returned. She never even knew he left the hotel room. "I never left her side."

"Do you think it a bit odd that a woman was murdered in the same way in Helen, hours away from

Jacksonville, around the time you would have been visiting the area?"

"I do." Jim thought hard about his next words, but now was the time to share what he knew about the one suspicious character he had kept to himself. "I think it's very strange. I've had a few strange things happen lately."

"Like what?"

"This man. He's homeless, I believe. Wears camo pants and sometimes a black T-shirt. I saw him at an unconnected murder weeks ago, and then I saw him again walking around UNF."

"Did you tell anyone?"

"There wasn't much to tell. I couldn't even be sure it was the same person."

"So why tell me now?"

"I think he's following me."

"What makes you think so?"

"The other night, some women in the neighborhood said they saw a man fitting that description walking down our street. Also, it appeared as if someone had been in my wife's car."

"Did you share this with anyone?"

"No. I had no reason to yet. I've been staying up and watching to see if he comes back. I first need to confirm that he's the same man I saw at UNF near the crime scene. Not to mention, there's a bit going on in my life right now. The man hasn't been a big concern until now."

"What changed?"

"If a murder happened when I was in Helen, that raises serious suspicions about a drifter intent on following me and who was seen at the last crime scene."

"You said the man wears camo."

271

Jim nodded.

"Tell me more about him."

"I've had two quick glimpses of him in weeks. I don't have much: a white man, brown hair, medium height, thin."

"Let's have you do a sketch." As Brent punched a number into his phone, a lump formed in Jim's throat. Why was he petrified of them finding this man? "Skylar," the special agent said, "I need all the names and addresses of shelters and VA hospitals around the Jacksonville area."

The woman on the other end of the phone spoke words Jim could not hear.

"Thanks. You're the best." She said something else. "I gotta go, but yes, I made the reservations." When Brent hung up, he had a hint of embarrassment on his face. "The troubles of working with your wife."

"Apparently, it's where you should meet your mate. Or at least it's where my wife met… Never mind."

Brent studied Jim for a moment. "Sorry, man. That's pretty tough."

"There are many things that not even a romantic weekend away can mend." Jim stood and grabbed his jacket. "I'm going to find the sketch artist. It's about time I meet this drifter face to face. I have a few questions I need answered." Jim walked calmly to the door while trying to hide the fact that his heart was slamming against the walls of his chest, and despite the air-conditioned room, sweat trickled down his collar.

Chapter 24

Present Day
Patient 541

Journal Entry
The next week, the nurse comes to my door and asks me if I want to meet with the chaplain. This surprises me due to my breakdown during our last visit. I don't answer, but I rise from the spot on my bed and follow her down the hallway. Her hair is up in a ponytail, and I study her skin and her vulnerability. I don't want to hurt her, but I know I can.

Chaplain Gregory doesn't greet me as cordially today. I can't blame him, except I can. He gave me the journal. He made the memories come back.

"Good morning," he says while gesturing to the chair.

I take my seat. "I should probably apologize."

"That's up to you. If it's not, then it's not really an apology, is it?"

"I suppose it isn't." He watches me, hands folded in front of him almost in prayer. I don't apologize. "I've written almost my whole story."

His eyebrow lifts quizzically. "Have you?"

"The war part."

"Has writing the words relieved you of any guilt?"

"Writing the words has made me guilty."

"How has writing made you guilty?"

"Because I remember. I remember everything."

A thick silence filled the room, almost as if the chaplain knew more than ever that he was sitting in front of a killer, like he was talking to the evil parts of me for the first time. Every second that ticked by made my anger rise. If I lost it again, I might not be able to come back. Did I care?

"Remembering is a good thing," the chaplain says.

I stare at him. "You have no idea what memories go through my mind now." My voice fills with rage. "What is replayed every time I close my eyes. I feel their skin beneath my fingers. I remember their eyes as they beg me silently to stop. How is that a good thing?"

The chaplain remains calm. If I'm frightening him, he doesn't show his fear. "You can't heal if you don't let the memories in first. I know this is painful, but it's a necessary step."

I have nothing to say. The clock ticks and we both look at it.

"You've had a visitor that you refuse to see." I look at the chaplain. He's staring back at me with intensity. "I think it's time you see him."

When I returned home, I took a taxi to my house. I carried one small suitcase. After paying the driver, I studied the home where my parents had raised me. Thoughts of my father filled my mind, overwhelming me with an array of emotions so broad I couldn't comprehend them at all.

I inhaled deeply and prepared myself for seeing my mother. During the months overseas, I never received a letter or gift package. The absence of such small niceties sent her message loud and clear: She was not proud of me. I contemplated walking away, but I had no place else to go, so I dragged my damaged self to the door, set down my bag, and rang the doorbell.

A dog barked, and I heard its nails on the hardwood as it raced to the door. A child giggled, and the curtain on the window moved slightly.

"Mom, there's a man here."

Before I could grab my bag and run, the door opened, and a stranger stood before me. She wore jeans and a casual top. Maybe mid-thirties, but her face looked worn down. A baby screamed in the background.

"Can I help you?"

My mind scrambled for a reply. "I don't think so."

She studied me. "Are you sure?"

"I was looking for the previous owner."

"Oh, I'm sorry." She looked down at my bag. Something told me that with one glance, she knew my whole story. Why would a man in camo show up at a door with his suitcase? Only one reason: He thought he was coming home. "I heard she moved to Georgia."

"Georgia." I put my hand in my pocket and released a long exhale. "Well, that makes sense."

"Did she have family there?"

"No." I picked up my bag. "And that's exactly why she moved there." I turned away and, over my shoulder, apologized for disturbing her.

"Oh, you didn't bother me. I'm sorry I couldn't help."

I gave her a wave and continued down the sidewalk. When I reached the road, I looked right and left, trying to decide which way to go. I turned right and started walking. I walked for miles and miles, and for years, many years, I believed I had chosen correctly. I only had to keep walking away from the past, and if I continued down the path I had chosen, everything would be fine. I didn't know that no matter how far I walked, the past still lingered around corners, and eventually, it would find me again.

****

2018
Jim

Jim spent an hour describing the man whom he had seen first in the crowd and then had seen walking down the road at UNF. When the sketch artist finished, Jim stared the ghost of the past in the eye, and for the first time, felt ready to see him face to face once again. But why had he not recognized the man from the crowd before now? The idea seemed implausible.

Gabe drove to the VA Hospital. They were halfway to their destination before he spoke.

"Why didn't you tell me about this guy?"

"There wasn't anything to tell until today." Jim thought back to when he'd seen the man in the crowd. "When we were at the crime scene in the park, I asked if you'd seen him, and you hadn't. I figured I was just being paranoid. There were dozens of people there to gawk at the body."

"I don't remember that."

"Why would you? It was a quick comment. I decided it wasn't anything of concern right after the words left my mouth. The second time I thought I saw him was at UNF after Bethany's body was found. I couldn't be sure it was the same man. You saw him, too, or you should have. I figured if he didn't catch your attention, he probably, once again, wasn't of concern.

"Maybe I should have mentioned someone was on my street, but again, I couldn't say for sure if it was the same man. I never even saw the guy in our neighborhood. It's just that now, the fact that he seems to be wherever I am, well, now I'm concerned."

Gabe seemed to contemplate the possibility that Jim was telling the truth. "I guess."

"That's all you have to say? You guess?" Jim huffed. "Damn it, Gabe. You know me. How are you even questioning me?"

"Maybe this whole serial killer thing is getting to me. Sorry, man."

"Whatever. Just drive."

They pulled into the VA Hospital, followed by Brent Foster.

"You have the sketch?" Brent asked.

"Yeah." Jim held the picture up, and Brent nodded.

"I can't imagine we'll be so lucky as to track this guy down in one stop, but here goes." When they entered, they walked to the check-in desk. Brent flashed his badge. "We need to speak to some of the employees who might recognize a sketch."

A middle-aged woman with reddish hair sat behind the desk. She didn't act surprised or impressed by the badge. She clicked the button on the device hanging from her neck. "Kim, can you come to the front?" Pointing to a small waiting area, the woman said, "She'll be right here. You can have a seat over there while you wait."

"Thanks," Brent said. The three men sat in the chairs as the clock ticked by five and then ten minutes. Finally, a nurse who looked to be in her fifties rushed down the hallway and stopped at the desk. The red-haired woman pointed toward them. Jim heard only a hushed conversation before the head nurse headed their way. She extended her hand to each of them and introduced herself.

"We're looking for a man we believe might be a veteran. We can't say for sure." Brent looked at Jim to prompt him to show the sketch. Kim nodded when she saw it. "You know him then?"

"I would love to help, but because of HIPAA, I can't discuss any information about the patients."

"But you seemed to recognize him," Gabe said.

"I'm sorry, but I can't help." She turned and walked down the hallway.

Jim and Gabe were almost out the door when a custodial worker called to them. They waited as the elderly man sauntered over to them while looking cautiously down the hallway.

"I heard you asking Kim about the man in the photo. Do you mind if I take a look at that picture?"

Gabe and Jim looked at each other, shrugged, and then Jim handed over the sketch.

"Something told me it would be him," the man said after studying the image for only a moment. "I know I probably shouldn't talk to you either, but I feel I should."

"Go on," Jim urged.

"His name's Tobias. He's been in and out of here for the past several months. New to the area, I guess."

"Is he dangerous?" Brent asked.

"Tobias is a mystery. I think that if he didn't need to come in here for meds, he would prefer to stay that way."

"Is he homeless?" Gabe asked.

"I don't believe so. I've seen him use a credit card, and he owns a newer smartphone. Sometimes it's the family members supporting them. Could be parents or a spouse."

"How often does he come in?" Gabe asked.

"He was here just a few days ago, so he won't need new prescriptions for some time. I can't say if he'll ever come back. I don't think he's from around here. He may have already headed home."

"Do you know how he travels around?"

"I believe he takes the bus. He seems mentally capable." The man glanced over his shoulder. No one stood within earshot of our conversation. "Several of us expressed concerns to each other about his last visit. He seemed…I don't know…angry, maybe. Something was just off about him."

Brent handed the elderly man his card. "If Tobias comes back in, you need to reach out to us immediately."

"You can be certain I will." He looked at the card. "Did he do something?"

"That's what we're trying to find out. But he is a person of interest." Brent turned to leave, and the other men followed suit. Then he stopped. "Tell the staff to be careful around him. We don't know what he's capable of yet."

They were almost to the car when the call came in from Larsen.

"Where?" Gabe said into his phone. "On our way."

Gabe's pace quickened. He didn't look Jim's way when he spoke. "They've got another S7."

"Where?"

"They found the body tossed in a pond off Pecan Park Road, near the airport."

The fourth Signal 7—the fourth dead body. The serial killer was becoming bolder and confident that he would not be stopped.

At top speed, the men raced to the area. By the time they reached the crime scene, the CSI team had already bagged the challenge coin. The young woman was blonde, just as the last three victims had been, and Jim could tell she had been attractive. Bruise marks covered her body, proving she had fought her assailant. But the bruising earned when she lost her battle formed a ring around her neck.

"We need to find this Tobias character today," Brent said to the air. Then he turned to Jim. "Did you happen to have a reason to be by the airport lately?"

"No. I haven't been this way in months."

"If it's Tobias, and he's following you, then why the girl at UNF?"

"Jim takes classes there," Gabe answered.

"Thanks, Gabe. I can answer for myself."

"Sorry. I guess the fact just jumped out at me."

"That's interesting." Brent paused. "And then you went to Helen, and the next woman was killed but found later."

"Yes." Jim shifted from one foot to the other. The conversation was making him feel uncomfortable, even if it was leading them to the killer.

"Then, you ate dinner at City Ale House, and the next day your waitress was murdered."

"Yes."

"Did you happen to see anyone suspicious in the restaurant?"

"I wasn't paying attention. I wish I had been."

"Do you have any connection to the airport?"

Jim hesitated.

"Jim, do you have a connection to the airport?" Brent asked again.

"My wife works at the airport." Jim looked at Gabe and then back at Brent. "And so does the man she's having an affair with."

"I think it's time Gabe and I speak to your wife and friend," Brent said.

Jim stared at the corpse. *What the hell was happening?*

Chapter 25

Present Day
Patient 541

Journal Entry
Months later, I received a Silver Star Medal for saving Marshall and Toby. Marshall attended the ceremony. His presence meant more to me than the medal itself. Seeing Marshall smiling up at me made me almost believe that I was worthy, that I could in fact be a hero in my story. Toby, as I said, went his own way. Just as Marshall's presence spoke volumes, Toby's absence screamed a message as well. He knew I didn't deserve recognition. Toby knew I was an imposter. One courageous moment did not erase the actions he found less admirable.

I chose to listen to Marshall's message and focus on my bravery and successes. The ability to do so was the glue I used to build a future from the remains of my past. My life became a portrait created from a million memories. From a distance, the picture is one of a successful man, but on closer inspection, a million smaller images appear. When the tiny pictures are studied, the truth can be seen.

For years, the glue held firm, and I walked around this world an undetected imposter. But the glue began to lose its adhesiveness the day I received the first letter. As

I opened the envelope and a challenge coin—fake, the kind bought online—fell onto the floor, my knees grew weak. The words on the page confirmed what I'd suspected to be true days before: The stranger from the crowd was anything but a stranger, and he had somehow discovered the truth about Dee's death.

My hands shook. Each of the letters, on its own, could mean anything. Placed together in specific sequences, they changed my world. Murderer. Secret. Guilty. My temple pulsed, and my eyes blurred, yet not with tears. The pressure of the once-seen images pressed against my corneas as if trying to escape.

The headaches and blackouts began shortly after that. My life was unraveling in many ways, but the letters, the message within the pages, the challenge coins that kept coming, those were responsible for the glue losing its hold and for all the messy pieces of me being released into the world.

Shortly after receiving the first letter, I fought with my then wife. God, she could drive me crazy. The next evening, I decided to stop off for a beer before returning home.

I was just ordering a second beer when a cute blonde girl came up beside me to get a beer. Just to be polite, I offered to buy her one as well. With the most condescending expression she could muster, she turned me down.

"I was just offering a beer. Don't get yourself all worked up over it."

"Don't you think you're a bit too old to be hanging out in a college bar offering to buy girls drinks? What's wrong with you?" Her stare dug into mine, and for a moment, she looked exactly like Dee.

"Calm down, lady. You can buy your own damn beer."

She walked over to some guy on the dance floor, and they looked my way. I slapped some money on the bar and walked out, not wanting any trouble. Or, more honestly, I didn't want to deal with explaining the trouble. As she said, I was way too old to be dealing with college students. I didn't want to go home yet, so I sat in my car and tried to push the memory of Dee out of my mind.

I don't know how much time had passed before the blonde walked out, arm in arm with the guy from the dance floor. She threw her head back in laughter, and he smiled down at her as if she were a gem he had just pulled out of the gutter.

My intention wasn't to follow them when I started my car, but that's what I did. I followed them straight to her building where he kissed her on the cheek and walked away. My wife texted that she was staying at her mother's house across town. They had some catching up to do, or so she said. Apparently, she didn't want to come home, either. The funny thing was that our fight wasn't even that big. If I were to be honest with myself, we were just becoming sick of each other. Maybe those are the worst fights of all. I parked my car and sat in the darkness while contemplating my marriage, my job, and the letter stuffed in my glove box.

I held the challenge coin in my hand, turning it around with my fingers the way Dee had shortly before she died. My head pounded. I don't remember falling asleep there, but I did. And for quite some time, I didn't remember waking up in the morning and seeing the blonde from the bar head out for her morning run.

Maybe my military training helped me cut her off on her route, but the task wasn't difficult.

Even now, when the memory is allowed to replay in my mind, I know that it wasn't that girl I killed in the woods. It was Dee. And as with all the unfortunate women who have crossed my path, I stuffed the sign of her "should-be loyalty" into her mouth. I ask myself why and have no definitive answer. With Dee, it was an impulse. I wanted her to choke on her disloyalty. But truly, in the moment, my hands just moved on their own.

Yet my actions never silenced Dee. She speaks to me still.

****

2018
Jim

The victim's name was Amy Pyle. She'd worked as a flight attendant and had been heading home for the night with what she thought might be the flu. She didn't tell her roommate that she had found someone to take her flight to Charlotte since they lived independent lives and mainly used each other to cut their rent cost in half. No one knew Amy was missing until some kids, trying to find a place to drink, found her body floating in the pond.

The day after finding her remains, Amy's car was found in the parking lot of a nearby gas station. The vehicle was parked behind a tree, and the video footage only picked up the car pulling into the spot. If the investigators zoomed in far enough, they could make out a blurred image of a person retreating from the car, but the image was too poor to decipher if the figure was a man or woman.

Jim wasn't allowed to sit in on the interview with

Paul, but he knew the outcome. Paul had an alibi: Gwen. He also had a hotel transaction to prove it. Investigators were still looking for evidence that the two of them had officially been together in a hotel room.

For days, Gabe, Jim, and Brent searched footage of the comings and goings at the airport. There were so many people that the detectives could very well have been staring right at Amy and whoever killed her but couldn't find them.

On the fourth day, Brent froze the screen. "Hold up." Everyone's attention turned to his screen. "Look here. There's a blonde woman in a dark skirt. The jacket covers the top so I can't tell if it's a flight attendant uniform, but it could be. Then watch." Brent let the video move forward several seconds. "Watch this guy in the sweatshirt. His hood is up, so I can't make out his face. Watch how he comes up behind her, and she doesn't look back at him."

"Okay?" Jim questioned.

"If someone you knew came up behind you and got that close, wouldn't you turn and address them in some way—a hug or a hello? She keeps looking forward. I think he has a gun in the front pocket of that sweatshirt."

"Shit, man. I think you're right." Gabe had his face inches from the screen. "There's something on that sweatshirt. Zoom in as far as you can."

Brent tweaked the image the best he could. "It looks like an airplane."

"Yeah. It does. Maybe it's someone who works with Paul." Gabe continued to stare at the screen.

"Let's get this video as clean as we can and see if Larsen wants to release it to the public. I think it's time folks know we have a serial killer on our hands." Gabe tapped the screen with his finger. "And I think that right there is our man."

****

Within hours, Larsen stood in front of dozens of news cameras and stated the facts the investigators knew. They'd decided to leave one out to prevent copycats from messing with the investigation. On the screen, the news channels displayed the frozen video of the man and described the blue, hooded sweatshirt with the yellow airplane logo displayed on the top right.

"If anyone recognizes this sweatshirt or has any knowledge of the crimes, please contact the hotline number at the bottom of the screen. We are asking young women, especially, not to walk alone at night. Check in with your friends and family members who might be living alone." Lieutenant Larsen looked directly into the camera. "There is a dangerous man out there, and it's up to all of us to keep each other safe and bring this monster to justice."

The newscast turned to the next headline as Jim walked in the kitchen door. Gwen stood at the counter, frozen. When she faced Jim, terror filled her eyes.

****

Present Day
Patient 541
Journal Entry

The letters and challenge coins kept coming. The writings were the unpublished articles of a would-be journalist. Within the pages, my relationship with Dee developed, fizzled, and exploded. The articles retold the story I had tried to forget. Dee told of our making love, a scene I believe she would never have published. Dee wrote of the conversations in the Humvee, the first battle, and the child she'd watched fall into a pool of blood. The final letter taken from her journal, each one an obvious copy, was only a few words: He tried to kill me.

Dee had faked her death. She hadn't died when I pressed my hand over her mouth. I'll never know if she bled out before the grenade hit her or if the grenade itself killed her, but I hadn't murdered her. I hadn't, but I might as well have. On the bottom of the page, the addresser of the letter had scribbled. I always knew the truth.

The words erased all my doubt.

Toby. I should have realized Toby was short for Tobias. He'd never understood me or what I needed to do to survive the war. I wanted to tell him that yes, maybe I had tried to kill her, but she'd been dying anyway. I saved the Marine. Why couldn't Toby focus on that fact? Why had he gone back into the building? We all saw the damage to it. We all knew that no one would have survived the effects of the grenade.

Why did Toby have to bring the past into the future? The dead should have stayed buried because the stench of their deaths proved contagious. Toby was as responsible for Bethany's, Tori's, Amy's, and Carrie's deaths as I was, only he would never see it my way. Toby, on his own with such little understanding of a damaged mind, had decided now was the time for my repentance. Unfortunately, repentance was not possible for a man so lost. Toby had the blood of those young women on his hands just as much as I did. Those women, yes, Toby murdered them right alongside me.

Maybe that's why I agreed to meet with him. He needed to know what he'd done.

Chapter 26

2018
Jim

"What are you watching?" Jim asked, even though he knew she was watching Lieutenant Larsen and seeing the picture of the man in a blue sweatshirt pushed up against the last victim.

"I was watching the…" Gwen swallowed hard.

"The news?"

"Yes. I was watching the news."

"I heard you had an alibi. That's good to know." Jim glared at his wife. His pulse beat against his temples.

"I'm sorry." Gwen's voice was small, like a child's.

"Of course you are." Jim filled a glass with water from the fridge and drank it down. "I'm surprised to see you here."

"I, um, I thought we needed to talk."

"I thought you might." Jim stood by the door as if her words would come easier if he knew he could run from them.

"It's just, I just think that you and I—well, we've always had our differences. What brought us together isn't enough to keep us together."

"Stop, Gwen. You don't get to be the one who ends this."

Gwen looked at the television screen. A commercial

for dog food was playing, but Jim suspected she was still envisioning the man in the sweatshirt.

"I don't think it's a good idea to go into everything."

"Oh, you don't? You don't think telling me that you're screwing the pilot is a good idea?" Jim's voice was close to a yell, but he knew better than to allow their fight to be heard from the street.

"Jim, please."

"Please what? Don't be angry that my wife is sneaking off behind my back? I don't get to be pissed about that?"

"Jim, this isn't all my fault. You forgot about me. You haven't even been here, or at least your mind hasn't been. You've been out in the garage with your damn Jeep and walkie-talkie." Gwen started to cry. "You aren't even you anymore."

"What do you know about the walkie-talkie?"

Gwen stared at him with fear in her eyes. "What do you mean? I was there with you when you bought it. Don't you remember?"

"It was you, wasn't it? You're trying to make me go crazy, so you can say it was my fault that you ran off with Paul." Jim's pulse pounded in his temples; his eyes blurred.

"Jim, you're scaring me. I don't know what you're talking about."

"You're lying, Gwen. You're lying to me just like you lied to me about you and Paul."

Gwen cried harder.

"Is he involved? Did you pay someone, or did you sneak out of the hotel room somehow?"

"Jim, you know I would never—"

"Do I? Did he steal his sweatshirt back?"

Something was happening. He had experienced this feeling before—several times.

"Jim, you have the sweatshirt. The hotel told me you picked it up when I called looking for it."

"What are you saying, Gwen?"

"You have the sweatshirt. Don't you, Jim?" Tears rolled down her cheeks, but he didn't sense sadness. Gwen was petrified. "It's you in the video, isn't it, Jim?"

He needed her to stop talking. When he turned to her again, he saw her through a foggy glass, but the strangest part was that he saw himself on the other side of that foggy glass beside her. He was watching a scene from his own life as it played out. How could that be? He was standing in place, yet he was also walking toward her. A blank emotion overtook him, and he watched.

When Jim refocused, he was in the garage, searching for the sweatshirt he had hidden there. Paul must have taken it back, and unless Jim pulled himself together, Paul and Gwen's plan of making him crazy would be successful.

"It's not here, Jim."

Jim's head jerked toward the walkie-talkie. "What? Who is that?"

He stared at the walkie-talkie, which remained silent. Then the light flickered. "You killed those women."

"Gwen, I know that's you. It's your voice. I know it."

"You can't silence all of us."

Jim snatched up the device and screamed into it. "Why are you doing this to me, Gwen?"

No one responded. Jim's heart pounded inside his chest. *What the hell was going on? Why would she be doing this to him? Why not just divorce him?*

Gwen's muffled screams from the kitchen reached him. Why was she muffled? What was happening? Perhaps the drifter had come into their home. Maybe he had forced her to say those things? Jim raced to the door and swung it open, ready to protect his wife. Gwen was tied to a chair, a towel stuffed in her mouth. Jim grabbed his gun from its holster and scanned the room. He darted throughout the downstairs and after finding the house empty, he ran back to his wife.

"Gwen," Jim cried, removing the towel, "are you okay?"

"Help," Gwen screamed. "Somebody, help me."

"Gwen, what the hell? I'm here. Stop screaming." But she continued. Jim stuffed the towel back in her mouth and ran back into the garage. Desperate to find what he was looking for, he tossed boxes about the area. Somehow, if he could locate the sweatshirt, everything would make sense again, even though he couldn't understand his reasoning himself. He shoved a cabinet over, and behind it, a dozen white envelopes drifted to the floor. They were all addressed to him with no return address.

From inside the house, Jim heard a loud crash. He raced back to the kitchen. The chair Gwen had been tied to had fallen over. By the time he reached her, her hands were almost out of the belt, his belt that had been used as handcuffs. As he leaned in to help free her, she kicked him with such force he lost his breath. Anger surged through him. Jim yanked the chair back to standing, and Gwen let out a cry of pain.

"Stop, Gwen. Just stop. You don't understand." She kept screaming through the cloth. Tears were flowing like rivers down her cheeks. "Damn it, Gwen. Just shut the hell up, so I can figure out what is going on." Her cries softened to a whimper.

"Someone is setting me up. They were talking to me in the walkie-talkie, and then that guy was following me."

Gwen stared at him in horror.

"Was it you? Please, just tell me."

Gwen only cried harder. She wasn't his wife. He wasn't her husband. They were something else entirely.

"Gwen, I don't know what's happening." And then, as his knees hit the floor, Jim began crying. He crawled to his wife and set his head in her lap like she was a mother who could fix everything. "I don't know what's happening." Jim's head throbbed. "I don't want to hurt you. I don't want to hurt anyone." He sobbed gut-wrenching sounds into his wife's lap. The cries were so loud that he almost missed the sound of her phone vibrating in her back pocket. But when the sound broke through, Jim went silent.

Slowly, he stood and went behind Gwen. He slid the phone from her back pocket and turned it over.

On the front screen was a text from Gabe: *We're on our way.*

"What have you done, Gwen?" Jim pulled his gun from its holster again and ran to the window. He stood off to the side and peered out quickly before ducking back, his gun at the ready. "I told you I just have to figure some things out."

Gwen was crying again.

"Stop. Please. I can't think. Think, Jim. Think." He leaned his back against the wall and breathed deeply before letting the air slowly seep out. "Gwen, I have a plan. If I untie you, will you stand by me?" Jim bent down next to her. "You owe me that. Don't you agree? You owe me a chance to explain, don't you think?"

Gwen nodded.

"Great." Jim went to the counter and set his gun down. "I'm going to untie you now, and you can wash your face and put on a smile." She nodded again. "Then, I'll let Gabe and Brent in, and we'll talk this out." Jim removed the towel from her mouth. "Can I trust you?"

She nodded again.

"No, I need to hear you say it. Can I trust you?"

"Yes." Gwen rasped.

Jim walked behind her and untied her hands. "Now run into the bathroom and wash your face."

Gwen retreated to the stairs, and all Jim could hope for was that in this matter, his wife wouldn't lie to him. She had to know that he wasn't a killer. She had to.

Outside, the sound of sirens split the air. Jim rushed to the window. "Holy shit," he said to the empty room. "Why are there so many damn cars?" He peeked out one more time. "Gwen, get down here. They're here."

A sound alerted him to her presence. He turned and saw her standing ten feet from him with his gun pointed straight at him. "Gwen, what the hell? I told you we're just talking to them. It's Gabe, for Christ's sake."

Her hands were shaking.

"Put down the gun, Gwen."

Tears rolled down her face as she cocked the pistol. "Gwen, you stupid—"

As Jim charged toward her, the splitting sound of the bullet filled the room, and then all went black around him.

****

Present Day
Jim

Jim entered the small room. The chaplain, instead of sitting behind the desk, had moved three chairs to form a circle. He motioned for Jim to take a seat.

At first, Jim only stood behind his chair and stared at the man sitting in the third chair. His heart pounded against his chest with anticipation. A million emotions bubbled to the surface, forcing Jim to either suffocate or let them all go. He let go of the fear, the anger, and the guilt and then stepped farther into the room to face his old friend.

"Hello, Toby."

Toby rubbed his palms on his cargo pants. He was clean shaven but haggard at the same time.

"Hello, Jim."

Jim sat, never breaking eye contact. "You're pretty brave coming here."

Toby swallowed hard and glanced at the chaplain. The chaplain nodded encouragement. Jim could tell by the parental gesture that they had spoken in the past.

"How did you know? About the challenge coin?" Jim asked. "How did you know?"

"When I was waiting to be shipped home, the medics spoke about finding one in Dee's mouth. I thought it was odd, but I didn't think you'd done it."

"Why the letters? Why now?"

"When I came home, I couldn't adjust. I ended up in and out of hospitals. Dee's journal, it was still safe when I went to..." He grimaced at the memory. "Anyway, I took it with me, but when I got home, I left my belongings at my mother's. She passed away. When I was going through her house, I came across it, and I found Dee's last words." Toby looked at Jim. "You tried to kill her, Jim. Why? I thought you loved her."

"She wouldn't stop talking. She…" Jim started crying. "Something snapped. I can't explain it. I can't believe I did it." He wiped his arm across his nose. "I was doing okay. I had a good life. You destroyed it by coming back."

"I just wanted to tell you I knew. I needed to know why. When I saw you at the crime scene, doing your job, being successful, I hated you. I despised you because you were shit, and you ended up okay, and I, well…I've never been okay. I sent you the letters because I wanted you to acknowledge what you did to Dee. That's all I wanted. I wasn't going to turn you in to the police because a part of me was crazy too, and crazy people do crazy things, but then I overheard the detectives at UNF talking about the challenge coin. I couldn't be sure, but I decided to look in the area. I really hoped it wasn't you. I really did."

"Go to hell, Toby. Go to hell. I had a good life."

"A person with secrets like yours does not have a good life. You needed to face what you'd done. Now you need to face what you did to the other women."

I had heard enough. I stood so quickly that my chair toppled.

A male nurse escorted me to my room where I paced until my legs ached, and then, exhausted by everything, I sat, picked up my pen, and wrote the final chapters.

Toby's words play in my mind like a recording. I need to come to terms with what I did. I need to own my actions.

I followed Bethany that morning. Toby's words were

with me when the second young woman crossed my path. The fact that I chose her was just bad luck on her part. Wrong place, wrong time, as they say. Add to that wrong hair color and blue eyes.

My weekend away with my wife had gone well until I checked her texts in the morning. It wasn't so much what was said but the familiarity that disturbed me. I watched Gwen sleeping for a bit, and I wanted to harm her. The healthy part of me wanted to punch her in the face. The hardest part of the whole betrayal wasn't worrying about my marriage ending but feeling like a fool.

The headache came on strong. I grabbed my shoes and found a trail behind the hotel. For a moment, I believed being surrounded by nature would be enough to chase away my frustration. I would run a few miles, go back to the hotel, and address the text: —Don't enjoy your weekend too much— *Maybe the message was nothing. Maybe I could stop the inevitable from happening.*

Losing myself in the rhythmic, running steps, I watched the ground beneath my feet. Each breath was deep and purposeful. Each exhale relieved the pressure building inside of me. My plan might have been successful if I had not tripped on a root. My legs buckled, and I caught myself with my hands. The jolt brought back all the frustration I was experiencing and added a bit more to the mix. I heard footsteps approaching and scrambled to my feet, but not quickly enough to avoid being seen by a young woman jogging effortlessly behind me. When she passed, she excused herself with a smirk on her face. The smirk could have been a polite smile, but not to me, not that day.

I jogged behind her for several hundred feet until the mind I depended on disappeared behind a veil. She met the same fate as the girl from the bar, but I had no recollection of the event. Even when I heard about the crime's location. The coincidence of the location sparked only a small interest in my mind, but I treated the evidence as I would for any other case. I was hardly aware that the coincidence had sparked interest in other people's minds as well, and they were not turning a blind eye to their suspicions any longer.

The next two women, well, I was angrier then. My life was falling apart, and I was becoming more disconnected. My blacked-out mind is still a mystery to me, but I believe I sought the victims out more.

Tori. Right when I felt a bit of hope that my marriage might not crumble, she insulted me. She made me look like a fool in front of my wife. I knew how to check for cameras, and I knew how to get lost in the shadows. Tori was singing on the way to the car, but she didn't sing for long. I was maturing as a killer, yet I also got sloppy. The sweatshirt gave me away.

The woman at the airport was different. The other women I killed to quiet Dee's voice in my mind. But the last woman wasn't Dee at all. When I think about the anger that caused me to seek her out, only Gwen's face comes to mind.

I set down my pen and close the journal. I am still far from free, but something inside me feels lighter, and for the first time in a very long time, I sleep peacefully.

****

In the months that followed, I learned that while Lieutenant Larsen held her press conference, Toby had walked into the police headquarters with a tale to tell. A tale about a Marine who held secrets. By the time Gwen sent her text, the detectives were already on their way.

After leaving the war, Toby spent years drifting in and out of therapy. He attempted suicide several times, but with medication, he doesn't feel the urge to end his life anymore. On occasion, Toby also kept in contact with Marshall. I learned Toby had rented a small apartment in town and received a small inheritance from his mother. He would be okay.

I know all this because Toby became a frequent visitor. For some time, I wanted to tear him apart, limb from limb, for making my life explode. But slowly, I came to realize Toby saved me. He made me face the parts of me that needed healing.

I work on myself. I talk to the chaplain, who tells me about a God who forgives. He assures me that my parents' teachings were misguided and harsher than God ever intended his words to be. I work on believing him.

I haven't spoken to Gwen since the day she shot me. The closest I've gotten to her is seeing her signature on the divorce papers I signed. Toby told me that she married Paul after he divorced Trish. Poor Trish. Sometimes, the world is harsh, even when we're not living in the middle of a war. I guess we manage to create our own personal battles to suffer through.

I've learned a great deal through my years in this facility. I've learned there's a wall between sane and insane, but sometimes the wall crumbles and needs to be rebuilt. I can almost visualize the gaping hole that needs mending. I can almost envision the sane parts of me leaking into the insane parts where the two blended until the wall was obliterated. All those feelings. All that anger…All I can say is that once the border was broken and whatever sat behind it had been set free, well, it was impossible to stop what flowed out of me.

And I've learned that if I try hard enough, Toby and the chaplain don't see the man who did those evil acts. But he's still there. Sometimes, when I lie in my bed at night, I study my hands, and I remember what they looked like wrapped around the women's necks. A surreal feeling overwhelms me as I curl and uncurl my fingers that don't seem to belong to me. The past can never be washed off them.

I tried to cover the corpses from the war with whatever recompense could conduct. One criminal at a time, locked behind bars, slowly erasing the black marks on my soul. I wasn't wrong to try to do better, but I couldn't just cover the rotten and believe it wouldn't taint the new. I had to fix what was broken and come to terms with the deeds I had done. My hatred, complete and deep-rooted, was never about Dee or insurgents or my father. My hatred was for myself. Did my father train me to despise myself? Absolutely. Was that his mission? I can't imagine it to be the case.

But whatever and whoever led me to the place where I am today, I'm left lost in a cloud of confusion. For even if my soul is not tarnished, the slate on which I write my life, my future, can never be wiped clean.

****

Another six months pass, and I once again meet with the ones paid to declare me safe for the outside world. Chaplain Gregory and Toby encourage me with their words. Toby has even offered me a place to stay while I get back on my feet. I smile and nod at the man who has become my only true friend. But I don't share his enthusiasm. I know my dark places. I know the war still

300

going on within my mind.

In the quiet of the night, I pray many prayers and beg the God I want desperately to believe in to forgive the unforgivable. I pray the people paid to decide if I am still dangerous will not trust the light they see in my eyes. It is merely a flicker. The darkness is strong within me, and my battle is best fought within the confines of this room. Despite my desire to walk in the sunshine once again, I pray that I stay tucked away behind these walls where the hands I clasp in prayer will never betray me again.

A word about the authors...

Tracy Tripp grew up in Upstate New York, where she earned her bachelor's degree in education with a concentration in English at the State University of New York at Oswego. She went on to earn her master's degree in education at Buffalo State College. After years of teaching, she decided to stay home with her three children and follow her passion for writing. Tracy Tripp has written four novels: Parting Gifts, Still Life, Something Like a Dream, and Awaken. She has also written two children's books: The Wealthy Frog and Sammy the Snowman. Tracy Tripp is a substitute teacher for grades K-12, plays tennis, and volunteers holding babies at the local children's hospital. She lives in Jacksonville, Florida, with her husband and three children. Read more about her works at www.tracytripp.com.

Dr. Edward Mickolus, after graduating from Georgetown University, wrote the first doctoral dissertation on international terrorism while earning an M.A., M.Phil, and Ph.D. from Yale University. He then served in analytical, operational, management, and staff positions in the Central Intelligence Agency for 33 years, where he was CIA's first full-time analyst on international terrorism; analyzed African political, economic, social, military, and leadership issues; wrote political-psychological assessments of world leaders; and managed collection, counterintelligence, and covert action programs against terrorists, drug traffickers, weapons proliferators, and hostile espionage services. For the following ten years, he was a senior instructor for SAIC and its spinoff, Leidos, Inc. He founded Vinyard

Software, Inc., whose products include ITERATE (International Terrorism: Attributes of Terrorist Events) text and numeric datasets and DOTS (Data on Terrorist Suspects). Clients include 200 universities in two dozen countries. His 50 books include a series of multi-volume chronologies and biographies on international terrorism; 31 book chapters; 100 articles and reviews in refereed scholarly journals and newspapers and presentations to professional societies; and 15 humorous publications. Topics include intelligence, inspiration, politics, fitness, education, public speaking, writing, creativity, the UN, and humor. He served as the Deborah M. Hixon Professor of Intelligence Tradecraft and Board of Advisors member at the Daniel Morgan Graduate School in Washington, DC and teaches at the University of North Florida and Jacksonville University. He is a recovering standup comic. He is working on a study of the honorees at State of the Union addresses, orchestrating a multi-author serial novel by 20 retired and serving CIA officers, continuing writing the terrorist events series, and addressing numerous writing groups and civic associations. He and his wife will soon become grandparents. Visit his author website at www.edwardmickolus.com.

Printed in the USA
CPSIA information can be obtained
at www.ICGtesting.com
LVHW020205160923
758204LV00007B/307

9 781509 248476